英文作文輕鬆得分指南

大學入學學測及指考英文作文解析

[2017修訂版]

深入淺出的寫作技巧傳授
＋ 最貼近實戰經歷的模擬練習
＝ 戰勝英文作文不二法門！

編著

前大考中心研究員
陳坤田

國家圖書館出版品行編目資料

英文作文輕鬆得分指南／陳坤田編著. －－臺北市：
書林, 2017.01
面；公分

ISBN 978-957-445-703-8 (平裝)

1. 英語　2. 作文　3. 寫作法

805.17　　　　　　　　　　　　　　　105014338

英文作文輕鬆得分指南（2017修訂版）

著　　　者	陳坤田
英 文 校 訂	Louise Crawford・Laura Stewart・Lynn Sauvé
執 行 編 輯	洪儷嘉・李虹慧
校　　　對	紀榮崧
出 　版　者	書林出版有限公司
	100台北市羅斯福路四段60號3樓
	Tel (02) 2368-4938・2365-8617　　Fax (02) 2368-8929・2363-6630
台北書林書店	106台北市新生南路三段88號2樓之5　Tel (02) 2365-8617
學 校 業 務 部	Tel (02) 2368-7226・(04) 2376-3799・(07) 229-0300
經 銷 業 務 部	Tel (02) 2368-4938
發 　行　人	蘇正隆
郵　　　撥	15743873・書林出版有限公司
網　　　址	http://www.bookman.com.tw
經 銷 代 理	紅螞蟻圖書有限公司
	台北市內湖區舊宗路二段121巷19號
	Tel (02) 2795-3656(代表號)　　Fax (02) 2795-4100
登 　記　證	局版臺業字第一八三一號
出 版 日 期	2006年一版，2017年1月修訂版
定　　　價	320元
I　S　B　N	978-957-445-703-8

序言

筆者對於高中學生英文寫作能力一向感到興趣，前後與大學教授合作進行過六項研究，探討英文寫作能力的命題和評量的方法。加上與研究數目相同的高中英文教學年資，發現高中學生英文寫作能力普遍欠佳；不論學測或指考，成績在十二分以上的（滿分二十分）不到總人數的百分之八。學生寫作能力普遍欠佳原因約有以下幾個：

第一，缺乏表達生活英文的語彙。學測或指考考的是「生活英文」，例如：中樂透之後要幫助誰？原因是什麼？都是相當生活化的英文。

第二，缺乏指導。學測或指考考的生活英文，要求學生簡短扼要地寫一百多字。由於文章短，又要結構完整，所以需要使用各種作文技巧：例如主題句、轉承語等。但是對於主題句的意義、寫法，和轉承語的用法，學生缺乏指導。難怪學生在 "Growing up means making my own decisions."（長大意謂自己作決定）之後就不知道要怎麼寫下去了。

第三，練習不夠。有些學校要求高一學生寫六篇作文，高二學生八篇，高三學生十篇。這已是最高的上限了。這麼少的練習，加上缺乏指導，進步有限。

有鑑於以上的原因，筆者寫了這本《英文作文輕鬆得分指南》，希望有助解決上述現象。

首先，加上歷屆大考英文作文試題的例文，本書共有八十多篇的生活英文作文。熟讀這些例文，對英文寫作，將是一大幫助。

第二，本書以大考英文作文評分指標為架構，詳細說明各種作文技巧：例如主題句、轉承語等，加上造句法，給予同學充分的作文指導。同學不致於看到 "Growing up means making my own decisions." 之後不知所措。

第三，本書第三章每單元的「輕鬆寫作」，給同學充分練習的機會。只要模仿參考範文，利用所提供的資料，同學就可以輕鬆寫好英文作文。

英文作文在學測或指考雖然只佔二十分，但學會作文的價值卻遠超過這個數字。首先，在學測或指考的英文試題中，「綜合測驗」、「文意選填」等有轉承語的試題，以及考句子連貫的「篇章結構」試題，其解法皆須用到本書第一章的說明。再者，懂得作文的組織，對閱讀的邏輯也有幫助。最後，熟讀本書，不但有助於以上三大題的得分，更由於整體英文程度提升，其他大題的得分也跟著提高。也就是說，英文作文分數的高低就是英文科得分高低的關鍵。

總之，筆者建議讀者花點時間來研讀此書。良好的寫作能力不但會讓讀者在考試時得到好成績，對於往後的學業或職業生涯也將助益良多。

2017 修訂版提供最新出題趨勢與參考範文，精進寫作能力，輕鬆應試。

編者 謹識
2017 於臺北

Preface

Through numerous research projects on the subject and six years of teaching, I have found that high school English writing students encounter three major difficulties. First, they don't know the basic skills for composing a short essay. Either their introduction is too long, or their sentences lack coherence, or they fail to address the topic appropriately. Worse still, very few of them know how to write an effective topic sentence.

The second is that they lack the proper vocabulary and expressions for communicating what they need to say on an exam. For example, some students write "big door" instead of "gate," "do problems" instead of "create problems," while others write "a classroom party" instead of "a class reunion," to mention just a few.

Third, very few of their sentences are grammatically correct.

The difficulties that high school students have can be attributed to several things. One of them is that students are not properly oriented. Very few teachers, if any, teach students composition. Another is that they don't spend adequate time practicing their writing. Even if they do, because of lack of proper orientation, their progress is rather limited.

In view of the above situation, I have written this book to help deal with the difficulties that high school students have. This book attempts to cope with the problem in the following ways:

First, it provides a detailed orientation. It includes basic skills needed for composing short essays, such as how to write effective topic sentences, methods for developing a narration, an exposition, and how to conclude, together with an ample amount of sample essays that demonstrate these skills. Among other features included, a section on how to construct compound and complex sentences and how to use transition words will help minimize grammatical mistakes.

Second, this book provides forty-five exercises in guided writing, which are similar to the writing tasks required on the university entrance exam, and which are meant to be a tremendous help to students in increasing their vocabulary, enriching their expressions, and enhancing their sentence making ability. Moreover, these exercises are designed with a view to familiarizing students with the format of composition, and most importantly, to help them with overall proficiency in English writing.

It is hoped that after finishing reading the orientation and doing the exercises, students will have eliminated many of their difficulties.

A good ability to write in English will not only help students cope with exams, it will also be useful throughout their lives. It is the authors' recommendation that students and teachers use this book and enjoy the countless benefits it offers.

本書使用法

致學生：

為了幫助讀者從本書獲得最大的益處，筆者在這裡多說幾句話。

第一：對自己要有信心。只要肯努力，就一定會進步。

第二：要親自動手研讀、做練習。

第三：先讀第一章，牢記每一個細節。特別是主題句寫法、轉承語用法等。

第四：再讀第二章，特別注意：

    (1) 完整句子的定義。

    (2) 從屬子句不可單獨存在。

    (3) 連接詞的用法。這也是綜合測驗、文意選填的考試重點。

第五：細讀第三章，特別注意：

    (1) 配合擬寫內容、重要的字詞及文法提示和寫作指導，確實了解參考範文的寫法，並盡量牢記範文內容，以提高自己用生活英文表達的能力。

    (2) 做造句練習，不要放過任何一題。

    (3) 做實力培養。要反覆練習，直到寫對每一空格為止。

第六：依提示或說明，做輕鬆寫作的部分。特別注意：

    (1) 不要恐懼或害怕。

    (2) 依參考資料的建議，勇敢寫作。

    (3) 寫完的作文留下來，不要丟棄。

    (4) 有空時，把自己寫的作文來出來看。隨著自己程度不斷提高，自己會逐漸有能力修改自己的作文。

進行到第六之(4)，你已經漸漸走上成功之路了，恭喜你！

致教師：

命題和批改是教英文作文的兩件費心力的事。本書作者建議英文教師使用本書第三章每一單元的「第8部份：輕鬆寫作」，既解決了命題的問題，又有寫作資料供學生參考寫作，在批改時也將輕鬆許多。第一、二章可擇要講解或指定學生自行閱讀。

感謝

在編寫此書時，筆者參考了前二本舊作《英文閱讀與寫作》和《英文作文典範》。在此要感謝前出版機構同意我引用部份舊作內容，改編成本書，由書林出版公司出版，與全國讀者分享。

此外，北一女退休老師林瑮珊女士和內湖高中李欣蓉老師二位，除負責中譯、注譯和造句練習之外，對本書編輯也提供很多寶貴意見。中英文稿則由楊寧和美籍 Louise Crawford、Laura Stewart 以及書林編輯群指正。

謹對以上諸君和機構致上萬分的謝忱。讀者有任何指教可以寄電子郵件至 ktchen35@yahoo.com.tw。

第三章　輕鬆學會英文作文

附　錄

英文作文題型和寫作方法剖析

第一章

　　本章根據大考中心英文作文命題原則和評分指標，詳細剖析英文作文，除說明英文作文的基本方法與技巧之外，也附重要的轉承語用法及示例，以幫助學生，使所寫的句子，更具有連貫性。

1 學科能力測驗和指定科目考試英文作文題型

　　以下題型系大考中心於民國81年研究確定，96年修訂。

一、指定科目考試題型

(1) 主題寫作

 請以 "Travel Is the Best Teacher" 為主題，寫一篇約120至150個單詞(words)的英文作文。第一段針對文章主題，說明旅行的優點，並在第二段舉自己在國內或國外的旅行經驗，以印證第一段的說明。

（改編自93年指定考試科目，見本書256頁）

(2) 主題句寫作

 提示：小考、段考、複習考、畢業考、甚至校外其它各種大大小小的考試，已成為高中學生生活中不可或缺的一部份。請寫一篇約120至150個單詞(words)的英文作文，文分兩段，第一段以Exams of all kinds have become (was) a necessary part of my high school life.為主題句；第二段則以The most unforgettable exam I have ever taken is (was)…為開頭並加以發展。

（改編自92年指定考試科目，見本書255頁）

二、學科能力測驗題型

(1) 簡函寫作

 高中生王治平收到美國筆友George的來信，告訴治平他要隨父母到台灣來住兩年左右，並問治平："Can you give me some advice and suggestions so that I know what I should do and what I should not do when I am in Taiwan?"現在請你以治平的身份，擬一封約100至120個單詞(words)適當的回信給George，歡迎他來台灣，並且針對他的問題，提出一些具體的建議。

（改編自84年指定考試科目，見本書245頁）

第一章

(2) 主題寫作

例 請以 "A Rainy Day" 為題，寫一篇約100個單詞(words)的短文，敘述你在某一個下雨天的實際經歷。 （例文見本書247頁）

(3) 看圖作文

例 請以下面編號1至4的四張圖畫內容為藍本，依序寫一篇約100至120個單詞(words)的文章，描述女孩與貓之間的故事。請注意，故事內容務必涵蓋四張圖意，力求情節完整、前後發展合理。 （例文見本書253頁）

註：以上的題型雖有所不同，基本上寫作方法（詳後文）是相通的。

② 英文作文命題原則

(1) 題意通常清楚明確。

(2) 作文的內容通常是考生所熟悉的生活或學習經驗。

(3) 對內容提示不會過於詳盡，避免考生照譯。

(4) 通常沒有限制段落數目與內容。

(5) 通常沒有限制作文之用字或用詞。

(6) 較抽象的議論文通常不會考。

(7) 寫作長度為100～120字（學測）；100～150字（指考）。

說明

① 英文作文該分幾段？由考生決定。該寫幾個字？通常依照題目要求，介於100至150字之間，即可滿足「英文作文評分指標」的要求。但超過150字沒關係。

② 命題原則告訴我們，英文作文考的是引導作文，而且較抽象的議論文不必費心去準備。

③ 分析過去數年的作文試題之後，發現在各種主要文體中，英文作文考的主要是敘述文（narrations）和說明文（expositions）。

❸ 英文作文評分指標

· 內容（content）：主題（句）清楚切題、並有具體、完整的相關細節來支持。（5分）

· 組織（organization）：重點分明，有開頭、發展、結尾、前後連貫轉承語使用得當。（5分）

· 文法（grammar）：全文幾無文法錯誤，文句結構富變化。（4分）

· 用字、拼字：用字精確、得宜，且無拼字錯誤。（4分）

· 體例（mechanics）：格式、標點、大小寫幾無錯誤（2分）

說明　必須滿足評分指標的要求，英文作文才有可能得到高分。內容切題與否分別如下列例子所示：

　　a. 不切題

How to Succeed in Life

There are winners and losers in life. If we don't want to be losers, we have to stop daydreaming. Daydreaming is not practical. As they say, money does not grow on trees...

　　b. 切題

How to Succeed in Life

To succeed in life requires several things. First, we have to know what we care about the most. If we really care about something, we will have the motivation and courage to face challenges and pay the price needed for success. Second, we must excel. By "excel" I mean be good at what we care about. For example, if we care about people and want to be doctors, we have to be good at medicine. Third, we must work hard. A taxi driver who works ten hours daily makes more money than one who works just two hours a day...

4 英文作文寫作基本原理

(1) 說明文：作者針對一個主題，寫出對這個主題的態度、認知、看法、想法或建議。

例 主題：Money
作者看法：Money is both a blessing and a curse.

Money

Money is both a blessing and a curse. If we have money, we can buy a nice car and a beautiful house, we can take a vacation and travel abroad, and we can do lots of other things with it. We can have many of our wishes fulfilled. Above all, we can enjoy life. This is why money is a blessing. On the other hand, if we have no money, we cannot have a decent place to live, and we cannot buy daily necessities, let alone take a vacation or travel abroad. We can hardly do anything. Our survival becomes a problem. This is why money is a curse. (108 words)

說明：作者說明有錢是幸事；沒錢是災禍。

(2) 敘述文：作者針對一個主題，寫出對這個主題的回憶及感想。

My Absent-minded Father

My father is often absent-minded. Here is an example:

One Sunday morning my father drove us kids up to the Yangmingshan National Park for an outing. After he parked his car, we got out and happily spent a pleasant morning there. We strolled in the woods and enjoyed looking at the beautiful flowers. Then it was time for us to leave. We walked back to our car, expecting to return home for the great lunch Mother had prepared for us. However, my father could not open the car door because he had left the car key in the ignition.

This time his absent-mindedness made us starve for nearly three hours before help finally came. My father learned a lesson.

> He started to bring a spare key with him. But I am afraid the next time he will forget the spare key as well. (143 words)

說明：作者回憶一件趣事及感想。

⑤ 大考英文作文寫作第一步驟

理論上，大考英文作文試題須給題目。但是，因大考主要考引導作文，因此，命題者有時認為有提示就夠了。因而忽略了給題目。在沒有給題目的情況下，如果考生能確定題目則更好，更能保證作文不會偏離主題。確定題目之後，則須擬定試題內容。

例如，九十四年指定科目考試英文作文試題為：「指定科目考試完畢後，高中同學決定召開畢業後的第一次同學會，你被公推負責主辦。請將你打算籌辦的活動寫成一篇短文。文分兩段，第一段詳細介紹同學會的時間、地點及活動內容，第二段則說明採取這種活動方式的理由。」就沒有給題目。這時如果能訂出題目為 "A Class Reunion"，不但能給閱卷教授一個好印象，更能幫助自己在寫作的時候不會偏離主題。

因此，英文作文寫作的第一步是決定主題（topic）和確定細節（details）。

練習 1

英文作文寫作的第一步是決定主題和細節。請根據提示，決定主題和細節。

1. 文章請以 "If I won two million dollars in the lottery, I would help..." 開始，敘述如果你或妳贏得臺灣樂透彩新臺幣兩百萬元之後，最想把全數金額拿去幫助的人、機構或組織，並寫出理由。

   Topic: _____

   Detail(s): _____

2. 你同意 "Laughter is better than medicine" 這種說法嗎？以你自己或親朋好友的經驗或你所知道的故事為例，加以說明。你的論點無論是正面或是反面都不會影響你的得分。

   Topic: _____

   Detail(s): _____

3. 每個人在不同的情況下對雨可能有不同的感受。請寫一篇短文，敘述你在某一個下雨天的實際經歷或看到的景象，並據此描述你對雨的感覺。

Topic: _____

Detail(s): _____

4. 請以自己的經驗為例，敘述當你感到不快樂或情緒低落時，（除了簡答題選文中所提及的方法外）你最常用哪一種方法幫自己度過低潮，並舉實例說明這個方法何以有效。

Topic: _____

Detail(s): _____

5. 指定科目考試完畢後，高中同學決定召開畢業後的第一次同學會，你被公推負責主辦。請將你打算籌辦的活動寫成一篇短文。文分兩段，第一段詳細介紹同學會的時間、地點及活動內容，第二段則說明採取這種活動方式的理由。

Topic: _____

Detail(s): _____

（參考解答請見附錄 I）

6 英文作文段落

英文作文的細節確定之後，接著是依提示寫就內容。以下討論如何寫就內容：含段落、開頭、發展、轉承語使用、結尾方法等。先討論段落：

(1) 界說：段落是作文的一個完整的部分。

(2) 分類：起始段落、轉承段落、發展段落、結尾段落。

(3) 發展段落 =「主題句 + 發展（局部或全部）」。

Why I Want a College Education

I have long hoped to become a college student. First, a college education will enable me to specialize in a certain field of knowledge, such as medicine or law, preparing me to become a professional. Second, it will help develop in me a strong character. In order to become a professional, I have to study a lot and pass many tests. I have to persevere in order to succeed. Therefore, as early as three years ago, I made up my mind to do my best in preparing for the university entrance examination. I hope I will do well on the examination. (101words)

① 主題句 "I have long hoped to become a college student." 是一個想法，後面的first, second等是鋪陳，一起構成一個段落。鋪陳短時，可以在一段中置放數個；鋪陳長時，一段只放一個。

② 一百多字的作文，不適宜有太長的引言，因此，起始段落通常很短或將它合併在發展段落中。

③ 故一個段落功用可不只一種。上例既為起始段落與發展段落，結尾也在其中。

④ 一篇作文也不一定包含各樣的段落。只要內容完整，有時只有一段也可以。

7 英文作文組織

(1) 說明文 = 作者的看法、態度或建議等加上解釋。

(2) 敘述文 = 作者回憶或詮釋過去的一個事件。

(3) 英文作文組織 = 開頭 + 發展 + 結尾。

Coming Down with a Cold

I came down with a cold last month and it was a painful experience. At the beginning, I felt dizzy. Then I developed a runny nose, I sneezed, had a sore throat and began coughing, and my head ached.

When my mother took me to see a doctor, my temperature was taken, and the doctor said I had a slight fever. The doctor said that there was no cure for colds except to get plenty of rest and drink a lot of liquids. He gave me some medicine to help with my coughing, my runny nose, my sore throat, and my headache. About a week later, I got over my cold.

Catching a cold was no fun. I didn't feel well physically, I couldn't study efficiently, nor could I go out with my friends. Accordingly, I have decided to take better care of myself so that I will not catch another cold. (151 words)

① 上文是敘述文，是作者對過去事件的回憶。

② I came down with a cold last month and it was a painful experience. 是開頭；Accordingly, I have decided to take better care of myself so that I will not catch another cold. 是結尾；其餘是發展，且每一段各為發展的一部分。

8 英文作文開頭寫法

通常將英文作文開頭第一句話寫成主題句。

(1) 主題句的意義

主題句告訴讀者行文的主題，並有帶動下文的作用。分三種情況討論：

(1-1) 行文為段落：以前文 "Money" 一文（見p.4）為例：

本文首句 "Money is both a blessing and a curse"，告訴讀者行文的主題是金錢，並帶動下文，告訴讀者即將說明的是金錢既是寶物也是禍因，即為主題句。本文只用一個主題句。

(1-2) 行文不只一段：以92年學測作文試題為例：

Music Is An Important Part Of Our Life

Music is an important part of our life. Many of us have never traveled abroad, but every one of us has some experience with music. For example, in school we learn to sing or to play a musical instrument. In our free time, we listen to music, or go to concerts for entertainment. We sing songs when we are happy. This is evidence that music is indeed an important part of our life.

The advantages that music brings are several. First, the beautiful sounds of music delight us. Second, the stories in popular songs touch us. Third, music reduces our tension and it releases our emotions.

In summary, music has so many advantages and it plays such an important role in our life that we simply can't do without it. (130 words)

本文有三段，第一段首句 "Music is an important part of our life." 告訴讀者行文的主題是音樂，並帶動下文，告訴讀者即將說明的是音樂的重要性，為第一段的主題句。第二段第一句 "The advantages that music brings are several." 告訴讀者行文的主題是音樂，並帶動下文，告訴讀者即將說明的是音樂的好處，為第二段的主題句。第三段為結論。

(1-3) 行文不只一段，但只有一個主題句：敍述文（narrations）通常只用一個主題句。

(2) 有效的主題句

有效的主題句必須：

(2-1) 是完整的句子（詳見第二章）。

(2-2) 暗示或明示主題。

(2-3) 要具有（容易）帶動下文的作用。

 題目：My Best Friend

有效的主題句：

John is my best friend because we have a lot in common.

 ① 是完整的句子。

② 明示主題為 my best friend。

③ 讀者期待 what does the author and John have in common，具有帶動下文的作用。

無效的主題句：

I have known my best friend John for a long time.

 ① 是完整的句子。

② 明示主題為 my best friend。

③ 但讀者不易看出下文的發展是什麼，此句不易帶動下文。

(3) 有效主題句的寫法。

(3-1) 條陳法：

 There are three reasons why we should learn English.

 本句用數字，預告後文「為什麼我們該學英文」有三個原因。

(3-2) 直說法：把對主題的態度、認知或看法直接寫在句中。

 Growing up means making my own decisions.

 本句主題為 "growing up"，作者對主題認知是「長大的意義在於自己做決定」。這句話可以帶動下文。

(3-3) 回憶法：對後文的敍述提出一個總的回憶或評價 (overall recollection or comment)（敍述文）：

 My last birthday was unforgettable.

Our last class reunion was a mess.

① 主題分別為 my last birthday 和 our last class reunion，總的回憶或評價為 unforgettable 和 a mess。

② 回憶或評價用字: surprising, interesting, shocking, disappointing, frustrating, embarrassing, etc.

(3-4) 用修辭問句（rhetorical question）

 What is kindness?

用修辭問句的目的在激發讀者的想像力或好奇心。作者在後文回答問題。所以用修辭問句是一種好的開頭方法。

練習 2

I. 判別以下的句子，是否為有效的主題句，並說明理由。

1. John goes to school every day.

2. Going to school is essential for children.

3. Mike has many friends.

4. Baseball is a popular sport in Taiwan.

5. Helping other people can be challenging sometimes.

6. I am afraid of strangers for two reasons.

7. My favorite book is *Harry Potter*.

8. It's useless to regret what has already happened.

9. The movie I saw last week was unforgettable.

10. There are many cars running on the street.

II. 請根據提示，決定主題和細節，並寫出第一句。

1. 請以 "A Happy Ending"（快樂的結局）為題，寫一篇約一百二十個單字的英文作文。你可以從你所讀過的故事、看過的電影或親身體驗中去找題材。描寫完快樂的結局以後，並寫幾句你的感想。答案請寫在「非選擇題答案卷」上。

   Topic: _____

   Detail(s): _____

   First sentence: _____

2. 請以 "A Daily Item" 為題，寫一篇約120～150個單字的英文作文說明你如何依賴日常生活中一件常用的物品。

   Topic: _____

Detail(s): _____

First sentence: _____

3. 請以 "Helping Others" 為題,寫一篇約120～150個單字的英文作文,說明你一次幫助他人的經過及感想。

Topic: _____

Detail(s): _____

First sentence: _____

4. 請以 "Examinations" 為題,寫一篇約120～150個單字的英文作文,說明你對高中學生考試過多的感想。

Topic: _____

Detail(s): _____

First sentence: _____

5. 每個人都有一些朋友。寫一篇約120～150個單字的英文作文,說明什麼樣的人適合做你要好的朋友。

Topic: _____

Detail(s): _____

First sentence: _____

（參考解答請見附錄Ⅰ）

⑨ 英文作文發展方法

　　除了主題句加說明之外,英文作文常用的發展方法有時間順序法（用於敘述文）、定義法、舉例法、條列法、歸納法、因果法（用於說明文）等,寫作時可以綜合各種方法,靈活運用。不過,大考是引導寫作,只要依提示寫作即可,故此不再贅述。

⑩ 英文作文結尾方法

　　英文作文常用的結尾方法有:(1) 以故事的教訓作為結尾;(2) 重述作文主旨;(3) 用訊號字（片語）如 "finally"、"to sum up"、"in summary"、"in conclusion"、"in brief" 等做結尾;(4) 對讀者提出邀請或警告;(5) 不著痕跡,自然結束。(6) 改變話題。詳細的用法及示例見第三章各單元的寫作指導。

⑪ 英文作文的轉承

使用轉承語的好處可從下例得知：

在 "The candidate was shot. _____, he did not die." 中，空格留白，並不影響文意。但如在空格中加入 "Luckily," 或 "Fortunately"，我們就知道作者和候選人（the candidate）為同一國的；反之，如空格中加入 "Unfortunately," 或 "Unluckily"，我們就知道作者和候選人不是同一陣線的人。

因此，轉承語的好處在於，它能使作者要表達的內容更為清楚。

作文常用的轉承語（畫底線的部分）分類並舉例說明如下。

(1) 有關次序、增加、累積的轉承語

例1 There are three reasons why I go to school. First (In the first place / First of all / For one thing), I go to school to learn. Second (In the second place, Then / Next / For another), I go to school to meet friends. Third (Finally), I go to school to prepare for my life.

（我上學的理由有三。第一，我上學是為了學習。第二，我上學是為了認識朋友。第三，我上學是為了為我的生活做準備。）

例2 My friend Jane has a nice personality. In addition, she works very hard.
My friend Jane has a nice personality; in addition, (besides / furthermore / moreover / what is more) she works very hard.

（我的朋友珍個性很好。此外，她非常努力。）

例3 We should work hard. Equally importantly, we should be frugal.

（我們應該努力工作。同樣重要地，我們應該節儉。）

例4 I lost my purse. To make it worse (To make matters worse/Worse still), I was a long way from home.

（我遺失了我的皮包。更糟的是，我離家很遠。）

(2) 表示比較或對照概念的轉承語

例1 Climbing Mt. Everest is difficult. However (Yet / Nevertheless / Nonetheless / But / Still), many people have succeeded.

（攀登聖母峰是很困難的。不過，很多人都成功了。）

例2 To learn to drive, we need a coach. Similarly (Likewise / In like manner), to learn to write, we need a teacher.

（為了學會開車，我們需要教練。同樣地，為了學習寫作，我們需要老師。）

例3 On the one hand, our body needs cholesterol. On the other hand, too much cholesterol is harmful to our body.

（一方面，我們的身體需要膽固醇。但另一方面，太多的膽固醇對我們的身體

有害。）

例4 John did pass the test. <u>At the same time</u>, he didn't know the subject very well.

（約翰的確通過考試了。然而，他對這個科目並不夠瞭解。）

例5 He didn't help his friend. <u>Instead</u>, (<u>On the contrary / Conversely / Rather</u>), he helped his enemy.
He didn't help his friend. <u>Quite the opposite</u>. He helped his enemy.

（他沒有幫助他的朋友。相反地，他幫助了他的敵人。）

例6 Mike is hardworking and frugal. <u>In contrast</u>, his brother Jack is lazy and wasteful.

（麥克勤勞又節儉。相形之下，他的哥哥傑克懶惰又浪費。）

(3) 表示例證或反覆的轉承語

例1 Jack has many hobbies. <u>For example</u> (<u>As an example / For instance / As an illustration / To illustrate</u>), he collects stamps.

（傑克有很多嗜好。例如，他收集郵票。）

例2 Many great men have risen from poverty. <u>Take</u> Lincoln <u>for example</u> (<u>for instance</u>).

（很多偉人出身貧窮。例如林肯。）

例3 One student is absent from class, <u>namely</u> John.

（有一個學生缺席了，就是約翰。）

例4 Mary is a good student. <u>That is to say</u>, she gets good grades in school.

（瑪麗是個好學生。也就是說，她在學校成績很好。）

例5 You say you took the book without his permission. <u>In other words</u>, you stole it.

（你說你沒有得到他的允許就把書拿走。換句話說，你偷了它。）

(4) 表示目的或結果等概念的轉承語

例 It rained heavily for hours on end. <u>As a result</u> (<u>Consequently / Therefore / Because of this / Accordingly / Hence, So</u>), the streets were flooded.

（連續下了好幾個小時的大雨。因此，街道都淹水了。）

(5) 表示時間的轉承語

例1 Jack is watching TV in the living room. <u>In the meantime</u> (<u>Meanwhile</u>), his father is cooking in the kitchen.

（傑克正在客廳看電視。同時，他的爸爸在廚房裡煮飯。）

例2　I will find a job and live independently after I graduate from school. For the time being (For now), I must stay with my parents.

（我畢業後將找個工作獨立生活。目前，我必須跟父母一起住。）

例3　He worked hard for many years. Finally (In the end / At last / Eventually), he succeeded in making a fortune.

（他努力工作了好幾年，最後終於成功地賺了一筆財富。）

(6) 有關強調的轉承語

例1　I don't like him. In fact (As a matter of fact / Actually / In effect), I hate him.

（我不喜歡他。事實上，我恨他。）

in fact 也可表示反駁：You didn't do your homework, did you? In fact, I have.

例2　Parents make the rules. To be sure, many of the rules are no longer appropriate today.

（父母親喜歡訂定規則。當然了，這些規則中有很多現在都不合適了。）

例3　There are many things we should know. Above all (Most important of all / In particular), we should know our limits.

（有很多我們應該知道的事。最重要的是，我們應該知道自己的極限。）

(7) 表讓步的轉承語

例　The university entrance examination is highly competitive. In spite of (Despite / Regardless of) that, many students hope to do well.

（大學入學考試競爭很激烈。儘管如此，很多學生希望能考得好。）

(8) 表結論的轉承語

例　To write well, first, you have to pay attention to grammar. Then you have to learn about organization. Third, you have to practice a lot. In summary (To sum up / In conclusion / In a word / In short / Finally), if you observe the points mentioned, you will soon be able to write well.

（為了要寫得好，首先，你必須注意文法。接下來，你必須學習組織。第三，你必須多練習。總之，如果你遵守上述各點，你將會很快能夠寫得好。）

(9) 其他的轉承語

例1　He is a bore. Frankly speaking, I don't like him.

（他很沒趣。坦白說，我不喜歡他。）

例2　Jack had a car accident. Luckily, (Fortunately / Unfortunately / Unluckily) he was unhurt.

（傑克出了車禍。幸好，他沒有受傷。）

例3 I've talked about the three aspects of living in Taipei. Incidentally (By the way), if you visit Taipei, be sure to experience the MRT and get a taste of the convenience it offers.

（我已經談論了生活在台北的三個層面。順便提一下，如果你來台北玩，一定要去體驗一下捷運，嘗試一下它所帶來的便利。）

例4 Many people like to watch TV. As far as I am concerned, I can do without a TV set.

（很多人喜歡看電視。就我而言，我可以不需要電視機。）

例5 People should respect each other. After all, no one likes to be looked down on.

（人們應該彼此尊重。畢竟，沒有人喜歡被看不起。）

例6 English is important. From what I have mentioned above, it is clear we should make an effort to learn it well.

（英文很重要。從以上我所提到的，很清楚的，我們應該努力把它學好。）

練習 3

I. 把最適當的轉承語（(A)至(J)選項）填入空格中。

1. I like the novel *Sons and Lovers*. _____, I have read it more than ten times.

2. One reason that John is liked by his friends is that he is generous with his time. _____ is that he helps his friends without asking anything in return.

3. To remain healthy, we should eat a balanced diet. _____, we should exercise our body.

4. My friend Richard has a nice personality. _____, he is very well-informed.

5. The car won't run without gas. _____, the body won't function without food.

6. Mary has many strange habits. _____, she sleeps during the day and works at night.

7. His performance did not reach the required standard. _____, he failed.

8. Jane doesn't know much about politics. _____, she doesn't care.

9. The naughty boy fell from a tree. _____, he was unhurt.

10. The team practiced a lot before the game. _____, it won the tournament.

(A) As a result	(B) Luckily	(C) Frankly speaking	(D) In other words
(E) For example	(F) Similarly	(G) What is more	(H) Equally important
(I) Another	(J) In fact		

II. 將文中的轉承語畫底線。

Helping Poor Students

If I won two million dollars in the lottery, I would help university students from poor families. First, I believe that students who are from poor families yet who managed to pass the highly competitive university entrance examination usually have great academic potential. Second, they have demonstrated the capacity to overcome difficulties caused by their poverty. If they are given a chance, they tend to cherish it and are more likely to do well academically.

The third reason for helping students from poor families is that my assistance will indirectly help the family they are from. They may have siblings who are struggling to get a good education. When they are helped, they are no longer a burden to their family and their siblings will have a better chance.

To sum up, if I won two million dollars in the lottery, I would help university students from poor families.

（參考解答請見附錄Ⅰ）

⑫ 英文作文保持連貫的方法

連貫是評分標準的要求。英文作文保持連貫的方法有：

(1) 使用代名詞：

在後句中使用代名詞，而以前句的單字、名詞、事實或概念為先行詞。

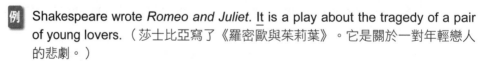 Shakespeare wrote *Romeo and Juliet*. It is a play about the tragedy of a pair of young lovers. （莎士比亞寫了《羅密歐與茱莉葉》。它是關於一對年輕戀人的悲劇。）

 "It" 指的是前句的 *Romeo and Juliet*。

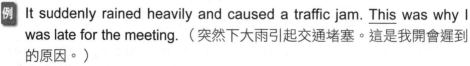 It suddenly rained heavily and caused a traffic jam. This was why I was late for the meeting. （突然下大雨引起交通堵塞。這是我開會遲到的原因。）

 "This" 指的是前句 "It suddenly rained heavily and caused a traffic jam." 的事實。

(2) 重複前句的單字、名詞、事實或概念。

 There was an accident on the road. <u>The accident</u> was caused by drunk driving and it killed five people. （路上有車禍。這場車禍肇因於酒醉開車，奪走了5條人命。）

説明　後句重複了前句的單字 "accident"。

(3) 前後句使用相同句型或平行結構。

 What kind of person is he? Once his mind is made up, <u>there is no one that can change his mind. There is nothing that can prevent him from fulfilling his wish.</u> （他為人如何？一旦他下定決心，沒人可以改變他的心意。沒人可以阻止他實現他的願望。）

説明　畫底線的部分為平行結構。

(4) 後句解釋前句的意涵。

 As students, our time is almost fully occupied. <u>We go to school during the day, and we do homework at night.</u> （做為學生，我們的時間全被佔滿了。我們白天上學，晚上做功課。）

説明　後句解釋前句「時間全被佔滿」的意涵。

(5) 後句舉證說明前句的觀點。

 People tend to believe that superstition is linked to ignorance, but this is not entirely true. <u>Many brilliant people have been superstitious.</u> （人們總是相信迷信與無知有關，但事情並不全然如此。很多有學問的人一直都是很迷信的。）

説明　後句舉證説明前句的觀點「事情並不全然如此」。

(6) 使用轉承語（transitional words）。

 Many people who achieved great things were superstitious. <u>For example</u>, Napoleon was afraid of cats." （許多有大成就的人都很迷信。例如，拿破崙怕貓。）

説明　兩句之間使用轉承語 "for example" 保持連貫。

練習 4

I. 利用保持連貫的方法，選出正確答案。

People tend to believe that superstition is linked to ignorance, but this is not entirely true. ___(1)___ Rousseau, a famous French philosopher, believed he had a ghost for a companion.

Superstitions usually arise when people try to find reasons for things that are beyond their comprehension. ___(2)___ People looked and wondered at the sky, then developed wonderful stories to explain the various clusters of stars.

___(3)___ A panic shook Europe when Halley's comet was expected to appear in 1910. ___(4)___ In 66 A.D., for example, its appearance coincided with the fall of Jerusalem. ___(5)___ They were so frightened that they even bought anti-comet pills and masks to protect themselves from deadly fumes.

(A) So the people of the twentieth century feared another catastrophe.

(B) It seemed that whenever this comet had appeared in the past, devastating events had taken place.

(C) Many brilliant people have been superstitious.

(D) Primitive societies created all kinds of fantastic explanations for illness, death, and natural events.

(E) Even the age of science has not destroyed people's beliefs in irrational things.

II. 閱讀以下作文後，調整句子的順序，並適度加轉承語，使其有較好的連貫。

Learning to Ride a Bike

Although learning to ride a bike was difficult for me, I didn't give up. At fifteen I learned how to ride a bike. I remember that it was a sunny day and it was a holiday. I took my new bike to the park near my home to learn to ride it. I frequently ran into a tree or I had to jump off my bike to stop it. I forgot I could use the brakes to stop the bike. I tried again and again. I often fell and got hurt. Finally, I learned how to ride it.

（參考解答請見附錄 I）

⑬ 英文作文的一致性 (unity)

英文作文的敘事觀點與內容必須一致。不論敘事觀點為第一人稱（I, we, our 等）或第三人稱（he/she, they），前後應保持一致。主題要前後一致，一篇文章只能寫一個主題。

練習 5

閱讀以下一篇作文後，做若干改寫，使敘事觀點一致。

Why We Should Learn English

There are many reasons why we should learn English. We learn English first because school teaches it and because university entrance examinations require it. Second, English is an international language. Learn it well, and you will be able to use it when you travel to other countries.

Besides the above reasons, you should learn English because you can use it to get new information. You may even find a job that requires English. To sum up, we learn English because of school, examinations, traveling, information, and job requirements.

（參考解答請見附錄Ⅰ）

⑭ 用字

(1) 用字清新（fresh diction）

 My grandfather is still as healthy as an ox.
我祖父依然壯得像頭牛。

 說明　「壯得像頭牛」這個片語過度使用，不清新。

My grandfather is healthy; he runs five miles every week.
我祖父很健康，他每星期跑五英里。

 說明　用「每星期跑五英里」來形容健康狀況，用字清新。

(2) 精確（accuracy）

 The building is several stories in height.
這幢建築有數層樓高。（模糊）

The building is ten stories in height.
這幢建築有十層樓高。（精確）

The perfume smells <u>sweet</u>.

這種香水很香。（模糊）

The perfume has <u>the sweetness of a rose</u>.

這種香水有玫瑰花的香味。（精確）

(3) 合乎習慣用法（idiomatic）

例 John is <u>positive in life attitude</u>.（不合乎習慣用法）

John <u>takes a positive attitude toward life</u>.（得宜）

約翰的人生態度積極。

⑮ 體例（格式、標點符號、大小寫）

(1) 格式（format）

每一個段落開頭要縮格（indentation）（通常5個字母）。第二行之後的每一行左側要對齊，右側是否對齊比較無所謂。

正確的格式：

> **Xxxx Xxx Xxxxxx**（標題）
>
>   Xxx xxxx xxxx xxxx. Xxxxxx xxxxxxxx xxxxxx xxxxxx xxxx xxxx xxx. Xxxxx xxxx xxxxxx xxxxxx xxxxx xxxxx xxxxx xxxx xxxx xxxx xxxx xxxx xxx x xxxx xxxx.
>
>   Xxx xxxx xxxx xxxx. Xxxxxx xxxxxx xxxxxx xxxxxxx xxxx xxx xx xx. Xxxxx xxxx xxxxxx xxxxxx xxxxx xxxxx xxxxx xxxx xxxx xxxx xx xxx xxxx xxxxxx xxxx.

錯誤的格式（一）：沒有縮格

> **Xx Xxxxxx**
>
> Xxx xxxx xxxx xxxx. Xxxxxx xxxxxxxx xxxxxx xxxxxxx xxxxxx xxxxxxx xxx. Xxxxx xxxx xxxxxx xxxxxx xxxxx xxxxx xxxxx xxxxx xxxx xxxx xxxx xxx xx xx xxxx xxxx.
>
> Xxx xxxx xxxx xxxx. Xxxxxx xxxxxxxx xxxxx xxxxxxx xxx xx xxxx xxx xx xxx. Xxxxx xxxx xxxxxx xxxxxx xxxxx xxxxx xxxxx xxxxx xxxx xxxx xxx xxx xx xx xxxxxx xxxx.

錯誤的格式（二）：沒有縮格，左側沒有對齊

Xxx xxxx xxxx xxxx. Xxxxxx xxxxxxx xxxxxx xxxxxxx.

　　Xxxxx xxxx xxxxxx xxxxxx xxxxx xxxx xxxx xxxxx xxxx xxxx

xxxx xxxx.

Xxx xxxx xxxx xxxx. Xxxxxx xxxxxxx xxxxxx xxxxxxx.

　　Xxxxx xxxx xxxxxx xxxxxx xxxx xxxx xxxxx xxxx xxxxx xxxx xxxx

xxxx xxxx.

(2) 標點符號（punctuation）

標點符號等同於一個字母，必須和之前的單字靠在一起，而不可和單字分開太遠，或甚至不在同一行：

正確的位置：句點緊跟 impossible
To learn English well in a week is impossible.

不正確的位置：相隔太遠
To climb up Mt. Everest in a day is impossible　.

不正確的位置：上一行因擠不下而放到下一行
It is impossible for anyone to learn English well in just a week
, just as it is impossible for anyone to climb up Mt. Everest in
just a day.

註：雙引號的前半「"」和長劃（dash）「—」為例外。

(3) 大小寫

(3-1) 標題

式一：標題第一字、最後一個字的第一個字母大寫，實詞（名詞、代名詞、形容詞、副詞、動詞、感嘆詞）第一個字母大寫，其餘的字母小寫。不定詞符號 "to" 第一個字母大、小寫均可。虛字（連接詞、介詞）若四個字母以上，第一個字母大寫。

例 Music Is an Important Part of Our Life

式二：將每一字的頭一個字母大寫。

例 Music Is An Important Part Of Our Life

式三：將每一字的每一個字母大寫。

例 MUSIC IS AN IMPORTANT PART OF OUR LIFE

(3-2) 其他

作文中每一個句子的第一個字母都大寫。引句中的引文如為句子，句子的第一個字母也大寫。專有名詞的第一個字母大寫。此外，句尾字不要拆成二字，寫不下時將全字寫在下一行。

練習 6

用第一種文法的大小寫規定，重寫標題。

1. how to save electricity

2. my favorite season

3. why I love dogs

4. one thing I have learned in high school

5. an appointment with my dentist

6. an interesting incident

7. taking a positive attitude toward life

8. should we help our enemy?

9. incident on a walk

10. how to remain healthy throughout life

（參考解答請見附錄Ⅰ）

 如何寫出正確的英文句子

如何寫出正確的英文句子？這是學寫作文第一重要的功課。本章扼要地介紹重點。

1 英文句子的定義

含有主詞與動詞，且形成一個完整的敘述、命令、感嘆、疑問或祈願的一群字，叫做句子。

例 Most high school students wish to go to university. （敘述句）
大部分高中生希望上大學。

(You) Turn in your papers next week. （命令句）
（你們）下星期交報告。

What an interesting story (this is)! （感嘆句）
這故事多有趣呀！

Can you tell me how to write an English composition? （疑問句）
你能告訴我如何寫英文作文嗎？

May you be always happy! （祈願句）
願你經常快樂！

注意：從屬子句（名詞、形容詞、副詞子句等）亦含主詞與動詞，但不是完整句子。

2 英文句子的要素

正如英文作文有主題，英文句子有主詞。正如英文作文有細節來支持主題，英文句子則由動詞來敘述主詞。主詞與動詞是英文句子最核心的要素。英文句子的要素分別如下：

(1) 主詞：敘述、命令、感嘆、疑問、祈願的對象。任何東西都可當主詞。

(2) 動詞：表示主詞怎麼樣的字。

(3) 主詞補語：幫助動詞，補充說明主詞怎麼樣的字或字群。

(4) 動詞受詞（簡稱受詞）：動詞所表達的意義的對象、結果或內涵。分直接受詞與間接受詞。

(5) 受詞補語：幫助動詞，補充說明受詞怎麼樣的字或字群。

例 (1) Jane smiled.（動詞smiled表示Jane笑了。）

(2) Jane seemed happy.（補語happy補充說明主詞快樂。）

（註：Jane seemed表意不完整，類似seem的動詞如look, appear, sound 等，需要受詞補語。）

(3) Jane loves her little brother.（受詞her little brother是loves所表達的意義的 對象）

(4) Jane made her little brother a toy.（直接受詞a toy是動詞made所表達的意 義的結果）

(5) The teacher forgave Peter his wrongdoing.（直接受詞his wrongdoing是 動詞forgave所表達的意義的內涵。）

(6) Jane made her little brother happy.（受詞補語happy補充說明受詞快 樂。）

（註：Jane made her little brother表意不完整。）

練習 7

找出各句的句子要素：主詞、動詞、受詞（直接、間接）、主詞（受詞）補語，並 畫底線標明。

1. The story is interesting.

2. The story interests me.

3. After searching for two days, the policemen finally found the stolen money.

4. The policemen finally found the stolen money buried in the woods.

5. Jim made a toy for his younger brother.

6. Jane made Michael a good wife.

7. Jane made Michael a good husband.

8. What has happened?

9. You can't deny him his rights.

10. He bought his son a new pair of shoes.

11. You saved me a lot of trouble.

12. Please tell me how to use this computer.

13. Please spare me my life.

14. They called their daughter Jamie.

15. Whether ghosts exist or not remains controversial.

16. She put on her coat.

17. From five to seven is the rush hour.

18. He who persists will win the race.

19. Please tell us whether you will come or not.

20. The sight of a huge spider in the kitchen surprised me.

（參考解答請見附錄Ⅰ）

❸ 英文句子的完整性

　　英文句子結構必須完整。是否完整，可以從判斷它是否要素俱全來決定。任何
一個句子，必須有主詞和（現在式或過去式）動詞。是否含受詞或補語等要素，則
視動詞（所表達的意義）而定。

例 (1) Do ghosts exist? （動詞exist（存在）不需受詞或補語）

　　(2) The man seems knowledgeable. （動詞seems需要受詞補語knowledgeable）

(3) *Harry Potter* fascinates many people. （動詞fascinate需要受詞many people）

但一些不含主詞、動詞，但意思清楚的片語，例如 "Quite the opposite." 稱為合理片句，用在作文中可以接受。除合理片句之外，<u>英文作文的每一個句子必須完整</u>。

 "How to talk with foreigners?" 不完整

改正：

(1) Many people don't know <u>how to talk with foreigners</u>.

(2) <u>How to talk with foreigners</u> is easy to learn.

 "How to talk with foreigners" 是一個名詞片語，只是一個要素，在上例中作主詞或受詞，所以不完整。

練習 8

判別以下各句是否為可接受的完整句子。是的打（○），不是的打（X）。

1. （　　）Owning a car is expensive.
2. （　　）The best way to learn English.
3. （　　）Spring is the most pleasant season of the year.
4. （　　）Going to college requires much more self-reliance than going to high school.
5. （　　）When I discovered my mother wasn't home.
6. （　　）What a beautiful flower!
7. （　　）Quite the opposite.
8. （　　）How to change a trie.
9. （　　）Though he is very tired.
10. （　　）The man who is standing there.
11. （　　）That he is an honest man.
12. （　　）This way, please.
13. （　　）Why not?
14. （　　）Certainly!
15. （　　）So much for the first point.
16. （　　）Because he woke up late.
17. （　　）Since we don't like it.
18. （　　）Whether you like it or not.
19. （　　）How to spell this word?
20. （　　）What I mean.

21. (　　) He has two goals in life. <u>To graduate from college and to establish himself in business</u>.（畫底線的部分）

22. (　　) After a long hard day of classes and studying.

23. (　　) Stand up.

24. (　　) Hide.

25. (　　) Take my advice.

26. (　　) Don't go.

27. (　　) Now another advantage.

28. (　　) My friend John, who is going abroad soon.

29. (　　) I to play basketball tomorrow.

30. (　　) I swimming yesterday.

31. (　　) I written a letter.

32. (　　) May you succeed.

33. (　　) Getting up early can do many things.

34. (　　) He made his mother.

35. (　　) I found John a good man.

36. (　　) Good day, class.

37. (　　) So much for now, until the next time.

38. (　　) Can you tell me the best way to learn English?

39. (　　) But I don't agree.

40. (　　) And the movie is interesting.

（參考解答請見附錄Ⅰ）

④ 合句的寫法

4-1. 對等連接詞

利用對等連接詞 and, or, nor, so, yet, but, for 等合併兩個單句。合併後的句子稱為合句。

(1) and

① 當兩個句子的內容性質相同或屬於同類時，用 and 合併：

Reading exercises our imagination. Reading enriches our mind.

→ Reading exercises our imagination and (it) enriches our mind.

閱讀激發我們的想像力，豐富我們的心靈。

I am 18. I am happy.

→ I am 18 and I am happy.

我十八歲，我很快樂。

② 當兩個動作連續時，用 and 合併：

I got up. I got dressed.

→ I got up and (I) got dressed.

我起身後穿好衣服。

③ 當後句為前句的結果時，用 and 合併：

She took some medicine. She got sick.

→ She took some medicine and got sick.

她服（錯）了藥，結果病了。

④ 當兩個觀點有連續性時，用 and 合併：

The cure for bad teaching is good teachers. Good teachers cost money.

→ The cure for bad teaching is good teachers, and good teachers cost money.

好老師是不良教學的藥方，此外，好老師是要花錢的。

(2) or

① 兩個句子表示兩種選擇，用 or 合併：

You can stay home. You can go out.

→ You can stay home, or you can go out.

你可以留在家裡，或者你可以出去。

② 當兩句子有因果關係，前句表條件時，用 or 合併，做「否則；不然」解：

Finish your job. You won't be paid.

→ Finish your job, or you won't be paid.

完成你的工作，不然你領不到錢。

(3) but

① 前後兩句表示對照時，可用but連接：

Michael has lots of friends. John has only a few.

→ Michael has lots of friends, but John has only a few.

Michael 很有多朋友，但 John 只有少數幾個。

② 當說話者為即將要說的話表示歉意時，先致歉意，再用 but 引出要說的話。

I am sorry. This is none of your business.

→ I am sorry, but this is none of your business.

抱歉，但這不干你的事。

(4) yet

yet的用法可和 but 互通，但當「前句為普通事實，後句卻令人驚訝」
時，用 yet 合併。

John doesn't eat much. He weighs 120 kilos.

→ John doesn't eat much, yet he weighs 120 kilos.

John吃的不多，但體重卻有120公斤。

(5) so

① 前句為因，後句有可能為一種結果時，用so合併：

I had a headache. I went home early.

→ I had a headache, so I went home early.

我頭痛，所以早回家。

② 前句為後句的一種預防措施時，可用so合併。

I brought some food. I wouldn't feel hungry on the way.

→ I brought some food, so I wouldn't feel hungry on the way.

我買了一些食物，以免在路上會肚子餓。

(6) nor

① 如果前句的否定敘述，也適用於後句的主詞，可用nor合併：

His story isn't true. Your story isn't true.

→ His story isn't true, nor is yours.

他的話不真，你的也不真。

② 前句為否定敘述，後句的補充說明也是否定時，可用 nor 合併：

Cooking up a quick dish doesn't mean you have to sacrifice flavor.
Fast food does not have to be junk food.

→ Cooking up a quick dish doesn't mean you have to sacrifice flavor,
nor does fast food have to be junk food. (Cobuild)

快速做一道菜並不表示你必須犧牲口味，速食也不一定是垃圾食物。

(7) for

前句表示推測，後句解釋可能原因時，用 for 合併：

It must have rained. The street is wet.

→ It must have rained, for the street is wet.

一定是下雨了，因為街道是濕的。

4-2. 功用與對等連接詞類似的轉承語（adverbial conjunctions）

(1)   besides   此外

(2)   moreover   此外

(3)   furthermore   此外

(4)   likewise   同樣地

(5)   however   然而

(6)   nevertheless   然而

(7)   otherwise   否則

(8)   therefore   因此

(9)   accordingly   因此

(10) consequently   因此

 這十個轉承語是副詞，雖有轉承作用，但不是連接詞。所以轉承語之前必須用具有對等連接詞功用的分號「;」，後面用「,」。

 He failed; however, he didn't give up.
他失敗了；但他不放棄。

4-3. 功用與對等連接詞類似的片語

(1) in fact   事實上

(2) in addition   此外

(3) on the contrary   相反地

(4) on the other hand   另一方面

(5) in other words   換句話說

4-4. 分號

分號的功用與對等連接詞類似，用以連接關係密切的前後二句。

 My mother won't let me go alone; she is afraid I might get hurt.
家母不讓我一個人去；她怕我受傷。

練習 9

I. 請在下面各題空格中，填入適當的對等連接詞：

1. Water the seeds _____ they will grow.

2. Work hard _____ you will succeed.

3. Work harder _____ you will fail.

4. You can continue your education _____ you can find a job.

5. I don't like baseball, _____ do I like basketball.

6. John worked hard before the test, _____ he did well.

7. John worked hard before the exam, _____ he did poorly.

8. He must be sick, _____ he is absent.

9. He doesn't talk much, _____ he talked endlessly for two hours this morning.

10. Marie will not go to the party, _____ she hardly knows anybody.

II. 請利用提示的轉承語，將二個句子合成一句，如第1題所示。

1. I don't want to go. I am tired. (besides)

→ I don't want to go; besides, I am tired.

2. He finished his work in time. He did it well. (moreover)

_____

3. The house isn't big enough for us. It is too far from the town. (furthermore)

_____

4. You must pack plenty of food for the journey. You will need warm clothing. (likewise)

_____

5. He received the invitation. He did not go. (however)

_____

6. He is not very smart. We like him. (nevertheless)

_____

7. Study hard. You may fail the course. (otherwise)

_____

8. He was late for school. He was punished. (therefore)

_____

9. They have spent a lot of time learning English. Their English is very good. (accordingly)

_____

10. The rain was heavy. The streets were flooded. (consequently)

_____

III. 請利用提示的介詞片語，將二個句子合併成一句，如第1題所示。

1. He likes her very much. He has decided to marry her. (in fact)

   He likes her very much; in fact, he has decided to marry her.

2. He does not mind. He is very pleased. (in fact)

   _____

3. My math teacher is a good guy. He teaches in an interesting way. (in addition)

   _____

4. John tops his class academically. He is not proud. (in addition)

   _____

5. Our teacher didn't say he would give us a test. He said he would let us watch a video. (on the contrary)

   _____

6. Father did not let us go to the movies last Saturday. He ordered us to stay home and help with housework. (on the contrary)

   _____

7. It is not cold. It is hot. (on the contrary)

   _____

8. My father is very kind to us. He has a quick temper. (on the other hand)

   _____

9. Patriotism is required of all. We must love our country. (in other words)

   _____

IV. 請用「；」將下面的句子合成一句，如第1題所示。

1. Try this one. It looks like your color.

   Try this one; it looks like your color.

2. Your car is new. Mine is eight years old.

   _____

3. I don't feel well. I can't go with you.

_____

4. Flora watches TV all night. She always comes to class late.

_____

5. Peter is very kind. He is always helping others.

_____

V. 改正下面各句的錯誤。

1. Peter is a very lazy student, he is always late for class.

_____

2. Study hard, otherwise, you won't make it to university.

_____

3. I don't want to go to his party, I don't like him.

_____

4. Because it was raining so we stayed indoors.

_____

5. Though he likes her but he does not dare to tell her.

_____

（參考解答請見附錄Ⅰ）

5 複句的寫法 (1)：含名詞子句的複句

5-1. 用連接詞 "that"

任何一個敘述句之前，加上 "that"，就變成名詞子句。名詞子句常作主詞或受詞。

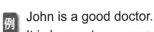 John is a good doctor.
It is known to everyone in town.

→ That John is a good doctor is known to everyone in town.
約翰是好醫生城裡的人都知道。

Students are afraid.

The university entrance examination is highly competitive.
→ Students are afraid that the university entrance examination is highly competitive.
學生害怕大學入學考試競爭激烈。

有時為使名詞子句做為主詞的結構更清楚，可在子句前加一個同位語：

The news that our baseball team had won third place in the World Cup surprised us.
我們棒球隊贏得世界杯季軍的消息讓我們感到驚訝。

The fact that I am fully occupied gives me little time for entertainment.
我的時間都排滿了的事實使我幾乎沒空娛樂。

The idea that one can succeed by working hard is not always true.
人可以經由努力而成功的主張並不總是對的。

名詞子句也可充當補語：

The truth is that nobody likes to be cheated.（畫底線的部分為補語。）

5-2. 用連接詞 "whether"

例 We may succeed on the examination. We may not succeed on the examination. It depends on how hard we work.
→ Whether we will succeed on the examination or not depends on how hard we work.
我們是否會通過考試，要看我們有多用功。

作受詞時， "whether" 和 "if" 意思相同：

I wonder **whether / if** my father will let me drive his car.
我想知道我爸會不會讓我開他的車。

5-3. 用兼有連接詞功用的疑問詞

1. It remains unknown.
   Who will be elected President.
   → **Who** will be elected President remains unknown.
   誰會當選總統仍然不知道。

2. **What** we need is a strong security force.
   我們需要的是堅強的防衛力量。

3. **When** the work will be finished is our concern.
   工作將於何時完成是我們所關切的事。

4. **Where** the kidnapper is hiding the child is what the police want to find out.
   綁匪把小孩藏在那裡是警方想知道的。

5. **Which** of the three goddesses was the most beautiful was for Paris to decide.

這三個女神哪一個最漂亮是巴利斯要決定的。

6. **How** he solved the puzzle is a secret.
他如何解謎是一項祕密。

7. He didn't tell us **why** he wanted to marry her.
他沒告訴我們他為什麼要娶她。

名詞子句有時會改變位置，原位則用 虛詞 "it" 替代：

1. **It** is true that we need a strong army.
我們需要一支堅強的軍隊是真的。

2. We believe **it** true that the earth is round.
我們相信地球是圓的是真的。

練習10

I. 在空格中填入適當的字。

1. It is not known _____ many people will come to the party.
2. The police are investigating _____ killed the girl.
3. It is true _____ the young man has been married four times.
4. _____ I will buy a car or not depends on _____ I have enough cash left.
5. _____ the criminal is hiding puzzles the police.

II. 運用名詞子句，將各句譯成英文。

1. 我不知道我是否能上大學。

_____

2. 但我知道我必須用功讀書。

_____

3. 我爸爸說我今年是不是能上大學無所謂。

_____

4. 可是我知道他希望我能通過考試。

_____

5. 我了解我該先做什麼。

_____

（參考解答請見附錄Ⅰ）

⑥ 複句的寫法 (2)：含形容詞子句的複句

含形容詞子句的複句由兩組句子結構結合而成。以下利用相加的方法說明形容詞子句寫法：

① 找出二句中相同的元素：單字、片語或子句。

② 決定哪一句要當作從屬的形容詞子句，哪一句要當主要子句。

③ 將形容詞子句與主要子句中相同的元素變成關係詞，如果相同的元素是「人」，則用 "who" 或 "that"，否則用 "which" 或 "that"，並考慮格（主格、受格、所有格）的問題。

④ 將關係詞置於形容詞子句開頭，使之引領形容詞子句。

⑤ 將關係詞引領的形容詞子句放入主要子句中相同元素的後面。

⑥ 適當調整新句中修飾語的位置，使之儘量靠近被修飾的字。

⑦ 若相同元素為子句、片語、地名、人名、形容詞或副詞時，關係詞前需加逗點。

例1 需要決定主從的情況：

(1) The pretty girl was dancing with a student.

(2) The student had a slight limp.

(A) 若句子主要敘述「girl」，則二句合併如下：

(1) + (2) → The pretty girl was dancing with a student who had a slight limp.

(B) 若句子主要敘述「student」，則二句合併如下：

(1) + (2) → The student who the pretty girl was dancing with had a slight limp.

例2 相同元素有格的問題：

(1) The mountain is very beautiful.

(2) Its top of the mountain is covered with snow.

(1) + (2) → The mountain whose top is covered with snow is very beautiful.

　　或　　→ The mountain of which the top is covered with snow is very beautiful.

例3 相同元素為片語：

(1) He wishes to learn English well in a month.

(2) To learn English well in a month is impossible.

(1) + (2) → He wishes to learn English well in a month, which is impossible.

例4 相同元素為子句：

(1) He said that he loved her.

(2) That he loved her was true.

(1) + (2) → He said that he loved her, which was true.

例5 相同元素為地名：

(1) He lives in Taichung.

(2) Taichung is located in central Taiwan.

(1) + (2) → He lives in Taichung, <u>which is located in central Taiwan</u>.

例6 相同元素為形容詞：

(1) He was kind.

(2) His brother never was kind.

(1) + (2) →He was kind, <u>which his brother never was</u>.

例7 比較複雜的情況：

(1) Richard knocked the vase to the floor.

(2) He did so carelessly.

(3) The vase was his mother's.

(4) She kept it on the top of her dresser.

(1) + (2) + (3) + (4) 並強調修飾語位置後得到：

Richard carelessly knocked to the floor his mother's vase which she kept on the top of her dresser.

例8 關係代名詞與關係副詞互換的情形：

(1) This is the house.

(2) He lives in the house.

(1) + (2) → This is the house which he lives in.

　　　　　→ This is the house in which he lives.

　　　　　→ This is the house where he lives.

例9 複合關係代名詞

關係代名詞的先行詞如為 something, the thing，可將之省略，改用 what 代 something that/which：

I will give you something. You want something.

→ I will give you what you want.

This is the thing. I want the thing.

→ This is what I want.

例10 關係代名詞的先行詞如有 any，則用-ever:

I will give you anything. You want anything.

→ I will give you whatever you want.

疑問句為例外：

Is there anything that you want?

例11 複合關係副詞：

You can come at any time. You want to come at any time.

→ You can come whenever you want.

練習11

I. 利用關係詞，將下面各題的句子合併。

1. The building has no elevator. I live in this building.

_____

2. Romeo and Juliet were two lovers. Their parents hated each other.

_____

3. There is a dictionary in my room. The dictionary was a gift from my sister.

_____

4. I was sitting in a chair. It suddenly collapsed.

_____

5. The party will take place on Saturday. More people can come on Saturday.

_____

6. Mr. Smith said he was too busy to speak to me. I had come especially to see him.

_____

7. His girlfriend turned out to be an enemy spy. He trusted her absolutely.

_____

8. This is the story of a man. His wife suddenly loses her memory.

_____

9. We'll have to memorize a lot of words. This will be difficult.

_____

10. The car crashed into a queue of people. Four of them were killed.

_____

11. I was waiting for a man. He didn't turn up. (The man...)

_____

12. I saw several houses. Most of them were quite unsuitable.

_____

13. Mr. Smith works in an office. This is the office.

_____

14. John did it by some means. He didn't tell us about the means.

_____

15. Saturday afternoon I will be free. You can call at that time.

_____

16. There are no students. The students do not have to take tests. (that... not = but)

_____

17. I lost a watch. This is the same watch. (as)

_____

18. The contest will be held on Sunday. More people can participate on that day.

_____

19. You sent me a gift. Thank you very much for it.

_____

20. I like to draw pictures of people. I meet the people.

_____

II. 儘量利用形容詞子句，將下列各句譯成英文。

 1. 我爸爸常說，從經驗中獲得的教訓很有用。

_____

 2. 例如，他告訴我們，不可以相信在面前稱讚你的人。

_____

 3. 這是我聽過的最有用的忠告。

_____

 4. 上個星期天，當爸媽忙著招待他們一年來一次的客人時，我去看了一場電影。

_____

5. 這部電影是關於一個有名的作家，被一個崇拜他的人劫持的故事。

（參考解答請見附錄Ⅰ）

7 複句的寫法 (3)：含副詞子句的複句

7-1. 利用表時間的連接詞

(1) 用連接詞 "when"

例 Dick was 15 years old.

An interesting thing happened to him then.

→ When Dick was 15 years old, an interesting thing happened to him.
狄克 15歲時，發生了一件有趣的事。

(2) 用其他表時間的連接詞

1. after, before 在～之後（前）

I will go to university after I finish high school.
高中畢業之後我將上大學。

You have to get a visa before you go abroad.
出國前你得先獲得簽証。

2. as soon as, the moment 一～就

I will let you know as soon as/the moment I find out the answer.
我一找到答案立刻就通知你。

3. next time 下一次

I will show you more places next time you are in Taiwan.
下次你來臺北，我帶你看更多地方。

7-2. 利用表地方的連接詞

例 He goes to places.

She goes to the same places.

→ She goes where he goes.
他去那裡，她就去那裡。

7-3. 利用表原因的連接詞

(1) 用連接詞 "**because, since**"

例 You did not apply.

We can not give you admission.

→ <u>Because</u> / <u>Since</u> you did not apply, we can not give you admission.
（因為你沒申請，我們不能給你入學許可。）

(2) 用連接詞 "**now that**"

例 Mike has arrived.

We can begin the lesson.

→ <u>Now that</u> Mike has arrived, we can begin the lesson.
既然麥克已經到了，我們可以開始上課了。

7-4. 利用表條件的連接詞

(1) 用連接詞 "**if**"

例 I pass the university entrance examination and go to a good university.

My father will buy me a motorcycle.

→ <u>If</u> I pass the university entrance examination and go to a good university, my father will buy me a motorcycle.
假如我通過大學入學考試而進入好大學，我爸爸將買一部摩托車給我。

(2) 用連接詞 "**unless**"

例 The shy boy will not speak to others.

He is spoken to first.

→ The shy boy will not speak to others <u>unless</u> he is spoken to first.
除非別人先開口，這個害羞的男孩不會和別人說話。

(3) 用連接詞 "**so long as, as long as**"

例 We can watch TV.

Watching TV does not affect our studies.

→ We can watch TV <u>so long as</u> / <u>as long as</u> it does not affect our studies.
只要不影響我們的功課，我們可以看電視。

(4) 用連接詞 "**in case**"

例 Mother said that we could order some pizza.
She came home late.

→ Mother said that <u>in case</u> she came home late, we could order some pizza.
媽媽説萬一她回家晚了，我們可以叫比薩。

7-5. 利用表讓步的連接詞

(1) 用連接詞 "**though, although**"

例 It was raining. The students continued playing basketball.

→ <u>Though</u> it was raining, the students continued playing basketball.
雖然下著雨，學生們繼續打籃球。

(2) 用連接詞 "**even if**"

例 A soldier should not betray his country. His life is in danger.

→ <u>Even if</u> his life is in danger, a soldier should not betray his country.
即使生命有危險，軍人不該背叛國家。

7-6. 利用表目的的連接詞

(1) 用連接詞 "**so that, in order that**"

例 John's parents work long hours. They can buy a new apartment.

→ John's parents work long hours, <u>so that</u> they can buy a new apartment.
約翰的父母每天工作很久，以便他們可以買新公寓。

(2) 用連接詞 "**for fear that**"

例 We feared we might be late. We started early.

→ We started early <u>for fear that</u> we might be late.
我們害怕遲到，很早出發。

7-7. 利用表結果的連接詞

(1) 用連接詞 "**so... that**"

例 The sight of the snake caused her much fear.
She fainted.

→ The sight of the snake caused her <u>so</u> much fear <u>that</u> she fainted.
她看見蛇害怕得暈過去了。

(2) 用連接詞 "**such... tha**t"

> 例 The question was a very easy one. Everyone got it right.
>
> → The question was <u>such</u> an easy one <u>that</u> everyone got it right.
> 題目如此簡單,大家都答對了。

7-8. 利用表比較的連接詞

(1) 用連接詞 "**than**"

> 例 There are 40 students in my class.
> There are 35 students in your class.
>
> → My class has more students <u>than</u> your class do.
> 我班上學生人數比你班上人數多。

(2) 用連接詞 "**the... the**"

> 例 You work harder. You accomplish more.
>
> → <u>The</u> harder you work, <u>the</u> more you accomplish.
> 你工作越賣力,你成就越多。

7-9. 利用表樣態的連接詞

用連接詞 "**as**"

> 例 You do it in this way.
> I do it in this way.
>
> → You do it <u>as</u> I do.
> 你照我的方式做。

練習12

將各句中文譯成英文。

1. 我十歲時,第一次參加演講比賽。

_____

2. 輪到我演講時,我慢慢地走到前方。

_____

3. 但是,等到我走到前方時,我突然想不起任何要說的內容。

_____

4. 我只好儘快走下臺。

_____

5. 奇怪的是，一旦回到座位上，我又想起了要說的內容。

___

6. 夫妻之間到底是誰帶頭呢？

___

7. 有人說，先生走到那，太太就跟到那。

___

8. 也有人說，太太走到那，先生就跟到那。

___

9. 就我而論，不論到什麼地方，夫妻都得同意才行。

___

10. 我們通常都照教練說的話去做。

___

11. 有一天，他看起來就像撞了鬼似的。

___

12. 當他叫我們跑一萬公尺時，我們都跑回家了。

___

13. 我爸爸說，如果在大學時像在高中時一樣用功，我們可以在學業上有了不起的成就。

___

14. 此外，我們的成就愈大，動機就愈強。

___

15. 因此，我決定上大學會盡可能用功讀書。

___

16. 做為學生，應該多讀書。這並不是因為別人的要求，而是因為讀書對我們有益。

___

17. 當我們讀書，我們獲得知識，而知識就是力量。

___

18. 既然明白這個道理，就該去實踐它。

___

19. 我哥哥買了一部車，以節省通勤所需的時間。

___

20. 他很小心開他的新車，因恐出意外。

___

21. 我的同學 John 人很好，大家都喜歡他。（such... that）

_____

22. 昨天上課時，他累的睡著了。（so... that）

_____

23. 假如我樂透中200萬，我要幫助我的爸爸。

_____

24. 除非下工夫學習，不可能學好任何事情。

_____

25. 只要活著，就有希望。

_____

26. 萬一下雨，我們怎麼辦？

_____

27. 倘若你能在二個星期內還給我，我就把書借給你。（provided that）

_____

28. 不論我們喜歡或不喜歡，我們都得學英文。

_____

29. 即使生病，我也要設法學點東西。

_____

30. 不論年齡多大，我們都不該停止學習。

_____

（參考解答請見附錄Ⅰ）

⑧ 其他應注意事項

8-1. 句子必須有一致性（統一性）

My good friend John is a good student, and he has a nice car.（不一致）

Having a nice car 與 being a good student 無關，不宜放在同一句中。

My good friend John is a good student, and he is not proud.（一致）

Being a good student 與 being not proud 講的都是人品，內容一致，可放在同一句中。

8-2. 句子要有長短變化

Mike is sick. Mike is weak. He cannot walk. I am sure of this.

 都是短句，沒變化。

→ Mike is sick. I am sure he is too weak to walk.

麥克病了。我確定他太虛弱，無法走路。

 把後三句合併，使有長短之變化。

8-3. 文法不要有錯

There is a strange disease suddenly break out in Asia called SARS.

 文法有錯。

→ A strange disease called SARS suddenly broke out in Asia.

 ① 文法無誤。
② 句子的主要結構為「主詞＋動詞」。原句的結構不清楚。修正後改正了這個缺點。

 第三章 **輕鬆學會英文作文**

最近幾年，寒假舉行的學科能力測驗的英文作文都出看圖寫作的題型。這種題型 81 年就已確定，因為等到 93 年才首度出現，因此大家就感覺比較陌生。我們在第三章一開始，先說明看圖寫作，助大家輕鬆了解看圖寫作的要領。其他的題型將輪流出現。

Unit 1 An Embarrassing Incident

題型：看圖作文

1. 試題

 說明
1. 依提示在「答案卷」上寫一篇英文作文。
2. 文長 120 個單詞 (words) 左右。

 提示
請根據以下三張連環圖畫的內容，以 "One evening,..." 開頭，寫一篇文章，描述圖中主角所經歷的事件，並提供合理的解釋與結局。

2. 擬寫內容

難為情的事件

　　一天傍晚，一件難為情的事發生在約翰身上。約翰去餐廳參加喜宴，在那裡他遇到一位老朋友。在喜見老友之時，約翰向他訴說了自己的不快樂；因為新娘以前是他的女朋友。他非常痛苦，喝了很多酒。

　　到了該回家的時候，他出了餐廳想攔計程車，卻攔下一部警車。因為他太醉了，無法告訴車裡的警察他要去那裡，就被載到警局去了。

　　第二天早上約翰醒過來之後，被警察勸戒。在了解所發生的事情之後，他感到很難為情。他決定儘快忘掉過去，也不再喝那麼多酒了。

3. 參考範文

An Embarrassing Incident

One evening, **something embarrassing happened to John**.[1] John went to a wedding feast **taking place**[2] in a restaurant, and there he met an old friend. He was very happy to see the old friend and told him how unhappy he was because the bride had previously been his girlfriend. He was so miserable that he drank a lot of wine.

When it was time for John to go home,[3] he left the restaurant and tried to stop a taxi. However, **he stopped a police car instead.**[4] **Being too drunk to tell the policemen**[5] in the car where he wanted to go, he was taken to a police station.

When John finally **came to**[6] the next morning, he was reprimanded by a policeman. After he realized what had happened, he felt very embarrassed. He decided to forget about his past and to drink less in the future.

4. 寫作指導

(1) 看圖作文需要想像力,將圖片內容作合理的解釋與結局。

(2) 這個題目的圖片須寫成敘述文 (narration),上文對敘述文的五個要素 where (at the restaurant and the police station), when (one evening), why (why he got drunk and ended up at the police station), how (John was taken to the police station) and what (happened to John) 等都有清楚的交代。

(3) 為方便敘述,可為圖中的主要人物取個名字。本題主要人物取名 "John"。

(4) 圖片上提供的資料要設法用在作文中,以使作文更為切題。例如圖一中有囍字,圖二有計程車、警車、以及主角酒醉樣子,圖三有警察局、時鐘、以及表示驚訝與不解的「!?」符號等,都可應用到作文中。

(5) 開頭用第一章所述敘述文開頭的方法:對過去的事件做一個總的回憶或評論。

(6) 結尾説 He decided to forget about his past and to drink less in the future.,提出事件對主角的教訓 (moral)。

(7) 以上是一個好的敘述文例子。

5. 重要的字詞及文法提示

(1) something embarrassing happened to John

有一件難為情的事發生在 John 身上。事發生在人身上：事 happen to 人

例 an accident happened to Mary

something unlucky happened to Mike

something unexpected happened to Richard

(2) taking place 發生，舉行

take place = hold 但用法不同

take place 用主動，主詞是「事情」：

例 The meeting will take place in July.

Our class reunion will take place in August.

hold 主動、被動都可以：

例 We will hold the meeting in July.

The meeting will be held in July.

(3) when it was time for John to go home

when it was time for N. / for sb. to V. 到了～的時候

例 when it was time for the test to be given

when it was time for the crops to be harvested

變化結構：

The time for us to take the exam has come.

(4) he stopped a police car instead

這句話等於

He did not stop a taxi. He stopped a police car instead.

前句省略了，但意思仍清楚。

(5) Being too drunk to tell the policemen

這個分詞結構表示原因，原結構是：

Because he was too drunk to tell the policemen，省去副詞子句的連接詞和主詞，並將動詞 was 改成現在分詞 being。

副詞子句、形容詞子句，和用 and 連接的對等子句，在意思明確時，大多可以省去子句的連接詞和主詞，並將動詞改成現在分詞。

(6) came to

指的是昏過去或酒醉之後醒過來。

例 The man fainted, but he soon came to after first aid.

6. 造句練習：將各句譯成英文。

(1) 今天早上一件奇怪的事發生在我身上。

(2) 我沒穿校服，卻穿便服上學。

(3) 但是，我班上的同學好像沒有注意到我沒穿校服。

(4) 到了放學回家的時候，校車司機不讓我上車。

(5) 幸好有警車經過，我把警車攔了下來。

(6) 好心的警察帶我回到家裡。

(7) 這件有趣的事原來是一場夢。

（參考解答請見附錄 II）

7. 實力培養

An Embarrassing Incident

One evening, something embarrassing happened to John. John went to a wedding feast _____, and there he met an old friend. He was very happy to see the old friend and told him _____ because the bride had previously been his girlfriend. He was so _____ he drank a lot of wine.

When _____, he went out of the restaurant and tried to stop a taxi. However, he _____. Being too drunk to tell the policemen in the car _____, he was taken to a police station.

When John finally _____ the next morning, he was reprimanded by a policeman. After he realized what had happened, he felt very embarrassed. He decided to _____ and to drink less in the future.

8. 輕鬆寫作

提示

請根據以上三張連環圖畫的內容，用你自己的版本，以 "One evening, ..." 開頭，寫一篇文章，描述圖中主角所經歷的事件，並提供合理的解釋與結局。

參考資料：

圖一

(1) a wedding banquet/feast

(2) a lot of people

(3) drinking

(4) a restaurant

圖二

(1) late at night

(2) stars and the moon

(3) the hero trying to stop a taxi

(4) a police car patrolling by

圖三

(1) eight o'clock the next morning

(2) the police station

(3) the hero came to

(4) a policeman reprimanding him

(5) The hero had no idea what had been going on.

Unit 2 Curiosity

題型：主題寫作

1. 試題

說明 請以 "Curiosity" 為主題，寫一篇英文作文，說明你對什麼事感到好奇。文長至少 120 字，最多不超過 170 字。

2. 擬寫內容

好奇心

我對很多事情都感到好奇。例如，我對異性永遠感到好奇。我想多了解他們一點：他們喜歡些什麼？他們為什麼是這個樣子？還有，最重要的是，如何與他們相處？所以我看很多書，希望能找到答案。看小說或戲劇的時候，我也會對它們的結局感到好奇。例如莎士比亞的《奧塞羅》中，大壞蛋伊亞格的下場會如何？我很高興最後正義得到伸張。

目前我對我的未來感到好奇。我能通過大學入學考嗎？我將上哪所大學？我的主修科目會是什麼？這些就是我感到好奇的一些事。我希望能很快得到所有的答案。

3. 參考範文

Curiosity

I am curious about many things. For example, I am forever curious about the opposite sex. I want to know more about them: **what they like**,[1] why they are the way they are and, **above all**,[2] how to get along with them. So I read books, **hoping to find out.**[3] I am also curious what the ending will be when I read a novel or a play. For example, what will happen to Iago, the villain in Shakespeare's *Othello*? **At the end**,[4] **I am glad that**[5] justice is done.

Right now I am curious about my future. Will I pass the university entrance exam? Which university will I be going to? What will my major be? These are a few things that I am curious about. I hope I will soon have all the answers.

4. 寫作指導

第一段：第一句是 topic sentence。之後舉例鋪陳。

第二段：第一句是 topic sentence。之後舉例鋪陳。最後用自答作結。

5. 重要的字詞及文法提示

(1) what they like

「疑問詞 S V」的構造是名詞子句，其主詞與動詞順序沒有變動。本文中類似的結構有：

why <u>they</u> <u>are</u> the way they are
　　　S　　V

what <u>the ending</u> <u>will be</u>
　　　　S　　　　V

what <u>will happen</u> to Iago
　S　　V

這種名詞子句可以當 (a) 主詞 (b) 受詞 (c) 補語。

例 (a) What you eat has a great effect on you.

(b) List on the paper what you eat for breakfast.

(c) The topic of this article is what we should eat.

(2) above all

above all（最重要的是）是一個轉承詞。

例 Living in the countryside, you can breathe fresh air, see beautiful scenery, and, above all, live at a slower pace.

(3) hoping to find out

這個分詞結構是由 and hope to find out 簡化而來。表示和主要動詞同時發生或進行的動作。

例 John would sit by the window, waiting for his son to come back.

(4) At the end

這是 at the end of the play 簡化來的。at the end 是指在某事物的結尾，in the end 的意思是 finally（最後），後面不可以有 of 片語修飾。

例 What will be left to you at the end of life?

She kept thinking, and in the end, she came up with a way to solve the problem.

(5) I am glad that

I am glad/surprised/happy/etc. + that 子句

I am glad that you are here.

I am surprised that Jane passed the exam.

6. 造句練習：將各句譯成英文。

(1) 閱讀有很多好處。最重要的是，它可以增廣我們的見聞。

(2) 你捐多少錢並不重要，重要的是心意。

(3) 這個小女孩對於她會得到什麼耶誕禮物感到很好奇。

(4) 電影最後，所有飛機上的乘客都被救了。

(5) 我們想知道的，是我們何時會用光自然資源。

（參考解答請見附錄 II）

7. 實力培養

Curiosity

I _____ many things. For example, I am forever curious about the opposite sex. I want to know more about them: _____, why they are _____ and, above all, _____. So I read books, _____ _____. I am also curious what the ending will be when I read a novel or a play. For example, what will happen to Iago, the villain in Shakespeare's *Othello*? At the end, I am glad _____.

Right now I am curious about my future. Will I pass _____ _____? Which university will I be going to? _____? These are a few things that I am curious about. I hope I will soon have all the answers.

8. 輕鬆寫作

 照本單元的命題，另寫一篇作文，舉出二至三個你所感到好奇的事物，並說明好奇的理由。可參考以下的資料：

Things that you may be curious about:

(1) Who will be your Mr. Right/spouse/ sweetheart?

(2) How long can you live?

(3) Will you have a successful career?

(4) Who will be the next President?

(5) Will Taiwan become independent?

(6) How many children will you have?

(7) What kind of job will you do?

(8) Will you become wealthy?

Unit 3 | What I Care about the Most

題型：主題句寫作

1. 試題

以 "What I Care about the Most" 為主題，說明目前你很在意的一件事，在意的原因，以及你將如何促成這件事。以 I care about _____ the most. 為起始句，文長至少 120 字，最多不超過 170 字。

2. 擬寫內容

我最在意的事

　　我最在意我的未來。我的未來對我及所有愛我的人來說，都是最重要的。如果我有光明的未來，我的家人就不必擔心我。他們反而會以我為榮。反過來，我會回報他們的愛和撫養我長大的仁慈。我也能對那些愛我的人有所幫助。

　　為確保我能有個光明的未來，我善加利用每一天。我儘可能地學習。我好好地照顧自己。我保持樂觀的人生觀。這是確保我擁有一個光明未來的唯一方法。

　　當我持續努力用功的同時，我期盼著那一天的到來。

3. 參考範文

What I Care about the Most

　　I care about my future the most. My future is the most important thing to me and to all the people who love me. If I have a bright future, my family will not have to worry about me. Instead, they will be proud of me. I will be able to give them something **in return**[1] for their love and kindness in **bringing me up.**[2] I hope I can **be of help to**[3] those who love me.

　　To make sure I will have a bright future, I make good use of every day. I study as much as I can. I take good care of myself. I maintain an optimistic view of life. This is the only way to make sure that I will have a bright future.

　　While[4] I **keep working hard,**[5] I **look forward to**[6] the coming of that day.

第三章

4. 寫作指導

(1) 在意的事有很多可以寫，要説得有説服力不容易。因此，有選擇材料的必要。本文以在意我的未來為內容，並説明原因，是可行的選擇材料的方法。

(2) 第一、二段符合命題要求。第三段以盼望作結。

5. 重要的字詞及文法提示

(1) in return

in return（作為回報）是個副詞片語。

例 What should I give my parents in return?

如果要表示「作為對某事的回報」，可以用 in return for sth.

例 I helped him repair his car, and he brought me a bottle of wine in return for my assistance.

(2) bring sb. up

bring sb. up（養育某人）相當於 raise sb.。

例 Raising five children in the twenty-first century is no easy task.

(3) be of help to...

be of help to sb.（對某人有幫助）也可以説成 be helpful to sb.。help 前可加上 great 來表示「有很大的幫助」。

例 Listening to radio programs in English is of great help/very helpful to me.

(4) while

while（在⋯的同時）是個連接詞，後面接子句，表示當該事正進行時，另一事情也同時在進行。

例 While my father was cleaning the floor, my mother was doing the laundry.

While they remained silent, their boss kept on complaining about their poor performance.

(5) keep working hard

keep（繼續）之後要接動名詞，也可説 keep on V-ing。

例 Jenny kept (on) singing as though nobody else were present.

(6) look forward to

look forward to（期待）這動詞片語之後要接名詞、代名詞、或動名詞。

例 Everybody is looking forward to the Lunar New Year.

They looked forward to seeing Michael Jordan.

6. 造句練習：將各句譯成英文。

(1) 大部分的父母盡全力地將子女養育大，而且不要求任何東西作為回報。

(2) 學習聆聽！他人的勸告可能對你很有幫助。

(3) 她沒有氣餒，相反地，她繼續做研究。

(4) Susan 在做蛋糕時，孩子們在廚房裡玩。

(5) Ted 這次考得很好，所以他期盼著收到成績單。

（參考解答請見附錄 II）

7. 實力培養

What I Care About The Most

　　I care about my future the most. My future is the most important thing to me and to ＿＿＿＿＿＿＿＿＿＿＿＿＿＿＿＿. If I have a bright future, my family will not have to ＿＿＿＿＿＿＿＿＿＿. ＿＿＿＿＿＿＿＿＿＿, they will be proud of me. I will be able to ＿＿＿＿＿＿＿＿＿ their love and kindness ＿＿＿＿＿＿＿. I can also ＿＿＿＿＿＿＿ those who love me.

　　To make sure I will have a bright future, I make good use of every day. I study as much as I can. I take good care of myself. I maintain ＿＿＿ ＿＿＿＿＿＿＿＿＿. This is the only way to make sure that I will have a bright future.

　　While I keep working hard, I ＿＿＿＿＿＿＿＿＿＿＿ the coming of that day.

8. 輕鬆寫作

提示

照本單元的命題，另寫一篇作文，舉出二至三個你所關心的人或事物，並說明關心的理由。可參考以下的資料：

Things you may care about:

(1) whether you are good-looking or not

(2) whether your friends like you

(3) your family's financial situation

(4) your parents' health

(5) whether you will be successful in the future

Unit 4 **What to Live For**

題型：簡函寫作

1. 試題

 最近你交了一個外國筆友。在你們的通信中，你們談到很多事情。現在請你寫一封信給對方，告知他（她）你的人生為何而活。以 "Dear Friend," 開頭，日期7月2日，以 "Your Friend" 署名。文長至少 120 字，最多不超過 170 字。

2. 擬寫內容

七月二日

親愛的朋友：

　　在人生不同階段裡，我們會為了不同目標而活。在能獨立之前，我認為人生的主要目標是達到長輩的期望。父母期待我們接受良好的教育，老師期望我們達到學業上的要求。在此階段，我們很少會懷疑為何而活。

　　然而，在獨立自主了之後，有時我們可能會懷疑為何而活。工作時，我們的目標是對雇主忠心及完成我們的責任。結了婚，我們的目標是愛我們的配偶及養家庭。但是閒暇時我們的目標又是什麼呢？應該花更多時間和家人在一起嗎？或者去當志工？我們該為何而活？這是每一個人必須為自己做決定的灰色地帶。

　　你的意見如何呢？盼望很快得到你的回音。

你的朋友 敬上

3. 參考範文

July 2

Dear Friend,

　　We live for different objectives during different periods of our life. Before we become independent, I think **the main objective of our life is to**[1] **live up to**[2] our elders' expectations. Our parents expect us to receive a good education, and our teachers expect us to meet their requirements academically. During this period of time, few of us ever wonder what to live for.

When we work, our objective is to be faithful to our employer, and to fulfill our duties. When we get married, our objective is to love our spouse and to support our family. But what about our free time? Should we spend more time with our family? Or should we volunteer to do social work? What should we live for? This is **a gray area where**[3] everyone has to decide for himself/herself.

What do you think? I look forward to hearing from you soon.

Sincerely,

Your Friend

4. 寫作指導

(1) 為何而活題目較大，故分階段處理。

(2) 書信寫作要注意格式：

    (a) 日期要放在右上角第一行

    (b) 不論寫給誰，用 "Dear Mr. Last name, Dear First name," 稱呼

    (c) 姓或名後用逗點，商業書信才用 "："。

    (d) 簽名放右下角。上一行可用 "Sincerely," 或 "Sincerely yours,"

5. 重要的字詞及文法提示

(1) the main objective of our life is to...

不定詞 to V 可當作主詞補語使用，說明主詞。

例 His goal is to serve his country.

本文中有很多這種結構。

(2) live up to

live up to（符合）表示做到了被期待或應允的事。

例 He works hard to live up to his parents' expectations.

(3) a gray area where...

where 引導的關係子句用來修飾前面的地方名詞。where 是關係副詞，本文中的此句是從下面兩句話合併而成：

This is a gray area.

Everyone has to decide for himself/herself in that area.

→ where

→ This is a gray area where everyone has to decide for himself/herself.

6. 造句練習：將各句譯成英文。

(1) 這個研究的目的是要了解男女在使用圖書館上的不同處。

(2) 這裡的風景不如預期。

(3) 如何保護野生動物是一個熱門的議題。

(4) 這篇文章的主題是如何增進記憶力。

(5) 他們還未決定在哪裡設立孤兒院。

（參考解答請見附錄 II）

7. 實力培養

We live for different objectives during different periods of our life. Before we become independent, I think the main objective of our life is to _____. Our parents expect us to receive a good education, and our teachers expect us to _____ _____. During this period of time, few of us ever wonder _____.

When we work, our objective is to be faithful to our employer, and to fulfill our duties. When we get married, our objective is to _____ _____. But what should be our objective for our leisure? Should we _____? Or should we _____? What should we live for? This is a gray area _____ for himself/herself.

What do you think of my view? I look forward to _____ _____.

8. 輕鬆寫作

提示

以 "Achieving Objectives" 為題，寫一篇英文作文，說明你一年內想要達成什麼目標，以及想要達成目標的理由。文長 120 至 150 之間。

參考資料：

What you may wish to achieve in one year:

(1) to get into a good university—to pursue an advanced education, to meet young people of the same age and interest

(2) to save a certain amount of money—to start making money and save it for future needs, to get a taste what it is like to work for money

(3) to go steady with someone you like—to prepare to be a spouse, to learn how to get along with the opposite sex

Unit 5 | Choosing Friends

題型：主題寫作

1.試題

說明

以 "Choosing Friends" 為主題，寫一篇英文作文，說明擇友應注意的事項。文長至少 120 字，最多不超過 170 字。

2.擬寫內容

擇友

　　擇友時，我們應遵守一項原則。也就是說，務必要避免那些有惡習的人，例如偷竊、說謊、酗酒、和吸毒。由於朋友通常會分享共同的喜好，假如我們與這種人為友，我們可能會受引誘去做他們做的事，我們就可能變成小偷、騙子、酒鬼或毒蟲。結果，我們的一生就可能毀了。

　　反之，我們應該與有好嗜好的人為友，像閱讀或畫畫，並結交正經、努力工作的人士。如此一來，我們就可以和朋友共享美好的事物，我們也可以改善生活。

　　總之，朋友可以幫助我們，也可以毀了我們，因此，我們宜慎選朋友。

3.參考範文

Choosing Friends

　　In choosing friends, we should observe one principle. That is, **by all means**[1] avoid those who have bad habits, **such as**[2] stealing, lying, drinking, or drug using. Since friends often share things in common, if we make friends with such people, we may **be tempted into**[3] doing the same things that they do. We may **end up**[4] thieves, liars, alcoholics, or **drug addicts**.[5] **Consequently**,[6] our life may be ruined.

　　Instead, we should make friends with people who have good hobbies, like reading and painting, and those who are decent and hardworking. In this way, we will share good things with our friends, and we will be able to **better**[7] our lives.

　　To sum up, friends can **either** help us **or**[8] ruin us, so we should choose friends carefully.

第三章

4. 寫作指導

擇友事關每一個人，注意事項選一些容易説明的。In choosing friends, we should observe one principle.是主題句，第二句用換句話説再説一遍，整段是主題句的鋪陳。第二段説出交友正面的注意事項。第三段為結論。

5. 重要的字詞及文法提示

(1) by all means

by all means（無論如何）的 means 有「方法」的意思，這個片語字面上來看是「用盡所有方法」，也就是「無論如何」。

例 They intended to reach their destination by all means.

(2) such as

such as（像是）用在列舉事物當例子時。

例 They visited some European countries, such as France, Germany, and Austria.

(3) be tempted into

be tempted into（被慫恿去做）表示被鼓動或勸説去做某事，into 之後可接名詞或動名詞。

例 She was tempted into an extramarital affair.

Short of money, he was tempted into gambling.

(4) end up

end up（結果（成為））這片語表示達到某狀態、到達某處、或採取某行動。

例 Fooling around all day, he ended up a loser.（接名詞）

Not used to the harsh weather, many immigrants ended up dead.（接形容詞）

If you keep stealing, you'll end up in prison.（接地方副詞片語）

He had intended to please her, but ended up annoying her.（接動名詞）

(5) drug addict

drug addict（有毒癮者）中 addict 是指上了某種癮或沈迷於某事物的人。

例 cocaine addict 　　古柯鹼成癮者

　　Internet addict 　　上網成癮者

　　game addict 　　　打電動成癮者

若要表示「對…上了癮」可用 be addicted to N。

例 He was addicted to drugs and alcohol.

(6) consequently

consequently（結果，因此）這個字的用法和 as a result、therefore 同，通常可放（子）句首以連貫上下文。

例 His car broke down; consequently, he was late for the meeting.

(7) better

better（改善）是個動詞，可說成 improve。

例 The employer hopes to better the conditions of the workers.

(8) either... or...

either A or B（不是 A 就是 B，A 或 B）除了如上文中表示兩者中有一個是真的，還可表示有兩個或兩個以上的選擇性。A、B 是對等的結構。

例 You can take either French or Spanish as a foreign language to learn.

6. 造句練習：將各句譯成英文。

(1) 政府正致力於改善農民的生活情況。

(2) 我受了慫恿買下了那部昂貴的車。

(3) 一個沈迷於電視的人會漸漸失去創意。

(4) 無論如何戰爭應該被避免。

(5) 由於他整日在外遊蕩，所以落得一事無成的下場。

（參考解答請見附錄 II）

7. 實力培養

Choosing Friends

In choosing friends, we should observe one principle. _____, by all means avoid those who have bad habits, such as stealing, lying, drinking, or drug using. Since friends often _____, if we make friends with such people, we may _____ the same things that they do. We may _____ thieves, liars, _____, or drug addicts. _____, our life may be ruined.

_____, we should make friends with people who have good hobbies, like reading and painting, and those who are decent and hardworking. In this way, we will _____, and we will be able to _____.

To sum up, friends can either _____, so we should choose friends carefully.

8. 輕鬆寫作

以 "An Ideal Friend" 為題，寫一篇英文作文，第一段說明你心中的理想朋友應具備的條件是什麼，第二段舉一個你認識的好朋友，來驗證第一段的說法。

參考資料：

qualities of an ideal friend:

(1) is honest—lying affects friendship because liars are not sincere

(2) is unselfish—selfish people think only of themselves, they don't make good friends

(3) has something in common with you—either you have the same hobby or have the same goals, so that you enjoy doing things together

(4) is helpful—gives you a hand in times of need

第三章

Unit 6　The Cell Phone

題型：主題句寫作

1. 試題

說明

手機已經成為一項生活必須品。以 "The Cell Phone" 為主題，寫一篇英文作文，第一段說明手機流行的原因，第二段說明使用應注意的禮貌。以 "The Cell Phone has been popular for several reasons." 為開頭，文長至少 120 字，最多不超過 170 字。

2. 擬寫內容

行動電話

　　行動電話會流行有幾個原因。第一是它的便利性。我們能隨身攜帶此小型機器。因此，我們幾乎能在任何地方聯繫他人，而別人也能聯繫到我們。第二是它的多功能。除了傳統電話的功能以外，行動電話能用來傳送與接收訊息、瀏覽網路、查生字、玩遊戲，甚至拍照。第三點是它容易買到。行動電話不是奢侈品。幾乎每個人都買得起，人手一機。

　　當我們享受行動電話帶給我們方便的同時，也必須注意使用的禮節。例如，在戲院裡或會議進行中，必須關掉行動電話，或改為震動模式，以免鈴聲干擾到別人。

3. 參考範文

The Cell Phone

　　The cell phone is popular **for several reasons**.[1] The first is convenience. We can carry this tiny device around. **As a result**,[2] we can reach others and be reached almost anywhere. The second, it has multiple functions. **Besides the functions**[3] that traditional telephones have, the cell phone can be used to send and receive written messages, to surf the Internet, to **look up**[4] words, to play games, and even to take pictures. The third is availability. Cell phones are not a luxury. Almost everyone **can afford**[5] one and has one.

　　However,[6] while we enjoy the convenience cell phones bring us, we have to observe some etiquette. For example, we should turn our cell

> phones off or change it to vibration mode when we are in a theater or in a
> meeting, or the ringing will bother other people.

4. 寫作指導

(1) 命題有提示主題句,後文說明一些原因即可。至於使用的禮節,關掉行動電
話或改為震動模式的表達方法要學會。

(2) 注意寫作要領的把握:表達觀點之後,要有所鋪陳。

5. 重要的字詞及文法提示

(1) for several reasons

for several reasons(由於幾個理由)常用來引介出某事成立的原因。

> 例 I want to go abroad to study for several reasons.

(2) as a result

as a result(結果,因此)這片語用來作為轉承語,表示後面的句子是前面句
子的結果,相當於 consequently、in consequence。

> 例 John spent every minute memorizing new words. As a result, he has a
> large vocabulary.

as a result 之後可以接 of + N,意思是「由於…」。

> 例 John was thinking about his weekend plan when he was driving. As a
> result of his absent-mindedness, he bumped into a big tree.

(3) Besides the functions...

besides(此外)這裡當介系詞,其後接名詞或動名詞。

> 例 Besides English, English majors have to learn another foreign language.
> Besides writing a letter to the old man, he sent him a gift.

(4) look up

look up(查詢)這片語表示查詢某件資料。

> 例 You can look up the word in the dictionary.

※注意:查字典是 consult the dictionary,不是 look up the dictionary。

(5) can afford

afford 常和 can, could 或 be able to 連用,表示「負擔得起…」,其後可接
名詞或不定詞。

> 例 They went on foot for they couldn't afford(to take)a taxi.

afford 另外可解釋為「有足夠的…」。

例 I'd like to go on a vacation, but I can't afford the expense nor the time.

(6) however

however（然而）是副詞，當轉承語用，在前後文表示對照時使用。可放在句首、句中、或句尾。

例 Driving on a rough road can be very unpleasant. However, the travelers found it exciting.

The travelers, however, found it exciting.

The travelers found it exciting, however.

---

6. 造句練習：將各句譯成英文。

(1) Mary 吃了醫生的處方藥，結果頭就不痛了。

(2) 行動電話有語音信箱，打電話的人可以留言。

(3) 我喜歡行動電話，因為它帶給我很多方便。

（參考解答請見附錄 II）

---

7. 實力培養

> 　　The cell phone is popular for several reasons. The first is _____. We can carry this tiny device around. _____, we can reach others and be reached _____. The second, it has multiple functions. Besides the functions _____, the cell phone can be used to send and receive written messages, to _____, to look up words, to play games, and even to _____. The third is availability. Cell phones are not a luxury. Almost everyone _____.
>
> 　　However, while we enjoy the convenience _____, we have to observe some etiquette. For example, we should turn our cell phones off or _____ while we are in a theater or in a meeting, or the ringing will bother other people.

---

8. 輕鬆寫作

提示　用英文寫一篇作文，第一段說明你使用行動電話的時機，第二段說明你對使用行動電話的感想。可參考以下的資料。

Occasions for using the cell phone:

(1) to ask for information—call your classmate to make sure what the assignment is

(2) to make appointments—call your friends for seeing each other, or for seeing a movie together

(3) to ask for help—call your mum to send you money or other daily necessities

(4) to gossip—chatting with your friends about trivial daily things

What you may think about the cell phone:

(1) it is expensive to talk over the cell phone—more expensive than using conventional telephones such as pay phones

(2) it is convenient—you can carry it around, not limited by space

(3) it is trendy—almost everybody has a cell phone

Unit 7　Life in 2100

題型：主題句寫作

1. 試題

說明

說明：人類科技不斷進步。請寫一篇英文作文，想像西元 2100 年時人類的生活和目前可能有那些不同。以 Human life in the year 2100 will be... 開始。文長至少 120 字，最多不超過 170 字。

2. 擬寫內容

西元2100年的生活

西元 2100 年人類的生活至少在三方面會比較好。第一，從醫學的觀點來說，人類壽命可能會比較長。目前無法治癒的疾病可能在距今一百年後可以治癒。因此，人類將享有較長的壽命。

第二，人類生活在政治方面將會比較好。今天世界上有些地方仍然沒有言論自由或宗教自由。距今一世紀後，我相信這些地方的人將享有這些人權。

第三，人類在物質上將會更富裕。人類將享受機器所帶來更多舒適。例如，機器人將進入家庭中負責處理家庭雜務。

總而言之，很難準確地想像 2100 年的生活將會怎樣，不過大概在很多方面都會比現在進步。

3. 參考範文

Life in 2100

Human life in the year 2100 will be better in at least three ways. First, medically speaking, mankind will enjoy a longer life span. Illnesses that are incurable today may be curable **one hundred years from now**.[1] Consequently, human beings will enjoy a longer life.

Second, human life will be better politically. Today, there is still no freedom of speech or of religion in some parts of the world. A century from now, I believe the people in these places will enjoy these human rights.

Third, man will **be better off**[2] materially. Man will enjoy more comforts brought by machines. For example, robots will enter the household and take care of the chores.

> In summary, it is hard to imagine **exactly what**[3] life in 2100 will be like, but it **is likely to**[4] improve in many ways.

4. 寫作指導

本題必須運用一些想像力。從醫學、政治、和物質三方面加以鋪陳，就可以滿足要求的長度。

5. 重要的字詞及文法提示

(1) one hundred years from now

one hundred years from now 字面上是「從現在算起一百年」，也就是「一百年後」的意思。請注意這裡不能說 after one hundred years 或 one hundred years later。這兩種說法只能用在談論過去的時候。比較下面兩種用法：

(a) Some scientists say a big earthquake will hit this island ten years from now.

(b) He entered the room alone. Five minutes later, the door locked automatically.

(2) be better off

better off（更富裕）是 well off 的比較級。

例 He can't afford the study tour because his family is not well off.

(3) exactly what...

exactly 常放在疑問詞引導的名詞子句之前。

例 Do you know exactly when he will arrive?

I don't know exactly where my father is.

(4) is likely to

be likely (to)（可能）有下面兩種用法：

(a) it is likely + that 子句：

例 It is likely that Mr. Li will win the election.

(b) be likely to + Verb (phrase)

例 Mr. Li is likely to win the election.

6. 造句練習：將各句譯成英文。

(1) 誰知道十年後這世界會是什麼樣子呢？

(2) 總之，保護環境需要每一個人的努力。

(3) 人類有可能在一千年後滅絕嗎？ (Is it likely...)

(4) 由於科技的進步，現代人生活更富裕。

(5) 沒有人知道他確實做了什麼。

（參考解答請見附錄 II ）

7. 實力培養

Human life in the year 2100 will be better in at least three ways. First, _____, mankind will enjoy a longer life span. Illnesses that are incurable today _____. Consequently, human beings will enjoy a longer life.

Second, human life will be better politically. Today, there is still no freedom of speech or of religion _____. A century from now, I believe the people in these places will enjoy these human rights.

Third, man _____. Man will enjoy more comforts brought by machines. For example, robots will enter the household and _____.

In summary, it is hard to imagine _____ _____, but it is likely to improve in many ways.

8. 輕鬆寫作

請寫一篇英文作文，想像二十年後你的生活和目前可能有那些不同。以 My life twenty years from now will be... 開始。文長至少 120 字，最多不超過 170 字。

參考資料：

(1) being dependent VS being independent—have a job, make your own living and your own decisions

(2) being single VS being married—may have fallen in love with someone, may have gotten married and established a family

(3) be a parent—fathering or mothering children

(4) many of your dreams may have come true—have pursued advanced studies, and accomplished other goals

| Unit 8 | **Movie Theaters or Home Videos** |

題型：主題句寫作

1. 試題

你喜歡到電影院或租錄影帶在家觀賞電影？寫一篇英文作文，先說明電影和出租錄影帶的流行，最後說明你的偏好。以 "Going to the movies has been a popular recreation." 為開頭，文長至少 120 字，最多不超過 170 字。

2. 擬寫內容

電影院或家庭錄影帶

　　到電影院看電影一直是流行的娛樂。當人們有時間和金錢享受他們喜歡的電影的時候，每個人都會很興奮。他們可以欣賞他們最喜愛的演員表演，或享受劇情。不論是什麼理由，到電影院看電影已成為人們的生活方式。

　　然而，自從可以買到或租借錄影帶，DVD 或 VCD 之後，很多人選擇在家，而不到電影院看電影。現在到處都有錄影帶出租店，這說明了為什麼看錄影帶愈來愈受歡迎。

　　就我而言，我比較喜歡在電影院看電影而不在家看錄影帶。一則，我不需要和家人搶遙控器。再者，我可以和我的好朋友一起度過一些時光。雖然到電影院看電影比較貴，但是值得。

3. 參考範文

Movie Theaters or Home Videos

　　Going to the movies is a popular recreation. Everyone is excited when they have the time and money to enjoy a movie. They may enjoy **watching their favorite stars performing**,[1] or they may enjoy the story itself. **Whatever the reason**,[2] going to the movies has become a way of life for people.

　　However, since videos, DVDs, and VCDs became available, many people have chosen to watch movies at home, **instead of**[3] going to the movies. Today there are video shops everywhere, which shows that watching DVDs is gaining popularity.

> **As far as I am concerned**,[4] I **prefer** watching movies in a theater **to**[5] watching DVDs at home. **For one thing**, I don't have to fight with my family for the remote control. **For another**,[6] I can spend some time with my friends. **Although**[7] going to the movies is more expensive, I think **it is worth it**.[8]

4. 寫作指導

根據事實說明電影院或家庭錄影帶流行原因，最後依題目要求提出個人偏好及理由。

5. 重要的字詞及文法提示

(1) watching their favorite stars performing

watch sb. V-ing 感官動詞的用法結構如下：

see watch hear listen to smell feel	+ O +	V （強調 V 這件事實） V-ing （強調 V 這進行的動作）

例 I saw him cross the street with an old woman.（強調 cross 這件事實）

I saw him crossing the street with an old woman.（強調 cross 的動作）

(2) Whatever the reason

Whatever the reason（不論原因為何）是 Whatever the reason is 省略 is 而來，也可說成 No matter what the reason is。Whatever 子句中，如果主詞是普通名詞，動詞是 be 動詞時，可省略 be 動詞；其他情況則不可省略動詞。

例 Whatever you like, I'll get it for you.

Whatever the present, it is the thought that counts.

(3) instead of

instead of（而不是…）這個片語用來表示某一事物取代了 instead of 之後接的事物。因為 of 是介系詞，所以後面要接名詞或動名詞。

例 He bought an old car instead of a new one.

Instead of studying in the library, he went to a movie.

(4) As far as I am concerned

as far as I am concerned（就我個人而言）通常用來表示說話者的看法。

例 As far as I am concerned, that proposal is unrealistic.

(5) prefer A to B

prefer A to B（喜歡 A 勝過於 B）中 to 是介系詞，A、B 是名詞或是動名詞。

例 He prefers classical music to jazz.

They preferred eating out to cooking by themselves.

(6) For one thing.... For another....

For one thing（其一）為轉承語，其用法與 first, in the first place, to begin with 類似，但如用 for one thing，則通常與 for another（其二）搭配。在寫作時，可用來列舉事項。

例 I like English for several reasons. For one thing, it is the most universal language today. For another, it expands my horizons.

(7) although

although（雖然）後接子句，也可用 despite 或 in spite of 後接名詞表示。

例 Although the weather is bad,

Despite the bad weather, ｜ they still sailed out to sea.

In spite of the bad weather,

要特別注意 although 已是連接詞，不可以和 but 一起出現，但可用 nevertheless, nonetheless, still, however 等副詞來表示「但是」的意思。

(8) it is worth it

be worth it（是值得的）是個固定片語。

例 I know you have to work very hard for success, but it is worth it.

worth（值得）是形容詞，其後可接（代）名詞、動名詞、數字等。

例 That job is challenging, but it is worth a try.

The museum is worth visiting.

This used car is still worth thousands of dollars.

6. 造句練習：將各句譯成英文。

(1) 我喜歡看蝴蝶在花叢中飛舞、聆聽鳥兒啼唱。

(2) 不管什麼理由，偷竊都是不對的。

(3) 讓我們很驚訝的，他沒有爭辯，反而聽從了她的勸告。

(4) 就我個人而言，沒有事情是不可能的。

(5) 他喜歡在家獨處勝過和朋友在外遊蕩。

(6) 雖然你必須把所有時間都花在這項研究上，但那是值得的。

(7) 不管他說了什麼，不要太當真。

(8) 這本書值得一讀。首先，故事引人入勝；其次，文筆優美。

（參考解答請見附錄Ⅱ）

7. 實力培養

Movie Theaters or Home Videos

Going to the movies is a popular recreation. Everyone is excited when they have the time and money _____. They may enjoy _____, or they may enjoy the story itself. _____, going to the movies has become a way of life for people.

However, since videos, DVDs, and VCDs became available, many people have chosen to watch movies at home, _____. Today there are video shops everywhere, which shows that _____ _____.

As far as I am concerned, I _____ watching movies in a theater _____ watching DVDs at home. For one thing, I don't have to fight with my family _____. For another, I can spend some time with my friends. Although going to the movies is more expensive, _____.

8. 輕鬆寫作

提示

用英文寫一篇作文，第一段以 "I like to go to the movies." 或 "I enjoy watching TV at home" 開頭，說明你喜歡的原因。第二段敘述上一次看電影或看電視的經過。

參考資料：

(1) reasons for going to the movies:

    (a) getting away from home for a while

    (b) spending time with friends

    (c) enjoying the crowd

(2) reasons for watching TV at home:

    (a) don't have to spend money

    (b) can spend time with your family

    (c) cheaper to watch a movie on DVD than at the cinema

    (d) some movies are only available on TV

Unit 9   How to Live Happily

題型：主題寫作

1. 試題

如何過快樂生活是很多人問的問題。有一天你和一群外國朋友聊天，談到這個問題。請就你日常生活觀察所得，寫一篇英文作文，舉例告訴這群外國朋友你對這個問題的看法。文長至少 120 字，最多不超過 170 字。

2. 擬寫內容

如何過得快樂

不同的人對於如何過得快樂有不同的看法。我對快樂的看法來自小孩。若去觀察小孩，我們可以得到一些有關快樂代表什麼，以及如何快樂生活的線索。

如果小孩沒有挨餓、生病，並有東西可以玩，他就會快樂。我們藉由看著他在育兒室到處跑並發出高興的聲音，就能感覺到他的快樂。相反地，當小孩飢餓、生病或寂寞時，他就會不高興。

同理，如果要活得快樂，就必須有方法維持我們的生活；要健康、要有樂於從事的事，並且，必須要有朋友。

3. 參考範文

How to Live Happily

Different people have different ideas on how to live happily. My idea of happiness comes from small children. If we observe a small child, we may get some clues **as to**[1] what happiness means and how to live happily.

The child will be happy if they are not hungry or sick, and **have something to play with**.[2] We can feel the happiness **by watching them**[3] running around the nursery room, and making happy sounds. On the other hand, the child will be unhappy when hungry, sick or lonely.

Likewise,[4] if we want to live happily, we must have the means to sustain our life, we must be healthy, we must have something that we enjoy doing, and we must have friends.

4. 寫作指導

(1) 參考範文第一段可視為 introduction。第二段借用小孩來界定快樂的意義。第三段指出正題。

(2) 「如何過得快樂」並不好寫。但用小孩沒挨餓、沒生病且有東西可以玩就會快樂來做比喻，就是恰到好處的說明。

(3) 第二段第一句是觀點，可視為主題句。因觀點很清楚易懂，所以沒有鋪陳。

5. 重要的字詞及文法提示

(1) as to

as to（關於）是介系詞片語，所以後面接名詞，也可說 concerning。

例 There are still some doubts as to whether this experiment was correctly conducted.

(2) have something to play with

不定詞片語 to play with 當形容詞用，放在名詞後，表示該名詞的功用。這句話是從下面句子簡化來的：

The child will be happy if he/she... has something that he/she can play with.

→ has something to play with.

這種不定詞的用法很常見：

例 She is hungry and needs something to eat.

The lonely child needs someone to talk to.

(3) by watching them

by（藉著）之後接動名詞表示藉著某種方式。

例 He learned English by listening to tapes.

(4) Likewise,...

likewise（同樣地）是轉承語，用來另外舉一個和前面的敘述類似的事實。

例 It takes a lot of practice to polish your basketball skills. Likewise, if you want to learn English well, you have to practice it every day.

6. 造句練習：將各句譯成英文。

(1) 不管是否有錢，你都可以幫助那些需要幫助的人。

(2) 他沒有提到關於改善工作環境的事。

(3) 你可以藉著少用塑膠袋來做環保。

(4) 我們需要一個可追隨的好的領導者。

(5) 你希望別人對你誠實；同樣地，你也不可以欺騙別人。

(6) 他喜歡挑戰，難怪他接受了這困難的工作。

(7) 由於缺少愛和關懷，他很難保持心理健康。

（參考解答請見附錄Ⅱ）

7. 實力培養

How to Live Happily

Different people have different ideas _____.
My idea of happiness comes from small children. If we observe a small child, we may get some clues _____.

The child will be happy if they are not hungry or sick, and _____ _____. We can feel the happiness by _____ _____, and making happy sounds. On the other hand, the child will unhappy_____.

Likewise, if we want to live happily, we must _____ _____, we must be healthy, we must have something _____ _____, and we must have friends.

8. 輕鬆寫作

 有一天你和同學聊天，各自發表如何做個快樂的學生的看法。現在請你把你的看法寫成一篇英文作文。

參考資料：

How to be a happy student:

(1) academically successful—get good grades in school

(2) socially welcome—able to establish good relations with other students

(3) a good child at home—don't make parents worry about you, honor your parents

Unit 10 | Happiness

題型：主題寫作

1. 試題

以 "Happiness" 為主題，寫一篇英文作文，說明一些你感覺快樂的時候，或舉例說明令你快樂的事情等。文長至少 120 字，最多不超過 170 字。

2. 擬寫內容

論快樂

快樂是一種感覺。一般來說，當我無憂無慮、沒有悲傷的感受時，便是處於快樂的狀態。

有些時候我感到特別快樂。首先，如果我能做想做的事，就會覺得快樂。可能是去國外旅行，或可能是買一只昂貴的手錶。如果我有時間和金錢那麼做，我會覺得快樂。再者，當我達成目標，我也會覺得快樂。例如，我想要讀完一本小說或書。當我做到時，不但覺得獲得了知識和娛樂，同時也覺得非常快樂。

總而言之，快樂是一種感覺，用錢買不到，只發生在當我們得到所想要的，以及當我們達到目標時。

3. 參考範文

Happiness

Happiness is a feeling. **Generally speaking,**[1] when I am **free from**[2] worries, or when I don't feel miserable, I am in a state of happiness.

There are times when[3] I am especially happy. For one thing, I feel happy if I can do what I want to do. I may want to take a trip abroad, or I may want to buy an expensive watch. I feel happy if I can afford the time and money to do that. For another, I feel happy when I accomplish my goal. For example, I want to finish reading a novel or a book. When I do, I **not only** feel informed and entertained, I **also**[4] feel happy.

In conclusion,[5] happiness is a feeling, which cannot be bought, but which **lies in**[6] being able to do what we want, and in accomplishing our goals.

4. 寫作指導

(1) 用平常的小事做例子，説明獲得快樂的方法，是高明的寫法。

(2) 第一段是 introduction。

(3) 第二段第一句是 topic sentence，其後是發展。

(4) 第四段是結論。

5. 重要的字詞及文法提示

(1) generally speaking

generally speaking（一般而言）這個片語常用在句首，來談論一般狀況，不考慮特殊情形。

例 Generally speaking, men are physically stronger than women.

(2) free from

free from sth.（無…的）表示不受某危險或不愉快的事物的影響。

例 A life free from fear and care is what she desires.

有很多動詞搭配 from 這個字，基本上意思都是「使免於某事物」：

keep sb./sth. from（使…無法；避免…）

stop sb./sth. from（使…無法；避免…）

prevent sb./sth. from（使…無法；避免…）

discourage sb. from（勸…不要…）

(3) There are times when...

There are times when...（有時）之後接子句，字面上意思是「有…的時候」。

例 There are times when a good listener is just what you need.

when 引導的是形容詞子句。

(4) not only..., but (also)...

not only..., but (also)（不但…而且…）常連接對等的詞組。

例 They need not only food but (also) medical supplies.

She not only wrote them letters but (also) sent them gifts.

She goes there not only on Saturday but also on Sunday.

如果連接兩個子句，also 要放在第二個主詞之後，這種情況下通常 Not only 放第一個子句句首，該子句倒裝；but 可省略，兩個子句間用分號。

例 Not only did they invite the poor man in, but they (also) offered him some food.

Not only did they invite the poor man in; they also offered him some food.

如果 not only 不放在句首，則不需要倒裝。

例　They not only invited the poor man in; they also offered him some food.

(5) in conclusion

in conclusion（最後）這個片語用來表示其後要講的是最後一點。

例　In conclusion, I'd like to thank everyone who has put their efforts into this business.

(6) lie in

lie in（在於）表示某抽象事物存在於另一事物上，或可在其中找到。

例　Happiness lies in contentment.

6. 造句練習：將各句譯成英文。

(1) 一般而言，老師受到很多的尊重。

(2) 她渴望過著不需害怕暴力的生活。

(3) 一個人會有需要面對死亡的時候。

(4) 這型的電腦不但貴而且不好用。

(5) 他不但照顧年老的雙親還撫養五個小孩。

(6) 真正的快樂在於欣賞自己所擁有的。

(7) 最後，要達到我們的目標需要每個人的努力。

（參考解答請見附錄Ⅱ）

7. 實力培養

Happiness

Happiness is a feeling. _____, when I am free from worries, or when I don't feel miserable, I am _____ _____.

There are times when I am especially happy. For one thing, I feel happy if I _____. I may want to take a trip abroad, or I may want to buy an expensive watch. I feel happy _____ _____ to do that. For another, I feel happy _____ _____. For example, I want to finish reading a novel or a book. When I do, I not only feel informed and entertained, _____ _____.

第三章

In conclusion, happiness is a feeling, which cannot be bought, but which lies in being able to do _____, and in accomplishing our goals.

8. 輕鬆寫作

提示　以 "The Happiest Moment of My Life" 為題，寫一篇英文作文，描述你一生中最感到快樂的一個時刻。

參考資料：

(1) Reasons for your happiness:

You have done something extremely well and were praised for what you have done, such as scoring high on an exam, successfully solved a problem, helped others, did others a big favor and were thanked, etc.

(2) Occasions when you may feel happy:

A lot of people come to celebrate your birthday, your success on something, or to see you for some particular reason.

Unit 11 The Generation Gap

題型：簡函寫作

1. 試題

最近你交了一位外國筆友。在你們的通信中，對方談到代溝的問題。現在請你寫一封信給對方，告知你對這個問題的看法。以 "Dear Friend," 開頭，日期 7 月 2 日，並以 "Your Friend" 署名。文長至少 120 字，最多不超過 170 字。

2. 擬寫內容

親愛的朋友：

　　我認為代溝主要是父母及兒女間意見的不同。如果意見的差異化解了，代溝就可以彌平。為了消除意見的不同，我認為父母和孩子都必須學習互相尊重及容忍。成熟且明智的父母必須了解，孩子並非他們所擁有。因此，當不同的意見真的出現，他們可以和小孩討論，而非命令小孩服從、不准問問題。即使無法達成協議，父母也必須聆聽並思考孩子們的意見。此舉將給孩子學習成長的機會。

　　同樣地，孩子應該了解父母心裏總是最關心他們，而且因為父母見過的世面較多，所以父母的忠告總是值得重視。

　　關於這個議題，我期待你的回音。

你的朋友 敬上
7月2日

3. 參考範文

July 2

Dear Friend,

　　I think the generation gap is mainly a difference of opinion between parents and children. The gap can be bridged if the difference of opinion is resolved. **To resolve**[1] the difference of opinion, I think both parents and children have to learn to respect and tolerate each other. Mature and wise parents should realize that they don't own their children. **Therefore**,[2] when a difference of opinion does occur, they can discuss it with their children, instead of ordering them to obey with no questions asked. **Even if**[3] an agreement cannot be reached, parents should listen to and consider their children's opinions. This will give the children a chance to learn and grow up.

Similarly, children should realize that parents always **have their best interests at heart**,[4] and that because their parents have seen more of life, parental advice **is always worthy of their attention**.[5]

I look forward to hearing from you regarding this issue.

Sincerely yours,

Your Friend

4. 寫作指導

(1) 本文先用定義説明代溝是什麼，接著申論。

(2) 用 look forward to hearing from you 是書信常見的結尾方法。

5. 重要的字詞及文法提示

(1) To resolve...

不定詞 to + V（為了）用來表示目的，可放句首或句尾。

例 He works out every day at the gym to keep fit.

To keep fit, he works out every day at the gym.

也可用 in order to。

例 In order to keep fit, he works out every day at the gym.

(2) Therefore,...

therefore（因此）是轉承語，表示結果。

例 He had lost his interest in politics. Therefore, he decided to resign.

(3) even if

even if（即使）中 even 是副詞，if 是連接詞（表示假設），所以後面要接子句。 even 本身後面不可接子句。

例 Even if you fail, that would not be the end of the world.

(4) have their best interests at heart

have sth. at heart（某事常在某人的心上）用來表示一個人常惦念著某事。

例 A good president always has his people's welfare at heart.

(5) is worthy of their attention

be worthy of（值得）後接名詞或動名詞。

例 His performance is worthy of praise.

This city is worthy of being visited.

6. 造句練習：將各句譯成英文。

(1) 即使不成功，他們的努力還是值得欽佩的。

(2) 為了達到共識，每個人都得做一些讓步。

(3) 員工的福利常在這雇主的心中。

(4) 他只看事情的光明面；因此，這世界對他而言總是美好的。

(5) 親子間有代溝；同樣的，師生間看法也會不同。

(6) 他的提議可行，值得考慮。

（參考解答請見附錄 II）

7. 實力培養

July 2

Dear Friend,

I think the generation gap is mainly _____
_____. The gap can be bridged _____
_____. To resolve the difference of opinion, I think
both parents and children have to learn to _____.
Mature and wise parents should realize that they don't own their children.
Therefore, when a difference of opinion does occur, _____
_____, instead of ordering them to obey with no questions
asked. Even if _____, parents should
listen to and consider their children's opinions. This will give the children
_____.

　　Similarly, children should realize that _____
_____, and that because their parents have
seen more of life, parental advice is always _____.

　　I look forward to hearing from you regarding this issue.

Sincerely yours,

Your Friend

8. 輕鬆寫作

提示 用英文寫一篇作文，舉一個例子說明你的意見和別人（同學、朋友、兄弟姊妹或父母等都可以）不同，以及獲取共識的經過。

參考資料：

(1) You want to go to an art school, but your parents want you to become a doctor.

(2) You want to go to a movie on the weekend, but your parents want you to study at home.

(3) You want to watch a certain program at night, but your brother wants to watch another program, so you fight for the remote control.

(4) You have a date with your friend. While you prefer to go a certain place, your date would rather go to another place.

第三章

Unit 12　Water

題型：主題句寫作

1. 試題

說明

以 "Water is both a blessing and a curse." 為開頭，說明水對生命的重要性及可能造成的禍害。文長至少 120 字，最多不超過 170 字。

2. 擬寫內容

水

　　水既是珍寶也是禍害。它是珍寶，因為我們每天都需要水。我們洗衣服需要水，清潔公寓時需要水，烹飪時同樣少不了水。我們需要喝水解渴；人體裡大部分都是水。水還可以調節氣候。最重要的是，我們需要水來種植作物。沒有水，我們便無法生存。

　　然而，水也可能危及我們的生命及財產。例如，雨下太多就會鬧水災。結果，農作物可能被損壞，建築物可能倒塌，人們可能溺死。這就是為什麼水是禍害了。

3. 參考範文

Water

　　Water is **both** a blessing **and**[1] a curse. It is a blessing because we need water every day. When we wash our clothes, we need water. When we clean our apartment, we need water. When we cook, we need water. We need to drink water to **quench our thirst**.[2] A large part of our body is water. Water also regulates the weather. **Most important of all**,[3] we need water to grow food. **Without**[4] water, we would die.

　　However, water can also destroy our life and property. For example, when it rains too much, there can be floods. As a result, crops may be spoiled, buildings may collapse, and people may drown. **This is why**[5] water is a curse.

4. 寫作指導

「水既是珍寶也是禍害」是 topic sentence。後文說明是祝福也是禍害的原因，即主題句的鋪陳。

5. 重要的字詞及文法提示

(1) both... and...

both A and B（既…也…）連接兩個對等詞語。

例 Mr. Lin is both friendly and generous.

Money can be both a blessing and a curse.

(2) quench our thirst

quench one's thirst（止渴）中 quench 是 put an end to 的意思。

(3) most important of all

most important of all（最重要的是）是個轉承語。

例 Education is valuable in many ways.... Most important of all, it helps us learn how to live.

(4) without

without（沒有）是介系詞，後接名詞或動名詞，形成副詞片語。

例 Without air, no creature could live.

這種句法也可寫成 If there were no air, no creature could live.

(5) This is why...

This is why...（這就是為什麼…）引導的句子是前述事項的結果。

例 Peter is generous with his time. This is why he is so popular among his friends.

6. 造句練習：將各句譯成英文。

(1) 他喝了一大杯柳丁汁來解渴。

(2) 沒有愛，這世界會是冰冷的。

(3) 他無法忍受城市的熙熙攘攘；這是他搬到鄉下的原因。

(4) 他既是工程師也是詩人。

(5) 颱風時下了太多雨，結果，到處都是水災。

(6) 我喜歡這部電影的情節及特效；最重要的是，它激勵我面對人生的挑戰。

（參考解答請見附錄 II）

7. 實力培養

Water

Water is both a blessing and a curse. It is a blessing _____

_____. When we wash our clothes, we need water. When

we clean our apartment, we need water. When we cook, we need water. We

need to drink water _____. A large part of our body

is water. Water also regulates the weather. _____, we

need water _____. Without water, we would die.

_____, water can also destroy our life and

property. For example, when it rains too much, _____.

_____, crops may be spoiled, buildings may collapse, and people

_____. This is why water is a curse.

8. 輕鬆寫作

提示

以 "Friends" 為主題,寫一篇英文作文,第一段以 "Friends can be a
blessing." 做開頭,說明朋友的益處。第二段說明結交損友的害處。文長
至少 120 字。

參考資料:

Friends can be a blessing, because they:

(1) share our sorrow

(2) keep us company

(3) provide timely help

(4) are like family members

Bad friends can be a curse, because they:

(1) tempt us to do bad things

(2) lead us astray

(3) have a bad influence on us

(4) should be kept at a distance

第三章

Unit 13　The Most Unbearable Thing

題型：主題寫作

1. 試題

以 "The Most Unbearable Thing" 為主題，說明一件令你最無法忍受的事是什麼，和無法忍受的原因。文長至少 120 字，至多不超過 170 字。

2. 擬寫內容

最不能忍受的事

　　我最無法忍受的事就是等待別人。第一，等人浪費我的時間。假如和我約好要見面的人不能來，他應該事先讓我知道。假如他能來，就要準時到，沒有理由讓我等。畢竟，我有其他的事要做。

　　第二，讓別人等是很不禮貌的。讓別人等可能表示不把別人當一回事，而且再怎麼說，不把別人當一回事是很不禮貌的。

　　第三，等人使我緊張，他為什麼還不來呢？是不是因為他不喜歡我呢？是因為發生了意料之外的事嗎？這些疑問都會叫我緊張。

　　總之，因為等人浪費我的時間，因為讓別人等不禮貌，也因為等人使我緊張，所以等人是我最不能忍受的事。

3. 參考範文

The Most Unbearable Thing

　　The most unbearable thing for me is to wait for other people. First, waiting wastes my time. If the person I am waiting for cannot come, they should let me know in advance. If they can come, they can come on time. **There is no reason to**[1] keep me waiting. **After all**,[2] I have other things to **attend to**. [3]

　　Second, it is impolite to keep people waiting. Someone who keeps people waiting may be **taking them for granted**.[4] And it is impolite to take people for granted, **to say the least**.[5]

　　Third, waiting makes me nervous. Why haven't they come? Is it because they don't like me? Is it because something unexpected has happened? These questions make me nervous.

> In summary, because waiting wastes my time, because it is impolite, and because waiting makes me nervous, waiting is the most unbearable thing.

4. 寫作指導

(1) 每個人所「最不能忍受的事」各有不同，因此，只要說得有道理就可以。本文第一句是 topic sentence，後文列出理由，支持 topic sentence。

(2) 結尾以重述觀點作結。

5. 重要的字詞及文法提示

(1) There is no reason to

There is no reason (for sb.) to V... 表示「（某人）沒有理由做出…」。

例 There is no reason for anybody to take another person for granted.

另一個常見句型是：There is no reason why S V...

例 There is no reason why you cannot succeed.

(2) after all

after all（畢竟）是個轉承語，用在為前面的敘述提出一個說明的理由時。

例 You don't need to feel bad about that mistake. After all, everybody makes mistakes.

after all 也可放在句尾，

例 You don't need to feel bad about that mistake. Everybody makes mistakes, after all.

(3) attend to

attend to sth.（處理某事）即 deal with 之意。

例 His job requires him to attend to all the financial matters of the company.

(4) taking them for granted

take sb. for granted 意思是「視某人做的一切為理所當然」。

例 Remember to show some appreciation to your parents. Do not take them for granted.

另外，take sth. for granted 的意思是「視某事為理所當然，不要認為…一定…」。

例 Don't take my patience for granted.

如果 sth. 是個子句，則移至 granted 之後，take 後可加上 it 作虛受詞。

例 The kids always take (it) for granted that their mother has to cook for the whole family.

(5) to say the least

to say the least 的意思是「保守的說」，用來表示還有更糟或更好的情況。

6. 造句練習：將各句譯成英文。

(1) 身為一個醫生，他必須處理病人基本的醫療上的需求。

(2) 他無法承擔這麼有挑戰性的工作；畢竟他已經七十歲了。

(3) 沒有理由期待每個人都順從我們。

(4) 他們把我的容忍視為理所當然。

(5) 我們直到必須獨立時，才會了解到：不應該認為父母所做的一切都是理所當然的。

(6) 保守的說，我們損失了將近三十萬美金。

(7) 不要認為你從大學畢業後一定找得到工作。

(8) 保守的說，這個週末我們過得不大愉快。

（參考解答請見附錄Ⅱ）

7. 實力培養

The Most Unbearable Thing

The most unbearable thing for me is to wait for other people. First, waiting wastes my time. If the person _____ cannot come, they should let me know _____. If they can come, _____ _____. There is no reason _____. After all, I have other things to attend to.

Second, it is impolite to keep people waiting. Someone who keeps people waiting may _____. And it is impolite _____, to say the least.

Third, waiting makes me nervous. Why haven't they come? Is it because they don't like me? Is it because _____ _____? These questions make me nervous.

In summary, because waiting wastes my time, because it is impolite, and because waiting makes me nervous, waiting is the most unbearable thing.

8. 輕鬆寫作

提示　幾乎每一個人都曾經等過別人。用英文寫一篇作文，第一段敘述你一次等人的經過，第二段說明對這個事件的感想。

參考資料：

Emotions when waiting:

nervous

feel bad

worry about accidents

How you might feel:

an unpleasant experience

being taken for granted

unhappy

Unit 14 Life Without a Goal

題型：主題句寫作

1. 試題

以 "Life Without a Goal" 為主題，說明一件令你最無法忍受的事。以 "I think the most unbearable thing is to live without a goal" 為開頭，文長至少 120 字，至多不超過 170 字。

2. 擬寫內容

生活沒目標

對我來說，最不能忍受的事就是生活沒目標。生活沒目標之所以最難忍受原因如下：第一，生活沒有目標就很乏味了。我們會什麼都不在乎，並且將無法有效地運用時間，生命也因此而浪費掉。

第二，生活沒有目標就好像航行沒有目的地。正如航行永遠到不了終點，我們也無法覺得快樂和滿足。

第三，假如我們沒有目標，生活將沒意義。生命是不斷努力的過程。沒有目標，我們就會不想努力，這樣就會使生活沒意義。

總之，沒有目標的生活既乏味又沒意義，當然就成了我最無法忍受的事。

3. 參考範文

Life Without a Goal[1]

I think the most unbearable thing is to live without a goal. Life without a goal is unbearable for the following reasons. First, life without a goal is boring. We don't care about anything, we don't use our time **constructively**,[2] and our life is wasted.

Second, life without a goal is like a voyage without a destination. Just as the voyage never comes to an end, we never **feel** happy and **satisfied**.[3]

Third, life is meaningless if we don't have a goal. Life is a continual process of effort. Without a goal, we wouldn't have to make any effort, and this would make life meaningless.

To conclude,[4] because life without a goal is boring and meaningless, it is consequently the most unbearable thing.

4. 寫作指導

(1) I think the most unbearable thing is to live without a goal. Life without a goal is the most unbearable for the following reasons. 也可以合併為 I think the most unbearable thing is to live without a goal for the following reasons.

(2) 原來的兩句之間用重複 life without a goal 作連貫的方法。

(3) 所提的三個理由中，第一個放在起始段落，其餘二個分別置於二、三段，最後以重述三個理由作結。

5. 重要的字詞及文法提示

(1) life without a goal

life without a goal（沒有目標的生活）中 without a goal 這介系詞片語當形容詞用，修飾其前的名詞 life。

例 Life without you would be like a desert.

　　A class without discipline is hard to teach.

類例：He finds women with long hair more attractive.

(2) constructively

constructively 的意思是「有建設性地」。

例 To really resolve the problem, you should complain constructively.

形容詞是 constructive。

例 constructive criticism

　　constructive advice

(3) feel satisfied

satisfied（滿意的）是指一種感覺。所有情緒動詞的過去分詞形式都是表示一種感覺。例如：interested, surprised, shocked, embarrassed, disappointed 等。

而情緒動詞的現在分詞則表示「令人產生某種感覺的」。例如：interesting, surprising, shocking, embarrassing, disappointing 等。

情緒動詞及其分詞形式的關係如下：

A + V + B　若「A 使 B 感到…」

A is V-ing.　則「A 是（令 B）…的」

B is V-en.　而「B（對 A）感到…的」

例 The game excited all my classmates.

The game was exciting (to all my classmates).

All my classmates were excited (about the game).

(4) To conclude

To conclude（總之）是用來下結論的，也可說 In conclusion。

例 To conclude, if we want future generations to enjoy natural resources as we do, we should try our best to conserve them.

6. 造句練習：將各句譯成英文。

(1) 這些政府官員常建設性地批評一些政策，並提供一些可行的建議。

(2) 沒有目的地的旅程常會造成時間上的浪費。

(3) 發現沒錢付帳時，他覺得非常尷尬。

(4) 總之，環保是當務之急，需要每個人的援助。

(5) 他那沈悶的演講令人非常失望。坐在我旁邊的男士半途就離席了。

（參考解答請見附錄 II）

7. 實力培養

Life Without a Goal

I think the most unbearable thing is to live without a goal. Life without a goal is unbearable _____. First, life without a goal is boring. We don't _____, we don't use our time constructively, and _____.

Second, life without a goal is like _____. Just as the voyage never _____, we never feel happy and satisfied.

Third, life is meaningless _____. Life is a continual process of effort. _____, we wouldn't have to make any effort, and this would make life meaningless.

To conclude, because life without a goal is boring and meaningless, it is _____ the most unbearable thing.

8. 輕鬆寫作

假如你的高中生活不是為升大學,而是毫無目標。請寫一篇英文作文,以 "My Boring School Life" 為題,說明上學的可能情況。

參考資料:

Going to school without a purpose—possible results:

(1) get bored because nobody cares about what you do or what you don't do

(2) doesn't matter whether you are late for school or not

(3) teachers not serious

(4) practically no discipline of any kind

(5) kids won't learn

Unit 15 | Why Lying Is Unbearable

題型：主題寫作

1. 試題

說明 以 "Why Lying Is Unbearable" 為主題，寫一篇英文作文，說明為何說謊令你無法忍受。文長至少 120 字，至多不超過 170 字。

2. 擬寫內容

為何說謊令人無法忍受

說謊之所以難以忍受的理由如下：

第一，說謊疏遠人與人之間的感情。為了圓一個謊言，我被迫說更多的謊言。結果人家會認為我虛假，最後對我失去信心。我就被疏遠了。

第二，說謊使我良心不安。說謊，我會不斷地擔心被揭穿。我再也無法心安理得。最後，我失去自我而變成一個完全不一樣的人了。

第三，說謊使我生病。就像我已經提過的，說謊產生恐懼，恐懼造成緊張，緊張一路累積到我生病為止。

總之，因為我不想被疏遠，不想變個人或生病，所以說謊是我最不能忍受的事。

3. 參考範文

Why Lying Is Unbearable

Lying is unbearable for the following reasons:

First, lying **alienates**[1] people. In order to **cover up**[2] a lie, I am forced to tell more lies. As a result, people **consider me untruthful**[3] and eventually lose trust in me. I become alienated.

Second, lying bothers my conscience. When I lie, I am constantly afraid of being found out. I no longer have a clear conscience. Consequently, I am no longer myself, and I become a totally different person.

Third, lying makes me sick. As I have pointed out, **lying generates fear,**[4] and fear builds up tension. The tension will accumulate **until**[5] I become sick.

In summary, because I don't want to be alienated, different or sick, lying is the most unbearable thing to me.

4. 寫作指導

(1) 不能忍受的事以說謊做發展，並舉出具體的原因。

(2) 第一段總起下文。

(3) 第二、三、四段各舉出一個具體的原因。

(4) 末段以重述原因作結。

5. 重要的字詞及文法提示

(1) alienate

alienate 使…疏遠。alienate A from B 表示「使 A 和 B 疏遠」。

例 His being too serious alienates him from his fellow workers.

Lying alienates us from others.

(2) cover up

cover up sth.（掩蓋）指的是掩蓋錯誤或不法的事情。

例 The government was trying to cover up those two cases of SARS.

(3) consider me untruthful

consider sb./sth. adj/n 表示「認為某人或某事如何如何」。

例 We consider his novel very imaginative.

Many people consider Hong Kong a paradise for shoppers.

也可說 consider sb./sth. to be adj./n.。

例 We consider his novel to be very imaginative.

表示對某事或某人的看法，還有下列常見的用法：

see	sb./sth. as adj./n.
view	
regard	
look on	
think of	

例 We regard Dr. Sun Yat-sen as the founding father of the Republic of China.

I view English as a useful language.

(4) lying generates fear

generate 意思是「產生」。

例 Water can generate electricity.

Success usually generates a sense of achievement.

(5) until

until（直到）可當連接詞，後面接子句；也可當介系詞，後面接名詞，指的是其前的動詞或狀態一直延續到某時才停止。

例 He stayed in the park until midnight.

He stayed in the park until all the lights were out.

not... until... 則是「直到…才…」的意思。

例 I won't leave until you ask me to.

6. 造句練習：將各句譯成英文。

(1) 種族歧視製造仇恨。

(2) 愛會產生很多力量。

(3) 我們直到發現他常幫助窮人之前都認為他很無情。

(4) 他對獨處的喜愛使他和社會脫節。

(5) 掩蓋自己的錯誤等於是又犯了一個錯。

(6) 貝克漢 (Beckham) 被認為是世界上最受歡迎的足球球員。

(7) 母親的愛一般認為是無條件的。

（參考解答請見附錄 II）

7. 實力培養

Why Lying Is Unbearable

Lying is unbearable for the following reasons:

First, lying alienates people. In order to cover up a lie, _____ _____. As a result, people consider me untruthful and eventually _____. I become alienated.

Second, lying bothers my conscience. When I lie, I am constantly _____ _____. I no longer have a clear conscience. Consequently, I am no longer myself, and I _____.

Third, lying makes me sick. As I have pointed out, lying generates fear, and _____. The tension will accumulate until _____.

In summary, because I don't want to be alienated, different or sick, lying is the most unbearable thing to me.

8. 輕鬆寫作

 提示 以 "Lying" 為主題，用英文寫一篇作文，敘述一次自己或他人說謊的經過及結果。

參考資料：

possible occasions for lying:

(1) you are afraid that what you have done might get you into trouble—such as being punished

(2) you are afraid that what you have done or have not done will displease your teacher or parents

(3) you are afraid of being laughed at

possible consequences of lying:

(1) you are caught lying and punished

(2) you are not caught lying, but constantly afraid of being caught

(3) you are nervous and under a lot of pressure

(4) you tell more lies until you cannot lie any further

Unit 16 Noise

題型:主題寫作

1. 試題

 以 "Noise" 為主題,寫一篇英文作文,説明你對噪音的感覺。文長至少 120 字,至多不超過 170 字。

2. 擬寫內容

噪音

　　噪音是令人無法忍受的。噪音之所以難以忍受有三個理由。第一,噪音使我無法專心。身為一個即將參加大學入學考的學生,我需要專心於課業。一旦分心,我便無法有效率地讀書。結果就會考不好。

　　第二,噪音影響我的睡眠。如果我睡不好,我就沒有體力讀書。第三,噪音使我煩躁,讀書時我需要平靜安詳的心情,我最最不想要的就是煩躁。因此我無法忍受噪音,因為它使我煩躁。

　　總之,因為噪音影響我的專注力和睡眠,又使我煩躁,所以噪音是我最不能忍受的事。

3. 參考範文

Noise

　　Noise is unbearable to me. It is unbearable for three reasons. In the first place, noise affects my concentration. As a student preparing for the university entrance exam, I need to concentrate on my studies. If I am distracted, I can't study **efficiently**.[1] Consequently, I don't do well on the exam.

　　In the second place, noise affects my sleep. If I don't sleep well, I don't have the energy to study. Third, noise upsets me. I need to feel calm and peaceful when I study. **The last thing I want is to be upset**.[2] Therefore, noise is unbearable.

　　To sum up, because it affects my concentration and my sleep, and because it upsets me, noise is the most unbearable thing.

4. 寫作指導

(1) 前二句合為「噪音之所以難以忍受有三個理由」，是 topic sentence。

(2) 之後以影響專注力、睡眠和使煩躁的觀點加以發展，並以重述主旨作結。

5. 重要的字詞及文法提示

(1) efficiently

efficiently（有效率地）不同於 effectively（有效地）。efficiently 指的是花最少的時間、精力、金錢而達到效果。而 effectively 指的是達到預期的效果。

例 Search engines help us search the Web efficiently. We don't have to visit each of the countless websites to find what we need.

Without interaction, we can't communicate effectively.

這兩個字的形容詞分別是：efficient 和 effective。

例 With so many efficient workers in his company, he makes a large profit.

Going on a diet is an effective way to lose weight.

(2) The last thing I want is to be upset.

the last thing I want 的意思是「最不想要的事、最不想做的事」，另外，the last person... 則是「最不可能…的人」。

例 Marrying him is the last thing I would like to do.

John is the last person who would steal something.

the last thing 和 the last person 之後接的是當形容詞用的關係子句或不定詞片語。

6. 造句練習：將各句譯成英文。

(1) 我最不可能放棄的就是我的家庭。

(2) 多閱讀是增加字彙最有效的方法。

(3) 一個自我中心的人是我最不想結婚的對象。

(4) 我們藉由互相合作很有效率地把那個研究計畫案完成了。

(5) 我最不想做的事就是傷害你。

（參考解答請見附錄 II）

7. 實力培養

Noise

Noise is unbearable to me. It is unbearable for three reasons. In the first place, noise _____. As a student preparing for the university entrance exam, I need to concentrate on my studies. If I am distracted, I can't study efficiently. Consequently, _____ _____.

In the second place, noise _____. If I don't sleep well, I don't have the energy to study. Third, noise upsets me. I need to feel calm and peaceful when I study. _____ is to be upset. Therefore, noise is unbearable.

To sum up, because it affects my concentration and my sleep, and because it upsets me, noise is the most unbearable thing.

8. 輕鬆寫作

 以 "Noise" 為主題，寫一篇英文作文，說明你所接觸到的噪音有那些，以及噪音如何影響你。

參考資料：

Kinds of noise:
(1) traffic on the streets
(2) airplanes flying overhead
(3) construction work
(4) gossip of fellow students
(5) radios blaring nearby
(6) TVs blaring nearby
(7) babies crying

How noise might affect you:
(1) makes you feel uncomfortable
(2) makes you nervous
(3) distracts your attention
(4) upsets you
(5) damages your hearing

Unit 17 Taking a Positive Attitude Toward Life

題型：主題寫作

1. 試題

以 "Taking a Positive Attitude Toward Life" 為主題，舉例說明人生應積極的理由，並舉一例支持你的觀點。文長至少 120 字，至多不超過 170字。

2. 擬寫內容

積極面對人生

我們應積極面對人生。當我們做任何事時，會有兩種可能的結果。一是成功，另一是失敗。失敗時，我們有可能就此放棄。但是，若以積極的態度來面對，我們就會願意從失敗中學習，再度嘗試，直到成功。因此，積極面對人生是成功的唯一方法。

我的父親以積極態度面對人生。例如，當他從商損失一百萬元時，我們都替他感到難過，並試著去安慰他。但他並未感到挫敗。相反地，他說他學到一個重要的教訓，並且說將來可以避免再犯相同的錯誤。

由於態度積極，他的事業發達。

3. 參考範文

Taking a Positive Attitude Toward Life

We should take a positive attitude toward life. When we attempt to do anything, there are two possible outcomes. One is that we succeed. The other is that we fail. When we fail, we may decide to give up. However, if we have a positive attitude, we are willing to learn from our failure and try again until we succeed. Therefore, taking a positive attitude toward life is the only way to succeed.

My father takes a positive attitude toward life. For example, when he lost a million dollars in business, we all felt sorry for him and tried to comfort him. But he was not frustrated. Instead, he said he had learned an important lesson and that he would **avoid making**[1] the same mistake again in the future.

As a result of[2] his positive attitude, **his business has prospered**.[3]

第三章

4. 寫作指導

作者先闡述人生應該要積極的道理，接著以他父親為例，說明積極的成果。

5. 重要的字詞及文法提示

(1) avoid making

avoid（避免）之後接名詞或動名詞。

例 She avoids his eye contact.

She avoids eating oily food.

(2) as a result of

as a result of... 字面上是「作為⋯的結果」，也就是「由於」的意思，其所引介的片語常放在表示結果的句子前。

例 As a result of his carelessness, he lost millions of dollars in his business.

如果原因已在前面敘述過，就只要用 as a result。

例 He drank and drove. As a result, he was fined for drunk driving.

(3) his business has prospered

prosper 可以指事業興隆或個人的成功。

例 With a good leader, this country prospered in a few years.

6. 造句練習：將各句譯成英文。

(1) 由於過勞及長期的壓力，他精神崩潰了。

(2) 我們應該避免把錢花在不必要的東西上。

(3) 自從分手後，他一直避開他的前任女友。

(4) 由於她的勤勉與能幹，生意日漸興隆。

(5) 常和小孩子玩在一起的人心態常保年輕。

（參考解答請見附錄 II）

7. 實力培養

Taking a Positive Attitude Toward Life

We should take a positive attitude toward life. When we attempt to do anything, _____. One is that we succeed. _____. When we fail, we may _____. However, if we have a positive attitude, we are willing to learn _____.

Therefore, taking a positive attitude toward life is the only way to succeed.

My father takes a positive view toward life. For example, when he lost a million dollars in business, we all felt _____. He was not frustrated. _____, he said he had learned an important lesson and that he would _____ in the future.

_____ his positive attitude, his business has prospered.

8. 輕鬆寫作

以 "Taking a Positive Attitude Toward Life" 為題,寫一篇英文作文。第一段說明 taking a positive attitude toward life 的好處,第二段舉一例驗證第一段的觀點。

參考資料:

Advantages of taking a positive attitude toward life:

(1) enables us to learn from our mistakes/failures

(2) helps us realize that failure is the mother of success

(3) gives us energy and motivation to try again

Possible examples you may have had:

(1) You didn't do well on a certain exam, you take a positive attitude, tried again and succeeded.

(2) You did not succeed in making an impression on someone you liked, so you tried again. Instead of feeling hopeless/frustrated, you succeeded in impressing the person and won their friendship.

(3) You wanted to prove to your parents that you were a good child and succeeded after several attempts.

(4) You wanted to prove to your friend that you had certain qualities and after several attempts, you succeeded.

第三章

Unit 18　My Favorite Subject in School—History

題型：主題句寫作

1. 試題

說明

以 "My Favorite Subject in School" 為主題，寫一篇英文作文，說明你最喜歡的一門科目。以 "My favorite subject in school is _____." 開頭，文長至少 120 字，至多不超過 170 字。

2. 擬寫內容

在學校我最喜歡的科目—歷史

在學校我最喜歡的科目是歷史。我喜歡歷史有三個原因。第一，歷史告訴我們來自何方、身處何處，以及將來會到哪裡。沒有歷史，我勢必會覺得迷失在時間的洪流裡。

第二，歷史提供心靈的饗宴。在歷史裡，我們看得到帝國的興衰、偉人的一生，以及人類文明的偉大成就。閱讀這些就好像在享受心靈的饗宴。因此，歷史豐富了我們的心靈。

最後，歷史是我們的良師。藉著研究歷史，我們可以避免犯下和祖先們所犯的同樣錯誤，變得更為睿智。

總之。因為歷史帶給我時間意識、提供心靈饗宴，也因為歷史是我的良師，所以在學校我最喜歡的科目是歷史。

3. 參考範文

My Favorite Subject in School—History

　　My favorite subject in school is history. I like history for three reasons. First, history tells me where I came from, where I am, and where I will be. Without history, I **could not bu**t[1] feel lost in time.

　　Second, history offers a **mental feast**.[2] In history, we can see the rise and fall of empires, lives of great men and women, and great achievements in civilization. Reading about these is like enjoying a mental feast. So, history nourishes our minds.

　　Finally, history is our guide. By studying history, we can avoid making the same mistakes our ancestors made. We become wiser.

第三章

> To sum up, because it gives me a sense of time, because it offers a mental feast, and because it is my guide, history is my favorite subject in school.

4. 寫作指導

以 I like history for three reasons. 作為主題句，每一個原因稍微鋪陳一下，就可以達到試題要求的長度。

5. 重要的字詞及文法提示

(1) could not but

sb. cannot but...（只好、不得不）之後接原形動詞。

例 Reading about his great feats, we could not but admire his courage.
另兩個類似的片語是

sb. cannot help + V-ing

sb. cannot help but + V

例 Seeing her husband wearing a funny hat, she could not help laughing.
　Seeing her husband wearing a funny hat, she could not help but laugh.

(2) mental feast

mental feast 的意思是「心靈的饗宴」。feast 原指「盛宴」（large meal），也可指一大堆我們可以做或看的好玩有趣的東西。

例 The summer camp will provide a feast of entertainment to suit everyone's tastes.

6. 造句練習：將各句譯成英文。

(1) 看著天上的繁星，我不得不驚嘆宇宙之大。

(2) 不論是一首樂曲或是一幅畫，藝術提供給我們豐富的心靈饗宴。

(3) 當我想到父母為我做的一切，我禁不住要說我愛他們勝過一切。

（參考解答請見附錄 II）

7. 實力培養

My Favorite Subject in School－History

> My favorite subject in school is history. I like history for three reasons. First, history tells me where I came from, _____

_____. Without history, I _____
_____.

Second, history offers a mental feast. In history, we can see the rise and fall of empires, _____, and great achievements in civilization. Reading about these is like enjoying a mental feast. So, history _____.

Finally, history is our guide. By studying history, we can avoid making the same mistakes _____. We become wiser.

To sum up, because it gives me a sense of time, because it offers a mental feast, and because it is my guide, history is my favorite subject in school.

8. 輕鬆寫作

提示 以地理作為你喜歡的科目，寫一封英文信，告訴美國筆友你喜歡地理的 原因：

參考資料：

Reasons for liking geography:

(1) studying the culture and landscape of different nations is fun

(2) getting to know the geography of different nations helps make us world citizens

(3) geography enables us to know the weather patterns of the globe, our place in the solar system, etc.

Unit 19　My Favorite Subject in School—English

題型：主題句寫作

1. 試題

說明　以 "My Favorite Subject in School" 為主題，寫一篇英文作文，說明你最喜歡的一門科目。以 "My favorite subject in school is ＿＿＿." 開頭，文長至少 120 字，至多不超過 170 字。

2. 擬寫內容

在學校我最喜歡的科目－英文

在學校我最喜歡的科目是英文，原因有三。第一，用英文和外國人溝通很刺激。很刺激是因為我們可以學到不同的文化和價值觀。

第二，會英文給我成就感。我的數學、地理或其他科目也許很棒，但是在日常生活中，我沒什麼機會炫耀這些科目的知識。相反的，我的生活週遭充滿英文。每當我看懂、聽懂或讀懂英文時，常覺得很有成就感。

第三，好的英文能力開啟無限的可能。我可以到國外旅遊或讀書，找到需要英文的工作，甚至可以教英文為生。

由於這三個理由，在學校我最喜歡的科目是英文。

3. 參考範文

My Favorite Subject in School—English

My favorite subject in school is English for three reasons. First, it is exciting to use English to communicate with foreigners. It is exciting because we can learn about different cultures and different value systems.

Second, **being able to use English gives me a sense of achievement**.[1] I may be good at math, geography, or other subjects. But in my daily life I don't have much chance to show off my knowledge in these subjects. **On the other hand**,[2] **I am surrounded by English**.[3] I often feel a sense of achievement whenever I understand what I see, hear, or read.

Third, **a good command of English**[4] opens unlimited possibilities. I can travel or study abroad, I can find a job that requires English, and I can even teach English to make a living.

For these three reasons, my favorite subject in school is English.

4. 寫作指導

以 My favorite subject in school is English for three reasons. 作為主題句,每一個原因稍微鋪陳一下,就可以達到試題要求的長度。

5. 重要的字詞及文法提示

(1) being able to use English gives me a sense of achievement

這是動名詞片語當主詞的句型,句中 being able to use English 是主詞,其後的動詞要用三單動詞。

例 Being able to communicate with people from other countries is not easy.
Teaching teenagers is a challenging job.

(2) On the other hand

On the other hand(另一方面)之後提出和其前敘述不同的另一種說詞。

例 He doesn't know if he should take the job. It offers a handsome salary. On the other hand, it is very demanding.

也可在第一敘述前加上 On (the) one hand。

例 On (the) one hand, the job offers a handsome salary. On the other hand, it is very demanding.

請記住:on the other hand 不是 besides 的意思,而比較接近 however 的意思。

(3) am surrounded by English

be surrounded by sth./sb. 意思是「被…所包圍;大量接觸…」。

例 Nurses are surrounded by sick people.

(4) a good command of English

a good command of English 是「精通英文」的意思。command 在這裡意思是「能力」。

6. 造句練習:將各句譯成英文。

(1) 能夠原諒別人帶來內在的平靜。
(2) 很自然地,大家都期望英文老師要能精通英語。
(3) 重複使用塑膠袋是保護環境的一種方法。
(4) 一方面他想吹冷氣;另一方面他又不想花太多錢。

(5) 精通四國語言為他帶來很多的工作機會。

（參考解答請見附錄 II）

7. 實力培養

My Favorite Subject in School－English

My favorite subject in school is English for three reasons. First, it is exciting to use English to _____. It is exciting because we can learn about different cultures and _____ _____.

Second, being able to use English _____ _____. I may be good at math, geography, or other subjects. But in my daily life I don't have much chance _____ _____. On the other hand, I am _____ _____. I often feel a sense of achievement _____ _____, hear, or read.

Third, a good command of English _____. I can travel or study abroad, I can find a job that requires English, and I can even teach English to make a living.

For these three reasons, my favorite subject in school is English.

8. 輕鬆寫作

提示 以 "My favorite subject in school is Chinese." 為主題句，說明你喜歡中文的原因。

參考資料：

Possible reasons why Chinese is your favorite subject:

(1) China has a five-thousand-year long history.

(2) Knowing the language is the key to understanding China.

(3) China is a large country, it has a population of over 1.2 billion.

(4) The Chinese people play an important role on the world stage.

(5) Chinese literature is worth studying.

Unit 20　My Hobby

題型：主題句寫作

1. 試題

說明

以 "My Hobby" 為題，寫一篇英文作文，第一段說明一項自己的嗜好是什麼，有什麼活動；第二段說明你的嗜好所帶來的好處。請以 "My hobby is..." 為開頭。文長至少 120 字，至多不超過 170 字。

2. 擬寫內容

我的嗜好

　　我從很小就喜歡畫畫。剛開始，我畫我接觸的人物，例如，可愛的小女孩，或者畫我看到的東西，譬如博物館裡的漂亮花瓶。漸漸地，我畫更複雜的。我畫見解、我的夢想、和我希望能去玩的虛擬地點。

　　畫畫有很多個好處。其一，畫畫幫我打發時間。每當我獨自一人時，我就畫畫。如此，我從來不覺得寂寞。其二，畫畫有助抒解我的情緒。譬如，當我生氣的時候，便藉由畫畫來抒解怒氣，也許畫些從未見過的怪獸。最後一點，畫畫使我快樂。每當畫畫時，我感到更貼近自己，這使我非常快樂。

　　畫畫做為嗜好很有樂趣。跟我一起畫畫，好嗎？

3. 參考範文

My Hobby

　　I have enjoyed **drawing**[1] **since**[2] I was very young. In the beginning, I drew pictures of people I met, like a cute little girl, or of things I saw, like a pretty vase in a museum. Gradually, my drawing became more complex. I drew about ideas, about my dreams, and about imaginary places that I wished to visit.

　　Drawing has several benefits. For one thing, drawing helps me kill time. **Whenever**[3] I am alone, I draw, so I never feel lonely. **In addition**,[4] drawing helps me release my emotions. **For instance**,[5] when I am angry, I release my anger in my drawing, perhaps by drawing a monster I have never seen before. Finally, drawing makes me happy. Whenever I am drawing, I feel close to myself. This makes me very happy.

> Drawing as a hobby is a lot of fun. Join me, won't you?

4. 寫作指導

第一段用時間順序發展，第二段以主題句 Drawing has several benefits. 開始，之後以轉承語 for one thing, in addition, finally 分別引出三個好處，並加以鋪陳，符合寫作原理。末段以邀請作結。

5. 重要的字詞及文法提示

(1) drawing

用鉛筆等畫東西；sketching 素描；painting 油畫

(2) since

現在完成式與 since 的用法

> 例 I have lived in Tainan since I was born.

(3) whenever

whenever 表「不論何時」之意，常用句法為 whenever S V, S V

> 例 Whenever I have time, I study English.

(4) In addition

表「此外」之意。表示附加的轉承語，除了 in addition 之外，還有變化結構 additionally，因為「介詞 + 副詞」可相當副詞。

In addition 也可寫成：

= Moreover

= Furthermore

= What is more

= Besides

這種轉承語可用於句首或句間：

> 例 John is kind. In addition, he works hard.
>
> John is kind; in addition, he works hard.

(5) For instance

表「例如」；這是一個轉承語，當後句為前句之舉例時使用。

類似的轉承語有：

For example

As an example

Take... for example

To give an example

6. 造句練習：將各句譯成英文。

(1) 人類初登陸月球距今有多久了？

(2) 只要你喜歡，不論什麼時候來看我們都可以。

(3) 我學英文已經六年了。我正在進步中。

（參考解答請見附錄 II）

7. 實力培養

My Hobby

I have enjoyed drawing _____. In the beginning, I drew _____, like a cute little girl, or of things I saw, like _____. Gradually, my drawing _____. I drew about ideas, about my dreams, and about imaginary places _____.

There are several benifits of drawing. _____, drawing helps me kill time. _____, I draw, so _____. In addition, _____. For instance, when I am angry, I release my anger in my drawing, perhaps by drawing a monster _____. Finally, drawing makes me happy. _____, I feel close to myself. This makes me very happy.

Drawing as a hobby is a lot of fun. Join me, _____ _____?

8. 輕鬆寫作

 依以上命題，寫一篇英文作文。

參考資料：

嗜好的種類：

(1) 創造性嗜好：drawing, painting, listening to music, playing a musical instrument, writing, reading

(2) 收集性嗜好：collecting things, such as stamps, hats, match boxes, dolls, baseball cards, coins...

培養嗜好的好處：helps to relax, helps in making friends, makes money, helps kill time, enriches knowledge, makes us happy, etc.

Unit 21 | Visiting with a Friend

題型：主題寫作

1. 試題

說明

以 "Visiting with a Friend" 為主題，寫一篇英文作文，敘述一次訪友的經過。文長至少 120 字，至多不超過 170 字。

2. 擬寫內容

拜訪朋友

前幾天我在朋友家度過了一個愉快的晚上。那天是約翰的生日，他邀請了一些朋友，大家幾乎同時到達。

我們先問候約翰的父母，然後他們外出，留下整個房子給我們。很快地，慶生會開始。巧克力蛋糕已準備好，我們點燃蠟燭。我們把燈關掉，並為約翰唱生日快樂歌，然後，他許願，接著吹熄蠟燭。蠟燭一吹熄，我們立刻又把燈打開，然後每個人都把帶來的禮物拿出來。約翰拆開禮物並謝謝我們大家。然後我們吃晚餐，玩遊戲和看電視影片。

最後，時間已晚，我們便離開。這真是一個愉快的夜晚。

3. 參考範文

Visiting with a Friend

I spent a pleasant evening at a friend's home the other day. It was John's birthday, and several friends were invited. Everyone arrived at about the same time.

We met John's parents first. Then they went out, **leaving the entire apartment to us**.[1] Soon the celebration began. A chocolate cake had been prepared, and we lit the candles. We turned off the lights and sang Happy Birthday. Then he made a wish, and blew out the candles. **As soon as**[2] the candles were blown out and the light was turned on again, we took out the presents we had brought. John opened the presents and thanked each of us. Then we ate dinner, played games and watched a movie.

Finally, it was getting late, so we left. It was **a very pleasant evening**.[3]

4. 寫作指導

(1) 這是一篇敘述文，依照時間順序發展即可，最後用離開朋友家結尾，很自然。

(2) I spent a pleasant evening at a friend's home the other day. 是主題句。

5. 重要的字詞及文法提示

(1) leaving the entire apartment to us

leave sth. to sb. 意思是「把某物託交給某人」。

例 If you have no time to complete the rest of the project, just leave it to me. I'll finish it.

leave sth to sb.也有「（死後）將某物遺贈給某人」的意思。

例 She left a big sum of money to her granddaughter.

(2) as soon as

as soon as S V, S V... （一…就…）中 as soon as 是個表示時間的連接詞。

例 As soon as he finished his homework, he went to bed.

as soon as 的子句也可放句中。

例 He went to bed as soon as he finished his homework.

類似的用法有

No sooner had S V-en than S V-ed...

Hardly had S V-en when S V-ed...

例 No sooner had he finished his homework than he went to bed.

Hardly had he finished his homework when he went to bed.

(3) a very pleasant evening

pleasant 表示「令人愉快的」，也可說 pleasing，如果要表示「感到愉快的」，必須說 pleased。

例 We were happy to have her around. She has a very pleasant/pleasing personality.

6. 造句練習：將各句譯成英文。

(1) 我很高興能聆聽那些世界聞名的鋼琴家的演奏。

(2) 她大學一畢業就出國深造。

(3) 那隻狗一聽到愉快的音樂，就會上下跳躍。

(4) 媽媽因為有同事來接她，所以就把她的車子交給我。

(5) 那位慈善家把所有的錢遺贈給那家療養院。

(6) 他一聽到那消息就跑出去了。（**No sooner...**）

（參考解答請見附錄 II）

7. 實力培養

Visiting With a Friend

I spent a pleasant evening at a friend's home the other day. It was John's birthday, and several friends were invited. Everyone arrived at about the same time.

We met John's parents first. Then they went out, _____ _____. Soon the celebration began. A chocolate cake had been prepared, and _____. We turned off the lights and sang Happy Birthday. Then he made a wish, and blew out the candles. As soon as _____ and the light was turned on again, we took out the presents we had brought. John opened the presents and _____. Then we ate dinner, played games and watched a movie on TV.

Finally, it was getting late, so we left. It was a very pleasant evening.

8. 輕鬆寫作

提示

你認識一個異性朋友。第一次去他／她家拜訪。寫一篇英文作文，敘述拜訪的經過。

參考資料：

(1) In writing a narration, you need to provide details such as when you paid the visit, where, why, how and what happened during the visit.

(2) You may begin your composition with something like "My girlfriend/ boyfriend invited me to visit her/him for the first time."

Unit 22　A Wonderful Thing

題型：主題句寫作

1. 試題

 以 "A Wonderful Thing" 為主題，寫一篇英文作文，說明一件發生在你身上的美好的事。以The most wonderful thing that has happened to me is ＿＿＿＿. 為開始。文長至少 120 字，至多不超過 170 字。

2. 擬寫內容

一件美好的事

　　我所遇過最美好的事就是出生在我的家庭。首先，我有最棒的父母。我的父母都很照顧我，時時心繫對我有益的事情。他們竭其所能地幫助我，支持我，並且幫忙我實現夢想，最重要的是，他們愛我。

　　其次，我有好兄弟姊妹。我哥哥是大學生，主修法律，他很聰明，總是協助我做功課。因為有他，我考試成績都很好。我姐姐也很聰明，她是醫院裡的護士，當我身體不適時，她很會照顧我。

　　總之，因為我有個很棒的家庭，所以我所遇過最美好的事就是出生在我的家庭。

3. 參考範文

A Wonderful Thing

　　The most wonderful thing that ever happened to me is that I was born into my family. First, I have wonderful parents. Both my parents care a lot about me. They both have my best interests at heart. They do all they can to help me, to support me, and to help make my dreams come true. Above all, they love me.

　　Second, I have wonderful **siblings**.[1] My brother is a university student, **majoring in**[2] law. My brother is intelligent, and always helps me with my schoolwork. Because of him, I do well on exams. My sister is also intelligent. She is a nurse at a hospital. When I **don't feel well**,[3] she takes good care of me.

> In summary, because I have a great family, the most wonderful thing that ever happened to me is that I was born into my family.

4. 寫作指導

只要言之成理,「我所遇過最美好的事」這個主題是很好發揮的。本文從惜福的角度出發,不失為一種方法。

5. 重要的字詞及文法提示

(1) siblings

siblings 指的就是「手足、兄弟姊妹」。

例 Your siblings are your brothers or sisters.

(2) majoring in

majoring in 主攻;主修…。在本文中是現在分詞片語,當形容詞用,相當於形容詞子句或另一個句子。此句構相當簡潔生動,可多應用。

例 My brother is a university student, majoring in law.

= My brother is a university student, who majors in law.

(3) don't feel well

don't feel well 覺得身體不適。well 作「舒服、健康、富有 (well off)」解時,是形容詞而不是副詞,其比較級仍是 better。

例 "How are you feeling today?" "Much better."

6. 造句練習:將各句譯成英文。

(1) 每當我身體不舒服時,我就去看醫生。

(2) 這班學生有一半將來要主修文學,另一半將主攻歷史。

(3) 真愛是不管對方是否富有。

(參考解答請見附錄 II)

7. 實力培養

> ## A Wonderful Thing
>
> The most wonderful thing that ever happened to me is _____
> _____. First, I have wonderful parents. Both my parents care a lot about me. They both have _____.

They do all they can to help me, to support me, and to help _____
_____. Above all, they love me.

　　Second, I have wonderful siblings. My brother is a university student,
_____. My brother is intelligent and always
helps me _____. Because of him, I do well
_____. My sister is also intelligent. She is a nurse at a
hospital. When _____, she takes good care of me.

　　In summary, because I have a great family, the most wonderful thing
that ever happened to me is that I was born into my family.

8. 輕鬆寫作

以 "A Wonderful Thing" 為主題，寫一篇英文作文，說明一件發生在你身上的美好的事，你的出生為例外。以 The most wonderful thing that has happened to me is _____. 為開始。文長 120～150 字之間。

參考資料：

(1) Some people consider falling in love a wonderful experience. You might write about your first love.

(2) Some people consider achieving success a wonderful experience. You might write about your success on an exam, an experiment, or attempt at something.

(3) Some symptoms of a wonderful thing:

　　(a) makes one feel content

　　(b) makes one very happy

　　(c) makes one feel worthwhile

　　(d) makes one feel useful

　　(e) makes one feel proud

Unit 23 | Life on Campus

題型：主題寫作

1. 試題

說明　以 "Life on Campus" 為主題，寫一篇英文作文，說明校園生活的內涵。文長至少 120 字，至多不超過 170 字。

2. 擬寫內容

校園生活

　　校園生活主要是學生和老師，以及學生與學生之間的互動。前者主要是教室活動，其中，老師身兼導演與演員的角色，他的主要工作就是把知識傳授給學生。老師講課、指導實驗、帶領討論、提出問題，或者指派作業。以教育之名，他得以採用各種不同的教法。

　　後者主要是課外活動。學生們參加社團，和其他的學生分享他們共同的愛好。在校園裡進行的所有活動都有一項共同點，那就是一切都是為了學習。學生學習將所知運用在生活中，並且在活動的過程中，他們成長且漸漸地變得獨立和成熟。

3. 參考範文

Life on Campus

　　Life on campus is mainly the interaction between students and teachers, and the interaction among students. **The former**[1] **consists** mainly **of**[2] classroom activities, in which the teacher is the director and actor whose main job is to **impart knowledge to students**.[3] The teacher may give a lecture, conduct an experiment, lead a discussion, ask questions, or assign homework. He may use all sorts of methods **in the name of**[4] education.

　　The latter[1] is made up mainly of extracurricular activities. Students participate in clubs, where they share things in common with **fellow students**.[5] All the activities that take place on the campus have one thing in common. That is, learning dominates. Students learn to apply what they know to life, and in the process, they grow up and gradually become independent and mature.

4. 寫作指導

　　"Life on the campus is mainly the interaction between students and teachers, and the interaction among students." 由這一句話作主題句，帶動下文，讓全文有緊密的組織。

5. 重要的字詞及文法提示

(1) The former...; the latter...

The former...; the latter... 表示「前者…；後者…」。

例 I owe a great debt of gratitude to Tom and Peter. The former gave me financial help when I was in need. The latter offered me spiritual support when I was down.

(2) consist of

A consists of B（A 由 B 組成）沒有進行式或被動式的用法。

例 Water consists of oxygen and hydrogen.

也可以說 be made up of

be composed of

例 Water is made up of oxygen and hydrogen.

Water is composed of oxygen and hydrogen.

(3) impart knowledge to students

impart sth. to sb. 意思是「將某資訊告知某人」。

例 He designed his own website to impart the latest news to basketball fans.

(4) in the name of

in the name of 在本文中是「為了某事物的緣故」(for the sake of)。

例 She did everything for him in the name of love.

(5) fellow students

fellow students（同學）中的 fellow 指的是同一種類型或身分的。

例 a fellow traveler（同遊者）

a fellow countryman（同胞）

6. 造句練習：將各句譯成英文。

(1) 成功是由一些小小的勝利組成的。

(2) 為了友誼的緣故，我不會欺騙你或占你便宜。

(3) 父母有責任將適當的價值觀傳授給孩子。

(4) 跟我一樣，同行的遊客都被那壯麗的風景震懾到。

(5) 工作和休閒都很重要。前者給我們實現自我的機會；後者幫助我們輕鬆一下。

(6) 王老師喜歡將最新的教學資訊告知同事。

（參考解答請見附錄 II）

7. 實力培養

Life on Campus

Life on campus is mainly the interaction between students and teachers, and the interaction among students. The former _____, in which the teacher is the director and actor _____ _____. The teacher may give a lecture, conduct an experiment, lead a discussion, ask questions, or assign homework. He may _____ in the name of education.

The latter is made up mainly _____. Students participate in clubs, where _____ _____. All of the activities that _____ have one thing in common. That is, _____. Students learn to apply what they know to life, and in the process, they grow up and gradually become independent and mature.

8. 輕鬆寫作

 以 "Participating in a Club" 為題，寫一篇英文作文。第一段說明你參加某社團的原因，第二段說明你參加某社團的好處。

參考資料：

(1) names of clubs:

The school band, the singing choir, the dancing club, the track team, the field team, the karate club, the guitar club, the English conversation club, etc.

(2) advantages of being a club member:

(a) getting to really know many people

(b) meeting friends with the same interests

(c) sharing things in common

(d) learning something useful for life

(e) leaving your studies for a while

(f) helping you relax

Unit 24 | Time

題型：主題寫作

1. 試題

說明

以 "Time" 為主題，寫一篇英文作文，說明你對時間的認知。文長至少 120 字，至多不超過 170 字。

2. 擬寫內容

論時間

時間是抽象的概念，看不到、聽不到也碰觸不到，但卻規範著我們的生活。它沒有開端，也似乎沒有盡頭。然而我們活在世界上的時間僅限於幾十年。

我們常常覺得時間不夠。我們需要時間完成我們的作業，我們需要時間準備期末考，我們需要時間和朋友相聚，我們需要時間和家人在一起，而且我們需要時間玩樂。除此之外，我們還需要時間休息。為了能夠生存，似乎我們需要更多的時間。

人生很短暫，但是我們仍需好好地利用時間，即使它是如此抽象、無形，以及難以定義。

3. 參考範文

Time

Time is an abstract concept, which cannot be seen, heard, or touched, but which **regulates**[1] our life. It does not have a beginning, **nor**[2] does it **seem to**[3] have an end. Yet our time in the world is limited to only a few decades.

We **are** often **pressed for**[4] time. We need time to finish our homework, we need time to prepare for the final exam, we need time to be with our friends, we need time to be with our family, and we need time to have fun. And after all that, we need time to rest. **It often seems that we need more time in order to survive.**[5]

Our life span is very short, so we should make good use of time, even though it is abstract, invisible and hard to define.

第三章

4. 寫作指導

(1) 時間這個抽象的概念，本來就不容易處理，但是用「看不到、聽不到也碰觸不到，但卻規範著我們的生活」來處理，卻頗貼切，用字也很簡單。這個題目告訴我們一個寫作方法：把困難的事變成簡單。

(2) 高中階段英文作文的要求，主要是能夠表達日常生活、週遭事物，所以把困難的事變成簡單是同學們要學習的。

5. 重要的字詞及文法提示

(1) regulate

regulate（使有規律，管理）是 regular（有規律的）的動詞型態。

例 regulate the flow of water

regulate the traffic

(2) nor

nor（也不）在這文章中是連接詞，意思是 and... not... either。其後的句子要倒裝，也就是要用疑問句的句型。

例 She can't walk, nor can she talk.

He doesn't understand his son, nor has he ever tried to.

(3) seem to

sth./sb. seem to（似乎）之後接原形動詞。

例 John seems to know the truth.

Her plan seemed to work.

此句型是從 It seems that S V 的句型簡化來的。例如以上兩句原是：

例 It seems that John knows the truth.

It seemed that her plan worked.

將 that 子句中的主詞提前，再稍做改變即可。

(4) be pressed for

be pressed for sth.（缺少某事物）即 not have enough of sth.。

例 We are very pressed for cash at the moment. Can we pay you next month?

(5) It often seems that we need more time in order to survive.

這句話也可說成 We often seem to need more time in order to survive.

請參見第 (3) 點說明。

6. 造句練習：將各句譯成英文。

(1) 那些缺少時間的人應該學會時間管理。

(2) 似乎沒有人在這場火災中倖存。

(3) 政府應制訂並執行更嚴格的法律來管理交通。

(4) 他沒做作業，也沒為考試作準備。

(5) 那個時候，逃跑似乎是唯一的一條路。

（參考解答請見附錄Ⅱ）

7. 實力培養

Time

Time is an abstract concept, which cannot be seen, heard, or touched, but _____. It does not have a beginning, nor _____. Yet our time in the world is limited to _____ _____.

_____. We need time to finish our homework, we need time to _____, we need time to be with our friends, we need time _____, and we need time to have fun. And after all that, we need time to rest. It often seems that we need more time _____.

Our life span is very short, _____, even though it is abstract, invisible and hard to define.

8. 輕鬆寫作

以 "Using Time Effectively" 為題，寫一篇英文作文。第一段說明有效使用時間的方法；第二段舉例驗證第一段的觀點。

參考資料：

Using time effectively:

(1) Don't put off until tomorrow what you can do today.

(2) Set priorities. Do important things first.

(3) Do one thing at a time.

(4) If you can't solve a problem at the moment, go on to something else. Give yourself time to think over your problem.

Examples:

You can't solve a math problem, so you move on to another. Later, when you come back, you find the solution to the difficult math problem.

Unit 25 | On Leisure

題型：主題寫作

1. 試題

 以 "On Leisure（論閒暇）" 為主題，寫一篇英文作文，說明你對運用閒暇的看法。文長至少 120 字，至多不超過 170 字。

2. 擬寫內容

論閒暇

　　每個人都會談論閒暇時間，但很少人認真去思考它。「閒暇」一詞的其中一個定義是「空閒時間」。依此定義，我們可能非常忙，但我們不會忙到完全都沒有任何閒暇時間。

　　我們工作以維持生活，但我們的命運卻決定於閒暇時間。例如，林肯原來是貧窮的鄉下農夫。然而，他利用他的閒暇時間儘可能地閱讀。結果，他不但通過了律師資格考試，最後還成了美國總統。

　　因此，讓我們利用閒暇時間至少培養一種嗜好。嗜好未必能帶來名譽與財富，但是會使我們過更快樂的生活。

3. 參考範文

On Leisure

Everybody talks about leisure, but few people think seriously about it. One of the meanings of the term "leisure" is free time. **Based on**[1] this definition, we may be very busy, but we will never be **so** busy **that**[2] we do **not** have any leisure time **at all**.[3]

We work to live, but our fate is determined by our leisure time. For example, Lincoln was originally a country farmer. However, he used his leisure time to read **as much as he could**.[4] As a result, he not only passed the Bar Examination, he ended up President of the United States.

So let us use our leisure time to at least cultivate a hobby. Our hobbies will **not necessarily**[5] bring us fame and wealth, but they will help us live a happier life.

4. 寫作指導

先定義「閒暇」一詞，再舉例說明「閒暇時間決定人的命運」，最後提出運用閒暇的建議。

5. 重要的字詞及文法提示

(1) based on

　　based on（根據）這片語放在句首，其後接名詞，表示其後句子所呈述的事實是以該名詞為根據；也可用 according to 來表示。

　　例 Based on/According to what he said, a new library is going to be constructed near the park.

(2) so... that...

　　so... that...（如此…以致於）這句型用來表示結果。so 之後接形容詞或副詞，that 之後接一個子句；that 這連接詞可以省略。

　　例 The weather was so cold（that）many people froze to death.

(3) not... at all

　　not... at all（一點也不…）這片語用來強烈否定某事。

　　例 He doesn't trust his employees at all.

　　也可將 at all 緊放在 not 之後。

　　例 He doesn't at all trust his employees.

　　　　That TV program is not at all informative.

　　也可說 not... in the least。

　　例 He doesn't trust his employees in the least.

(4) as much as he could

　　as... as one can（盡可能…）片語中，第一個 as 之後可接形容詞或副詞，如果形容詞之後有名詞，需放在一起。

　　例 You have to be as careful as you can.

　　　　Chased by a fierce dog, Michael ran as fast as he could.

　　　　They were asked to read as many English books as they could to improve their reading ability.

　　也可以說 as... as possible。

　　例 Please drive as carefully as possible/you can.

(5) not necessarily

　　not necessarily（未必）這個片語表示「某事不一定全然是事實」。

　　例 Rich people are not necessarily happy.

6. 造句練習：將各句譯成英文。

(1) 根據這本書，人類在五年後將面對資源缺乏的危機。

(2) 他氣得全身發抖。

(3) 她一點也不喜歡他的陪伴。

(4) 這些學生被要求在課堂上盡可能使用英語。

(5) 他上課不專心；因此，他沒聽到老師提到的很多重點。

(6) 他們一直往南開，結果到了高雄。

(7) 如果你每個月存一萬塊，最後將成為一個百萬富翁。

(8) 有學問的人未必是一個成功的老師。

(9) 他年輕時沒有培養嗜好；因此，退休之後他覺得很無聊。

（參考解答請見附錄Ⅱ）

7. 實力培養

On Leisure

Everybody talks about leisure, but few people think seriously about it. One of the meanings of the term "leisure" is free time. _____, we may be very busy, but we will never be so busy _____ _____.

We work to live, but our fate is _____. For example, Lincoln was originally a poor country farmer. However, he used his leisure time to read _____. As a result, he not only passed the Bar Examination, he ended up President of the United States.

So, let us use our leisure time to at least cultivate a hobby. Our hobbies will not necessarily bring us fame and wealth, but _____ _____.

8. 輕鬆寫作

提示　以 "How I Use My Leisure" 為主題，寫一篇英文作文。第一段說明閒暇給人的好處；第二段說明你如何運用閒暇。

參考資料：

Advantages of leisure:

(1) leisure enables us to take care of personal business

(2) leisure helps us relax

(3) leisure offers us time to do whatever we please

How to use leisure:

(1) going to cram school

(2) strengthen your English, math, physics

(3) prepare for the university entrance examination

(4) enjoy a hobby

Unit 26 | How SARS Affected My Personal Life

題型：主題句寫作

1. 試題

說明

以 "SARS affected my personal life greatly." 為主題句，寫一篇英文作文，説明 SARS 對你的生活所造成的影響。文長至少 120 字，至多不超過 170 字。

2. 擬寫內容

SARS 如何影響我的個人生活

SARS 大大地影響我的個人生活。第一，我必須依靠我父親開車往返學校，而不是搭乘公共運輸。第二，出門時我必須戴口罩。如果我沒有戴口罩，人家不讓我進入公共場所。第三，必須每天量兩次體溫以確定我沒問題（很健康）。

SARS 也影響了我的心理。一者，我必須非常小心以免被感染。再者，台灣成為感染區的這種情況使我感到不安。

對於 SARS 我幾乎無能為力。我所能做的是遵守醫學專家的建議（例如常洗手及睡眠充足）以及希望 SARS 儘早遠離我們。

3. 參考範文

How SARS Affected My Personal Life

SARS affected my personal life greatly. First, instead of taking public transportation, I had to rely on my dad to take me to and from school in his car. Second, I had to wear a mask whenever I went out. **If I didn't, I would not be allowed into public places**.[1] Third, my body temperature was taken twice a day, to make sure that I was okay.

SARS affected me psychologically, too. For one thing, I had to be very careful, **in order not to**[2] be infected. For another, I didn't feel good about the whole situation of Taiwan being an area of the epidemic.

There was almost nothing that I could do about SARS. **All that I did was follow the advice of medical experts**[3]—wash my hands often and get plenty of sleep—and wish SARS to leave us **as soon as possible**.[4]

4. 寫作指導

用淺顯的英文字句，分別從生活上、心理上說明 SARS 對個人的影響，最後以「希望SARS 趕快結束」作結。

5. 重要的字詞及文法提示

(1) If I didn't, I would not be allowed into public places.

非現在事實的假設，句中用過去式，句型為：

If S 過去式, S would 原形動詞…

could

might

例 I don't have much money now. If I had a lot of money, I would buy that car.

If 子句中的動詞如果是 be 動詞，常常用 were。

例 If I were you, I would avoid going to public places.

(2) in order not to...

in order not to（為了不要）是從 in order to（為了）來的，兩者之後都接原形動詞，說明做某事的原因。

例 She jogs every morning in order to keep fit.

He avoids eating ice cream in order not to put on weight.

(3) All that I did was follow the advice of medical experts...

that I did 是關係子句，用來限定 All，that 這個關係代名詞可以省略。be 動詞後要接原形動詞。

例 All (that) he does every day is hang out with his friends.

(4) as soon as possible

as adj/adv as possible 盡可能…

例 Please come as early as possible.

Read as many English books as possible.

也可說成 as adj./adv. as one can。

例 Please come as early as you can.

Read as many English books as you can.

6. 造句練習：將各句譯成英文。

(1) 讓你的生活盡量簡單。

(2) 你現在能夠做的就是遵從醫生的建議。

(3) 如果我得了 SARS，我就必須待在家裡。

(4) 這次的失敗對他來說是個打擊，不過，他卻得到了一個很好的教訓。

(5) 很多人把 SARS 視為無藥可救的病。 (incurable disease)

(6) 如果我是你，我會說實話而不會撒謊。

(7) 捷運被視為最方便的公共運輸工具。 (regard)

(8) 為了不要花太多錢，他搭公車上班。

（參考解答請見附錄Ⅱ）

7. 實力培養

How SARS Has Affected My Personal Life

　　SARS affected my personal life greatly. First, _____ _____, I had to rely on my dad to take me to and from school in his car. Second, I had to wear a mask _____ _____. If I didn't, I _____. Third, my body temperature was taken twice a day, to _____ _____.

　　SARS affected me psychologically, too. For one thing, I had to be very careful, _____. For another, I didn't feel good about the whole situation of Taiwan _____.

　　There was almost nothing that I could do about SARS. _____ _____ follow the advice of medical experts—wash my hands often and get plenty of sleep—and wish SARS to leave us as soon as possible.

8. 輕鬆寫作

提示

用英文寫一篇作文，説明你一次生病對生活的影響。

參考資料：

common diseases: a cold, the flu, an ulcer, pneumonia...

How diseases may affect your life:

(1) You feel uncomfortable.

(2) You cough, you have a runny nose, you have a fever.

(3) You feel dizzy and you are unable to concentrate.

(4) You cannot study effectively.

(5) You cannot go to school.

(6) You cannot take part in social activities.

Unit 27 What Does the Lunar New Year Mean to Me?

題型：主題寫作

1. 試題

說明

以 "What Does the Lunar New Year Mean to Me?" 為主題，寫一篇英文作文，說明農曆新年對你的意義。文長至少 120 字，至多不超過 170 字。

2. 擬寫內容

農曆新年對我有什麼意義？

　　農曆新年對我而言具有幾項意義。第一，它代表一段可以休息的時間。身為一個正準備著大學聯考的學生，我每天做的事就是讀書。我很少有時間休息。農曆新年是我能暫時將讀書拋在腦後，並且享受與家人朋友在一起的唯一時機。

　　第二，農曆新年代表成熟。既然我在新年以後多了一歲，我必須比前一年更為成熟。我必須更有教養、更善良並且更能體貼別人。

　　最後，新年代表愛。在農曆新年期間，家人團聚在一起。它是分享愛的時刻。此外，我們也會探訪我們的親戚和朋友以祝福他們健康。它是表達愛的時刻。

3. 參考範文

What Does the Lunar New Year Mean to Me?

　　The Lunar New Year means several things to me. First, it means a time for resting. **As a student**[1] preparing for the university entrance examination, all that I do every day is study. I seldom have time to rest. The Lunar New Year is the only occasion **when I can temporarily leave my studies behind**[2] and enjoy being with family and friends.

　　Second, the Lunar New Year means maturity. **Since**[3] I am one year older after the New Year, I have to become more mature than I was the previous year. I have to be nicer, kinder, and more considerate to others.

　　Finally, the New Year means love. During the New Year, family members get together. It is a time for sharing love. We also visit our relatives and friends to **wish them well**.[4] It is a time for love.

4. 寫作指導

「農曆新年對我而言具有幾項意義」是主題句。把內容摘述在一句中是個開始全文的實用方法。

5. 重要的字詞及文法提示

(1) As a student...

as（身為）是一個介系詞，後面接身分。

例 As a parent of a disabled child, Mrs. Lin had a tough life.

也可將整個片語放在句尾。

例 What can I do as a parent?

(2) when I can temporarily leave my studies behind...

when 是個關係副詞，引導一個關係子句，修飾限定其前的時間名詞。這個句子是從下面兩句合併而成：

The New Year is the only occasion.

I can temporarily leave my studies behind on the occasion.

→ The New Year is the only occasion when I can temporarily leave my studies behind.

例 Thanksgiving is a time when everybody shows their gratitude.

(3) Since...

since（既然、因為）接一子句，說明主要子句的原因。

例 Since you have asked, I'll definitely let you know.

(4) wish them well

wish sb. well（祝福某人好運）是個固定片語，如果是希望某人倒楣，可以說 wish sb. ill。此外，wish sb. sth. 則表示祝福某人享有或得到某個好東西。

例 I wish you a Merry Christmas.

　　I wish you happiness.

6. 造句練習：將各句譯成英文。

(1) 既然你知道時間就是金錢，就應該善加利用。

(2) 在他們啟程前往美國之時，我們祝福他們好運。

(3) 除了名利外，他還贏得了友誼。

(4) 暑假是一段學生們得以探索新興趣的時光。

(5) 運動讓我們放鬆；此外，還可以幫助我們保持身體健康。

(6) 身為老師，他盡力照顧班上每一個學生。

（參考解答請見附錄 II）

7. 實力培養

What Does the Lunar New Year Mean to Me?

The Lunar New Year means several things to me. First, it means a time for resting. As a student preparing for the university entrance examination, _____ is study. I seldom have time to rest. The Lunar New Year is the only occasion _____ _____ and enjoy being with family and friends.

Second, the Lunar New Year means maturity. Since I am one year older after the New Year, I have to become more mature _____ _____. I have to be nicer, kinder, and _____ _____ others.

Finally, the New Year means love. During the New Year, family members get together. It is a time for sharing love. We also visit our relatives and friends _____. It is a time for love.

---

8. 輕鬆寫作

提示

以 "How I Spend the Lunar New Year" 為題，寫一篇英文作文。第一段
説明你都是如何過新年的；第二段説明你對過新年方式的感想。

參考資料：

(1) How you might spend the New Year

    (a) visit your relatives with your family

    (b) visit your good friends

    (c) travel with your family to a remote place

    (d) eat a lot of food

    (e) watch a lot of TV

(2) How you might feel

    (a) feel relaxed

    (b) feel excited

    (c) feel happy being with your family

Unit 28　My Motto

題型：主題寫作

1. 試題

說明

以 "My Motto" 為題，寫一篇英文作文，說明你的座右銘是什麼，以及選此座右銘的原因。文長至少 120 字，至多不超過 170 字。

2. 擬寫內容

我的座右銘

"Just do it" 這句話可以解釋為：一有任何事需要完成，便應該儘快去做，不應該耽擱或拖延。我喜歡這句話，並且將它當作我的座右銘。

人們常常會耽擱，他們總認為能趕上最後期限就可以了。但是耽擱至少有兩個缺點。第一，會耽擱的人浪費時間在擔心，因此他們承受不必要的壓力。第二，他們無力招架任何偶發事件；一旦有偶發事件發生，他們將難以趕上最後期限。

另一方面，一旦實踐 "Just do it" 的哲學，將可以擺脫不必要的憂慮和壓力，而且也不會有趕上最後期限的問題。甚至有時間可以放鬆一下。這就是為什麼 "Just do it" 是我的座右銘。

3. 參考範文

My Motto

One interpretation of the sentence "Just do it" is that if there is anything that needs to be done, you should do it as soon as you can. You should not procrastinate or put it off. I like this expression and have **made it my motto**.[1]

Procrastination is common. People think that if they meet the deadline, they will be okay. But there are at least two disadvantages of procrastination. The first is that people who procrastinate **spend** a lot of **time worrying**.[2] Therefore they suffer from unnecessary pressure. The second is that they cannot afford any surprises. If anything unforeseen happens, they will **have difficulty meeting**[3] the deadline.

第三章

> On the other hand, if you practice the philosophy of "Just do it," you can free yourself from unnecessary worry and pressure, and will not have problems meeting the deadline. You will even have time to relax. This is why "Just do it" is my motto.

4. 寫作指導

Just do it. 可譯成「儘快做」。本文提出一些理由，說明如果有任何事需要完成，應該儘快做。

5. 重要的字詞及文法提示

(1) made it my motto

make A B（使 A 成為 B）中 make 後面接受詞，再接受詞補語來說明受詞。

例 The mother made her son a good citizen.

B 也可以是形容詞。

例 He always makes me happy.

(2) spend time worrying

spend + time/money + V-ing，只能用人或機構當 spend 的主詞。

例 Ted spent two hours fixing the bicycle.

Kathy spent $10,000 decorating her new apartment.

(3) have difficulty meeting

have difficulty 之後接動名詞表示做某事有困難，其實之後本有一介系詞 in，但可以省略。

例 The old man has difficulty (in) remembering names.

類似結構有：

have problems　V-ing

have trouble　　V-ing

have fun　　　　V-ing

have difficulty 之後也可接 with 再接名詞。

例 She has difficulty with English pronunciation.

6. 造句練習：將各句譯成英文。

(1) 有些小孩學習說話有困難。

(2) 當他十幾歲時便想服務人群，並以此為人生目標。

(3) 他的粗心大意常惹太太生氣。

(4) 他將大部分的時間都花在照顧年邁的雙親上。

(5) 她希望能盡快忘掉那次不愉快的經驗。

(6) 若想要精通英文，必須盡量多看英文書。

(7) 他在了解抽象概念上有問題。

(8) 他在用英語溝通方面沒有困難。

（參考解答請見附錄 II ）

7. 實力培養

My Motto

　　One interpretation of the sentence "Just do it" is that if there is anything that needs to be done, you should do it as soon as you can. You should not procrastinate ＿＿＿＿＿＿＿＿＿＿＿＿＿＿＿＿. I like this expression and I have ＿＿＿＿＿＿＿＿＿.

　　Procrastination is common. People think that if they ＿＿＿＿＿＿＿, they will be okay. But there are at least two disadvantages of procrastination. The first is that people who procrastinate ＿＿＿＿＿＿＿＿＿＿＿＿＿＿. Therefore they ＿＿＿＿＿＿＿＿＿＿ unnecessary pressure. The second is that they cannot ＿＿＿＿＿＿＿＿＿＿＿＿＿＿. If anything unforeseen happens, they will have ＿＿＿＿＿＿＿＿＿＿＿＿＿＿.

　　On the other hand, if you practice the philosophy of "Just do it," you can ＿＿＿＿＿＿＿＿＿＿＿＿＿＿ the unnecessary worry and pressure, and you will not have problems meeting the deadline. You will even ＿＿＿＿＿ ＿＿＿＿＿＿＿＿＿. This is why "Just do it" is my motto.

8. 輕鬆寫作

以 **My motto is "Whatever you do, do it well."** 為開頭，寫一篇英文作文，說明你選這個座右銘的理由。

參考資料：

Reasons for whatever you do, do it well:

(1) if you do everything well, you will be trusted

(2) if you do everything well, you will have fewer regrets

(3) if you do everything well, you will build up a reputation

(4) if you do everything well, you are more likely to succeed

Unit 29　Smoking

題型：主題寫作

1. 試題

 說明　以 "Smoking" 為主題，寫一篇英文作文，說明你對抽煙的看法。文長至少 120 字，至多不超過 170 字。

2. 擬寫內容

抽煙

　　很多人即使知道抽煙對自己和別人都有害，他們還是抽煙。雖然抽煙的人都有不同的理由這麼做，但是他們必須認真地重新考慮是否應該繼續抽煙。

　　根據研究，抽煙對吸煙者造成嚴重的傷害。我們都知道抽煙會引起呼吸方面的問題。除此之外，已知抽煙會傷害胃且可能會引發肺癌，或甚至早死。

　　抽煙也對別人造成傷害。抽煙污染空氣。因此對抽煙者周圍的人來說，是健康的威脅。研究也顯示那些吸二手煙的人比沒有吸到的人更可能得到與抽煙相關的疾病。

　　依據以上幾點，我們知道抽煙不只危害抽煙者，也會危害到他們周圍的人。抽煙的人該戒煙了。

3. 參考範文

Smoking

　　Many people smoke **even though**[1] they know that smoking is harmful both to themselves and to others. Although smokers have different reasons for smoking, they should seriously reconsider **whether**[2] they should continue smoking.

　　According to[3] research, smoking causes great harm to the smoker. We all know that smoking may cause breathing problems. Besides that, **smoking has been known to harm the stomach**[4] and it may cause lung cancer, or even early death.

　　Smoking causes harm to non-smokers, too. Smoking pollutes the air. It is consequently a health threat to those around the smoker. Research also shows that **those exposed to smoke**[5] **are more likely to**[6] get smoke-related

> illnesses than those who are not.
>
>   Based on the above, we know that smoking not only harms smokers but the people around them. For those who smoke, it is time to quit.

4. 寫作指導

例舉一些事實，說明抽煙對自己造成嚴重的傷害、也對別人造成傷害。因此，最後以建議戒煙作結。

5. 重要的字詞及文法提示

(1) even though

even though（即使）中 even 是副詞，though 是連接詞，所以後面要接子句。even本身後面不可接子句。

例 Even though he failed the exam, he was not discouraged.

(2) whether

whether（是否）是連接詞，其後接名詞子句，可放在動詞後當受詞用。

例 He didn't know whether he should resign.

可配合 or not 一起用。

例 He didn't know whether he should resign or not.

He didn't know whether or not he should resign.

(3) according to

according to（根據）用來表示資訊來源。

例 According to the weather forecast, there will be a brief shower tomorrow afternoon.

(4) smoking has been known to harm the stomach...

這個句子是從下面這兩句話簡化來的：

People have known that smoking harms the stomach...

→ 改成被動句：

It has been known that smoking harms the stomach...

→ smoking 提前當主詞：

Smoking has been known to harm the stomach...

英文中很多「認知」動詞都可有這種變化。

例 Formosa black bears are believed to be the largest mammals in Taiwan.

He is said to be the richest man in the world.

(5) those exposed to smoke

those exposed to smoke 是從 those who are exposed to smoke 簡化來的。
英文裡常用分詞片語當形容詞用。

例 The woman sitting next to our boss is his secretary.
This is one of the books written by Jane Austen.

(6) are more likely to

be likely to（可能）有下面兩種用法：
It is likely that Mr. Li will win the election.
Mr. Li is likely to win the election.
be more likely to 比較有可能

6. 造句練習：將各句譯成英文。

(1) 即使他很有可能會輸，他還是全力以赴。
(2) 常接觸書本的人知識較豐富。
(3) 狗很忠心是大家都知道的。
(4) 根據很多報告，吸煙的人比不吸煙的人有可能罹患肺癌。
(5) 雖然他損失了一大筆錢，但是卻贏得朋友的信任。
(6) 我不知道是否該繼續讀研究所。
(7) 她怕看到血，除此之外，她對病人沒有耐心。
(8) 根據她的觀察，這些熊只有在受到驚嚇時才會攻擊人們。
(9) 據說這工廠排放的廢水會對我們的身體造成很大的傷害。

（參考解答請見附錄Ⅱ）

7. 實力培養

Smoking

Many people smoke _____ they know that smoking is harmful both to themselves and to others. Although smokers have different reasons for smoking, they should seriously reconsider _____ _____.

According to research, smoking causes great harm to the smoker. We all know that smoking may cause breathing problems. _____, smoking _____ and it may cause lung cancer, or even early death.

Smoking causes harm to non-smokers, too. _____
_____ . It is consequently a health threat to _____ .
Research also shows that those exposed to smoke _____
_____ smoke-related illnesses than those who are not.

Based on the above, we know that smoking _____
_____ . For those who smoke, it is time to quit.

8. 輕鬆寫作

提示

你 (Jack) 同年的筆友 Peter 染上抽煙的習慣。請你寫一封英文信，勸他戒煙。

參考資料：

Excuses for smoking:

(1) helps one relax

(2) makes one look more mature

(3) helps one concentrate

(4) helps one become more sociable

Reasons for quitting smoking:

(1) smoking hurts the smoker and those around the smoker

(2) seek other means for relaxing

(3) true maturity lies in having wisdom

(4) seek other means for concentration

(5) when you are offered a cigarette, have the courage to turn it down

Unit 30　My New Year Resolutions

題型：主題寫作

1. 試題

說明 以 "My New Year Resolutions" 為主題，寫一篇英文作文，說明你今年的計畫。文長至少 120 字，至多不超過 170 字。

2. 擬寫內容

我的新年新希望

　　年初，我計畫在今年年底前完成三項目標。第一，今年要存十萬台幣。因為我有兼差，而且父母會給我零用錢，所以要達成這個目標應該沒有問題。我會把這筆錢存起來上大學用。

　　第二，我打算讀完一本文法書，而且儘可能多學些單字。我的英文老師說，每個學英文的學生都應該從頭到尾讀完一本文法書，所以我決定今年來做這件事，希望能藉此增進我的英文能力。

　　最後，我要花更多的時間陪我的祖父母。他們年紀大了，總喜歡我們陪在身旁。我要儘可能地多陪陪他們。

3. 參考範文

My New Year Resolutions

At the beginning of the year,[1] I decided to accomplish three objectives **by the end of this year**.[2] First, I want to save NT\$100,000 this year. As I am working part time and get pocket money from my parents, I should have no problem with this goal. I will save this money for my college education.

Second, I plan to **finish reading my grammar book**[3] and learn as many new words as I can. My English teacher says that every student of English should read at least one grammar book from cover to cover. So I **am determined to**[4] do it this year. I hope in this way I can improve my English.

Finally, I will spend more time with my grandparents. They are getting old, and enjoy having us around. I want to be with them as much as I can.

第三章

4. 寫作指導

「新年新希望」這個主題可以寫的有很多，只要能條列二至三件事，並加以鋪陳即可。

5. 重要的字詞及文法提示

(1) at the beginning of the year

at the beginning of... 表示「在…開始的時候」，注意介系詞用 at。in the beginning 是 at first（起初）的意思，之後不可有 of 引導的片語。

> 例 At the beginning of the semester, he made a resolution to study hard.
>
> In the beginning, I thought English was very hard, but now, it is a piece of cake.

(2) by the end of this year

by 加上時間，即 not later than 的意思。可能在那時間之前，也可能剛好那時候。

> 例 Please hand in your assignment by this Friday.

(3) finish reading my grammar book

finish 之後接動名詞。

> 例 When I arrived, she'd finished polishing all the shoes.

類似用法的動詞：

enjoy, keep, avoid, practice

(4) am determined to

be determined to 表示「下定決心去做某事」。

> 例 She is determined to go to graduate school.

6. 造句練習：將各句譯成英文。

(1) 我已下定決心要將一生奉獻給教育。

(2) 他將在明天前寫完那首要獻給母親的歌。

(3) 人們總是在一年的開始訂定新年新希望。

(4) 我們年輕時應該盡可能的多學些東西。

(5) 他決定要盡早結婚。

(6) 我希望在今年年底前我家附近的捷運系統能夠完工。

(7) 該環保團體將設法保護瀕臨絕種的動物，使其不被獵捕。

（參考解答請見附錄 II）

7. 實力培養

My New Year Resolutions

At the beginning of the year, I decided to accomplish three objectives _____. First, I want to save NT$100,000 this year. As I am working part time and get pocket money from my parents, I should _____. I will save this money _____ _____.

Second, I plan to finish _____ and learn _____ new words as I can. My English teacher says that every student of English should read at least one grammar book _____ _____. So _____ to do it this year. I hope in this way I can improve my English.

Finally, I will spend more time with my grandparents. They are getting old, and _____. I want to be with them as much as I can.

8. 輕鬆寫作

提示 你是個高三生，再過一年就要上大學了。用英文寫一篇作文，說明你將如何運用這一年。

參考資料：

Possible ways to spend the last year in high school:

(1) get well prepared for the university entrance examination

(2) stop fooling around and begin to be serious about your future

(3) try to find out what you really want from the university

第三章

Unit 31　My Dream

題型：主題寫作

1. 試題

 以 "My Dream" 為主題，寫一篇英文作文，說明一件你夢想擁有的東西，以及想擁有的理由。文長至少 120 字，至多不超過 170 字。

2. 擬寫內容

我的夢想

　　如果我能隨心所欲，我夢想要有一間自己的大臥房。首先，我要我的房間完全隔音；也就是說，聲音傳不進也傳不出房間。如此一來，我就不會打擾到別人，也不會被別人打擾。

　　第二，我要房間裡有電腦和電視，這樣我就可以連線上網，聽我喜歡的音樂，看我喜歡的影片和新聞節目。

　　第三，我要房間裡放滿我喜歡的書，書架上要放一套完整的百科全書，所有著名的文學作品等等。

　　最後，除了床和書桌外，我想要一個餐桌，以便招待來訪的朋友。

　　總之，擁有一間大臥房是我的夢想。

3. 參考範文

My Dream

　　If I could **have my own way**,[1] I would like to have a large bedroom **of my own**.[2] First, I would like my bedroom to be soundproof; that is, noises would neither come into nor go out of my room. In this way, I wouldn't disturb others or be disturbed.

　　Second, I would like to have a computer and a TV in my room, **so that**[3] I can surf the Internet, listen to my favorite music, and watch my favorite movies and news programs.

　　Third, I would like my room to be full of books that I like. I want an encyclopedia on my shelves, all the famous literary works, **and so forth.**[4]

　　Finally, besides my bed and a study desk, I would like a dining table so that I can entertain my friends when they come for a visit.

In summary, having a large bedroom is my dream.

4. 寫作指導

第一句是主題句，之後用四點來鋪陳，最後再把夢想重述一次作結論。

5. 重要的字詞及文法提示

(1) have my own way

have one's (own) way（為所欲為）也可以説 get one's (own) way。

例 If everybody has their own way, the world would be chaotic.

(2) of my own

of one's own 意思是「（屬於）自己的」。

例 How he wants a car of his own!

而 on one's own 則是「靠自己」的意思。

例 You have to learn to live on your own. Don't depend on others.

(3) so that

so that（以便，為的是）之後是一個表示目的的子句，也可以用 in order that。句型為

S V... so that S V...

例 Although she is very busy, she spends time talking with her kids so that they can have good communication skills.

這種句型如果兩個子句的主詞相同，也可改用下列句型：

S V... so as (not) to/in order (not) to V...

例 She got up early so as to /in order to catch the first train.

She walked quietly so as not to /in order not to wake up the baby.

如果是 so adj/adv that... ，則是「如此…以致於…」，that 之後接一個表示結果的子句。

例 She is so generous that we all love her.

(4) and so forth

and so forth（等等）也可用 and so on 或 etc.。請注意這些用詞前所列舉的項目之間只需逗點隔開，不需要再有 and 相連。

例 She bought a dictionary, two novels, some pens, and so forth/on.

She bought a dictionary, two novels, some pens, etc.

6. 造句練習：將各句譯成英文。

(1) 他慢慢說為的是讓每個學生都了解他的解釋。

(2) 我想要建立一個屬於自己的網站。

(3) 一個老是為所欲為的人無法體貼別人。

(4) 為了禦寒，你需要毛衣、外套、厚襪子等等。

(5) 他態度非常強硬，沒有人能說服他改變心意。

(6) 當你到一個新的地方時，必須靠自己處理所有的問題。

（參考解答請見附錄Ⅱ）

7. 實力培養

My Dream

If I could have my own way, I would like to have a large bedroom of my own. First, I would like my bedroom to be soundproof; _____, noises would neither come into nor _____. In this way, I wouldn't disturb others or _____.

Second, I would like to have a computer and a TV in my room, _____ I can surf the Internet, listen to _____, and watch my favorite movies and news programs.

Third, I would like my room to be full of books _____. I want an encyclopedia on my shelves, all the famous literary works, _____ _____.

Finally, besides my bed and a study desk, I would like a dining table so that I can entertain my friends _____.

In summary, having a large bedroom is my dream.

8. 輕鬆寫作

提示

寫一篇英文作文，說明你夢想著能擁有什麼事物，並提出理由。

參考資料：

Possible items you may want:

(1) a room of your own

(2) a car of your own

(3) a motorcycle

(4) a large sum of money

(5) an apartment as a birthday present

(6) a very close friend

(7) a very good friend of the opposite sex

Unit 32 My Idol

題型：主題寫作

1. 試題

說明

以 "My Idol" 為主題，寫一篇英文作文，說明什麼樣的人是你的偶像以及理由。文長至少 120 字，至多不超過 170 字。

2. 擬寫內容

我的偶像

就某方面來說，搖滾歌手艾薇兒和電影明星湯姆漢克斯是我的偶像，因為我崇拜他們在歌唱和戲劇上幾近完美的表現。以湯姆漢克斯為例，他以《阿甘正傳》一片榮獲奧斯卡最佳男主角，因而成為眾所週知的演員。

我自己並不真正喜歡歌唱和演戲，但我真的希望有一天，當我離開家裡，自我獨立的時候，我可以在我所從事的行業表現優異，就如同艾薇兒在歌唱方面表現優異，湯姆漢克斯在戲劇上表現優異一樣。我也希望我能成為知名人物。

以更廣的角度來看，任何在自己工作上表現優異的人，都是我的偶像。雖然我還不是很確定未來要做什麼，但我可以確定，只要下定決心，我將不遺餘力地讓自己成為值得驕傲的人。

3. 參考範文

My Idol

In a way[1] rock singer Avril Lavigne and movie star Tom Hanks are my idols. They are my idols because I envy them their near perfection in singing and in acting. **Take Tom Hanks for example**.[2] He won the best actor Oscar Award for *Forest Gump*. Tom Hanks is therefore a well-recognized actor.

I do **not necessarily**[3] like singing and acting myself. But I do hope that someday when I leave home and am independent, I can be good at what I do just like Avril Lavigne is good at singing and Tom Hanks is good at acting. I hope that I will be well recognized **as well**.[4]

In a broader sense,[5] anyone who is good at what they do is my idol. I am not absolutely sure what I want to be in the future yet, but I am sure that

第三章

> **once**[6] I have decided, I will **spare no effort**[7] to make myself someone that I can be proud of.

4. 寫作指導

不同於一般人所認定的偶像，作者以「在自己工作上表現優異的人」做為努力的目標。

5. 重要的字詞及文法提示

(1) in a way

in a way（在某點上）表示從某個方面來說。

例 Your argument is right in a way.

(2) Take Tom Hanks for example.

Take sb./sth. for example（以某人或某事物為例）單獨成一句，句尾用句點。用來引出下面的舉例。

例 Exercise helps lose weight. Take my uncle for example. He worked out every day at the gym and lost two pounds in one month.

(3) not necessarily

not necessarily（未必）表示某件事不一定全然是事實。

例 Rich people are not necessarily happy.

(4) as well

as well（也）也就是 too，常放句尾。

例 He speaks English and French as well.

(5) In a broader sense...

in a broader sense（較廣義的說）中 sense 是「意義」(meaning) 的意思。

例 in a broad sense 廣義上
　　in a narrow sense 狹義上

(6) once...

once（一旦）後接一子句，只要此子句的敘述的事實發生，主要子句的事實就會發生。

例 Once he gets to know the truth, he will be shocked.

(7) spare no effort

spare no effort（不遺餘力）後面可接不定詞，表示全力地去做某事。

To reform the educational system, he spares no effort to convince people of the importance of education.

6. 造句練習：將各句譯成英文。

(1) 一旦下定決心，就應該要堅持到底。

(2) 新任市長取締販毒不遺餘力。

(3) 較廣義的說，學校也可以算是一個社區。

(4) 希望我也能夠對國家有很多貢獻。

(5) 先到的人未必會受到最好的服務。

(6) 在某方面，我們的校長是個偉大的教育家。

(7) 美麗的女人不一定受歡迎。拿我的室友當例子，她很漂亮，但卻非常自私。

(8) 一旦成為一個家喻戶曉的人，就會失去一些自由。

（參考解答請見附錄 II）

7. 實力培養

My Idol

In a way rock singer Avril Lavigne and movie star Tom Hanks are my idols. They are my idols because I _____ in singing and in acting. _____ Tom Hanks _____. He won the best actor Oscar Award for *Forest Gump*. Tom Hanks is therefore a _____ _____.

I do not _____ like singing and acting myself. But I do hope that someday when I leave home and am independent, I can be good at what I do just like Avril Lavigne _____ and Tom Hanks is good at acting. I hope that I will be _____.

In a broader sense, anyone who is good at _____ is my idol. I am not absolutely sure what I want to be in the future yet, but I am sure that _____, I will spare no effort to make myself someone that I can be proud of.

8. 輕鬆寫作

以 "The Person I Admire the Most" 為題，寫一篇英文作文。第一段說明你最仰慕的人是誰，以及仰慕的原因；第二段說明你在那些方面受到他的影響。

參考資料：

People you may admire:

(1) your parents

(2) your teacher

(3) a great public figure

(4) an actor

(5) an athlete

(6) an artist

(7) a dancer

(8) a writer

(9) a statesman

Reasons for your admiration:

(1) career achievement

(2) contributions made to society

(3) personal charm

(4) unusual circumstances relating to you

第三章

Unit 33　How to Write Well

題型：主題寫作

1. 試題

說明　以 "How to Write Well" 為主題，寫一篇英文作文，說明如何寫作。文長至少 120 字，至多不超過 170 字。

2. 擬寫內容

如何寫作

　　想要文章寫得好，有四件事是必要的。第一，我們無論何時遇到單字或片語，我們必須學會如何去用它。例如，很多學生寫 "I afraid of dog" 而不是 "I am afraid of dogs"。一旦知道如何正確地使用單字，就可以避免作文裡的錯誤。

　　第二，我們需要指導。不論是從作文課本或是從老師那裡，我們需要學會一些事情，例如如何去寫有效的主題句、如何發展段落、文章如何組織，以及如何維持敘事觀點的一致性。

　　第三，我們需要練習。學習寫作就像學游泳或學開車。如果我們不握方向盤或不跳入水裏，便永遠無法學會。

　　最後，練習時我們需要教練的協助。所以好教練也是必要的。

3. 參考範文

How to Write Well

　　Four things are required if we wish to write well. First, **whenever**[1] we **run across**[2] a word or phrase, we should learn **how to use it**.[3] For example, many students write "I afraid of dog" instead of "I am afraid of dogs." If we know how to use words correctly, we will avoid mistakes in our compositions.

　　Second, we need guidance. **Be it from composition books or from teachers**,[4] we need to learn things like how to write an effective topic sentence, how to develop a paragraph, how to organize an essay, and how to **remain consistent**[5] in point of view.

Third, we need practice. Learning to write is like learning to swim or learning to drive. If we don't sit behind the wheel or jump into the water, we will never learn.

Finally, when we practice, we need a coach to help us. So a good coach is also essential.

4. 寫作指導

第一句是主題句，之後用四個觀點來說明主題句，每個觀點再略為鋪陳。

"Finally" 是用做結尾的訊號字。

5. 重要的字詞及文法提示

(1) whenever...

whenever（每當）用來連接兩個子句，表示每當某件事發生時，另一件事也出現。

例 Whenever I hear the music, I think of the time we spent together.

(2) run across

run across 意思是「碰巧發現或遇到」，也可說 come across。

例 When you run/come across a new word while reading, don't stop to look it up in the dictionary. Try to guess its meaning.

(3) how to use it

疑問詞 (how, when, where, what, who, which) 接不定詞成為名詞片語，可充當 (a) 主詞 (b) 受詞 (c) 補語。

例 (a) How to live a happy life is not an easy question to answer.（主詞）

(b) In this book, he wrote about how to live a happy life.（受詞）

(c) My topic today is how to live a happy life.（補語）

(4) Be it from composition books or from teachers...

這是 Whether it is from composition books or from teachers 的另一種說法。這個子句也可放在主要子句之後。

例 Those children play happily, be it rainy or sunny.

Be it rainy or sunny, those children play happily.

(5) remain consistent

remain（維持、保持）之後接形容詞或名詞，當主詞補語，說明主詞。

例 He decided to remain single.

He decided to remain a bachelor.

6. 造句練習：將各句譯成英文。

(1) 每當他覺得尷尬時，都會臉紅。

(2) 當他在公園裡慢跑時，巧遇一個童年的朋友。

(3) 學生必須學習如何獨立思考。

(4) 好朋友彼此分享經驗，不論是快樂的還是悲傷的。

(5) 當面對危險時要保持冷靜。

(6) 雖然他們身處異地，卻依舊是朋友。

(7) 在清理抽屜時，我無意中發現我所收到的第一封情書。

(8) 每當我覺得氣餒時，這句格言都鼓勵我繼續前進。

（參考解答請見附錄Ⅱ）

7. 實力培養

How to Write Well

Four things are required if we wish to write well. First, whenever we _____ a word or phrase, we should learn _____. _____, many students write "I afraid of dog" instead of "I am afraid of dogs." If we know how to use words correctly, we will _____ _____.

Second, we need guidance. Be it from composition books or from teachers, we need to learn things like how to write _____ _____, how to _____ a paragraph, how to _____ an essay, and how to _____ in point of view.

Third, we need practice. Learning to write is like learning to swim or learning to drive. If we don't sit behind the wheel or _____ the water, we will never learn.

Finally, when we practice, we need a coach to help us. So a good coach is also essential.

8. 輕鬆寫作

提示 用英文寫一封信給你 (Mike) 的同年筆友 (Richard)，告訴他你對學習作文的認知。

參考資料：

When you write, you should

(1) first, choose the topic you can deal with easily

(2) brainstorm

(3) write an outline

(4) write a draft

(5) modify your draft

(6) correct all the mistakes

(7) maintain a consistent point of view

(8) use effective topic sentences

(9) make it well organized

Unit 34　Good Qualities of a Friend

題型：主題寫作

1. 試題

以 "Good Qualities of a Friend" 為主題，寫一篇英文作文，說明在你心目中，好朋友應具備什麼樣的好特質。文長至少 120 字，至多不超過 170 字。

2. 擬寫內容

朋友的好特質

在許多可期望於朋友的特質中，也許最重要的是不自私。我們可以為了各種理由而和某人做朋友，但是我們大概不會和自私的人永遠在一起。

另一個好的特質是有見識。有見識的人擁有豐富常識、判斷能力佳又有好品味，每個人都喜歡和這樣的人相處。

第三是誠懇。誠懇會帶來慈悲與同情。當別人需要幫助時，不誠懇的朋友將不會慈悲或同情。

最後，如果朋友和我們有同好是最棒的。朋友通常會花時間聚在一起，並且分享各自的見解。如果他們有許多共同愛好，他們會有許多可以談的，這將可強化他們的友誼。

3. 參考範文

Good Qualities of a Friend

Among the many qualities[1] that can be desired in a friend, perhaps the most important one is unselfishness. We can make friends with someone for **all sorts of**[2] reasons, but we probably won't stick forever with someone who is selfish.

Another good quality is being knowledgeable.[3] Everybody enjoys being around someone who has good common sense and shows good judgment or taste, a result of being knowledgeable.

The third is sincerity. From sincerity come compassion and sympathy. A friend who is not sincere will not be compassionate or sympathetic when others are in need of help.

> Finally, it would be good if the friend **has something in common**[4] with us. Friends often spend time together, and share their ideas. If they have a lot in common, they have a lot to talk about, and this will reinforce their friendship.

4. 寫作指導

本篇範文用 one, another, the third, finally 等轉承語來鋪陳，使全文有很好的連貫。其中 finally 兼具結尾的功能。

5. 重要的字詞及文法提示

(1) Among the many qualities...

among（在…之中）也可寫成amongst，後接複數名詞或代名詞，可指包括在一群人或事物中。

例 Among the books written by Jane Austen, I like *Sense and Sensibility* best.

也可指被一群人或事物圍繞。

例 The teacher sat among the students and answered their questions.

(2) all sorts of

all sorts of（各式各樣的）是 all kinds of 的意思。

例 He likes all sorts of Japanese food.

(3) Another good quality is being knowledgeable.

形容詞不可以當同位性質的補語，必須要在前面加上 being。

(4) has something in common

have something in common（有些共同點）所衍生的片語包括：

have a lot in common	有許多共同點
have little in common	沒什麼共同點
have nothing in common	沒有交集
have anything in common	有何共同之處（用在疑問句或否定句）

例 Do you and Jane have anything in common?

6. 造句練習：將各句譯成英文。

(1) 在那家精品店裡，你可以買到適合各種場合的衣服。

(2) 善解人意是她個性上的一個特質。

(3) 沒有共同點的兩個人可以成為好朋友嗎？

(4) 雖然我父親和我母親相似的地方不多，但他們可以互補。

(5) 在這個工作的所有條件中，最少人符合的是願意加班。

(6) 因為他們有很多相同處，所以彼此都知道對方在想什麼。

(7) 他最大的缺點是優柔寡斷。

（參考解答請見附錄 II ）

7. 實力培養

Good Qualities of a Friend

  Among the many qualities that can be desired in a friend, perhaps the most important one is unselfishness. We can make friends with someone _____, but we probably won't _____ who is selfish.

  Another good quality is _____. Everybody enjoys being around someone _____ and shows good judgment or taste, a result of being knowledgeable.

  The third is sincerity. From sincerity come compassion and sympathy. A friend _____ will not be compassionate or sympathetic when others are in need of help.

  Finally, it would be good if the friend _____. Friends often spend time together, and share their ideas. If they _____ _____, they have a lot to talk about, and this will reinforce their friendship.

8. 輕鬆寫作

以 "My Best Friend" 為主題，寫一篇英文作文，列舉你最要好的朋友（男生請用 Jason，女生則用 Ruth）具有的特質。

參考資料：

Does your friend have the following qualities?

(1) hardworking—studies many hours a day

(2) friendly—is popular among fellow students

(3) helpful—often offers to help when necessary

(4) kind—treats fellow students nicely

(5) considerate—always thinks for others

Unit 35　The Greatest Advice

題型：主題寫作

1. 試題

說明 以 "The Greatest Advice" 為主題，寫一篇英文作文，說明你認為最棒的一個忠告 (advice) 是什麼，並用一些具體事實來驗證。文長至少 120 字，至多不超過 170 字。

2. 擬寫內容

最棒的忠告

　　在所有我曾獲得的忠告中，最棒的是「堅持你的目標」。這個忠告一直對我很重要，因為它幫助我達成我的目標。

　　例如，我一直想要增進英文能力。自從有了那個目標，我就一直勤奮地研讀英文。無論多麼忙碌，我都會設法每天學習一點英文。我研讀教科書，記生字及片語，研讀文法，並且收聽英文廣播節目以改進我的聽力。漸漸地，我的英文能力提升了。

　　未來我有更多目標要達成。例如，我想唸研究所，並達成我的生涯目標。我相信只要堅持目標，終究會達成的。這就是為什麼「堅持你的目標」是我所曾得到最棒的忠告。

3. 參考範文

The Greatest Advice

Of all the advice I have gotten,[1] I think the greatest is "Stick to what you aim at." This advice has been great for me because it has helped me accomplish my goals.

For example, I want to improve my English. **Since**[2] I set that goal, I have been studying English diligently. **However busy I may be,**[3] I **manage to**[4] learn some English each day. I study the textbook, I memorize new words and phrases, I study grammar, and I listen to English programs on the radio to improve my listening comprehension. Gradually, my English has improved.

I have **many more goals**[5] to achieve in the future. For example, I want to pursue a graduate education, and I want to attain my career goals. I believe that **so long as**[6] I stick to what I aim at, I will achieve my goals **in the long run.**[7] This is why "Stick to what you aim at" is **the greatest advice I have ever gotten.**[8]

4. 寫作指導

本文談最棒的忠告，只用了一個理由：因為它幫助我達成我的目標。接著舉自己學英文的例子來説明此忠告所帶來的影響，再加上對未來的期盼。全文切合命題要求。

5. 重要的字詞及文法提示

(1) Of all the advice I have gotten,

of（在…之中）也可用 among。這裡要注意 advice 不可數，所以不加 -s，如果是可數名詞，需用複數形。

例 Of all the girls I know, Tracy is the smartest.

(2) Since...

since（自從）可以當連接詞，引導一子句，表示主要子句動詞起始的一個過去的時間點。主要子句通常要用現在完成式，since 子句用過去式。

例 I have been learning to play the piano since I was three.

since 也可當介系詞，之後接名詞。

例 I have been learning to play the piano since 2000.

(3) However busy I may be

however busy I may be（不管我可能有多忙）也可説 no matter how busy I may be，句型為：

However adj/adv S V..., S V....

例 However hard you may try, you cannot learn a new language in a week.

However easy it may seem, you have to practice many times to dance well.

(4) manage to

manage to（設法辦到）之後接原形動詞。

例 Although the work was tough, she managed to finish it on time.

(5) many more goals

　more 常放在數詞或數量字後，表示「還有、再」的意思。

　例 The coffee is fantastic. Can I have one more cup?

(6) so long as

　so long as（只要）也可說成 as long as，作連接詞用。

　例 As long as you stick to your goal, you will succeed.

(7) in the long run

　in the long run（終究，最後）表示某事實雖非現在馬上發生，但未來某時一定會成真。

　例 Your hard work will pay off in the long run.

(8) the greatest advice I have ever gotten

　最高級之後常接一完成式子句，表示「曾經…之中，最…的」。

　例 She is the most beautiful woman I have (ever) seen.

　子句中的動詞也可用過去式。

　例 She is the most beautiful woman I (ever) saw.

---

6. 造句練習：將各句譯成英文。

(1) 自從他回去美國，我就沒有聽說過他的消息。

(2) 在所有的職業中，我認為當老師最有挑戰性。

(3) 不論你可能有多緊張，你最好假裝很有自信的樣子。

(4) 我雖然很生氣，但還是設法成功的控制了我的脾氣。

(5) 只要你不斷地努力，夢想終會成真。

(6) 因為來的人將比預期的多，我們還需要再十五張椅子。

(7) 這是我去過中最有趣的國家。

(8) 自從他輟學後，就在一家家具工廠工作。

（參考解答請見附錄 II）

---

7. 實力培養

The Greatest Advice

　　Of all the advice I have had, I think the greatest is "Stick to what you aim at." This advice has been great for me because ＿＿＿＿＿＿＿＿＿＿

＿＿＿＿＿＿＿.

　　For example, I want to improve my English. ＿＿＿＿＿＿＿＿＿＿, I

have been studying English intelligently. _____,
I manage to learn some English each day. I study the textbook, I memorize
new words and phrases, I study grammar, and I listen to English programs
on the radio _____.
Gradually, my English has been improving.

    I have many more goals to achieve in the future. For example, I want
to pursue learning, and I want to _____. I believe
that _____ I stick to what I aim at, I will achieve my goals
_____. This is why "Stick to what you aim at" is the
greatest advice _____.

8. 輕鬆寫作

 你的學弟妹向你討教一個忠告。寫一篇英文作文，說明你認為最棒的一
個忠告 (advice) 是什麼，告訴他們這個忠告最棒的原因。

參考資料：

Some good advice:

(1) honesty is the best policy

(2) a bird in the hand is better than two in the bush

(3) seize the day

(4) always be kind to others

(5) look before you leap

(6) beauty is only skin-deep

(7) believe in yourself

(8) whatever may happen, don't give up

Unit 36　What Does It Mean to Be a Good Child?

題型：主題寫作

1. 試題

以 "What Does It Mean to Be a Good Child?" 為主題，寫一篇英文作文，說明你心中的好孩子應該具備什麼特質。文長至少 120 字，至多不超過 170 字。

2. 擬寫內容

做個好孩子是什麼意思

　　雖然每個人都喜歡好孩子，但是人們對於好孩子應該是什麼樣子，可能有完全迴異的意見。很多人喜歡他們的小孩聽話，但又不喜歡小孩太被動。很多人希望他們的小孩有創意，但又不希望小孩的創意失去控制。

　　雖然意見似乎很難達成一致，我認為每個人大概都會同意下列幾項。第一，好孩子體貼他的父母。這可能意味著分擔家庭雜務，例如洗碗盤和洗衣服。

　　第二，好孩子不會向父母提出不合理的要求。好孩子是在父母所能供應的範圍內生活。

　　最後，好孩子努力學習獨立。雖然父母總是保護他們的孩子，但是他們會樂於看到孩子能夠獨立。

3. 參考範文

What Does It Mean to Be a Good Child?

While everybody likes a good child,[1] people's ideas may differ greatly regarding what a good child is. Many people **like their child to be obedient,**[2] but they don't like the child to be too passive. Many people like their child to be creative, but they don't want the child's creativity to get out of control.

Although a consensus is hard to reach,[3] I think everyone would agree with the following observations. First, a good child is considerate of their parents. This may mean sharing household chores, such as dish washing and doing the laundry.

Second, a good child does not make unreasonable demands on their parents. A good child lives within the limits of their parents' standard of living.

Finally, a good child **makes an effort to**[4] become independent. Although parents are always protective of their children, they are usually glad to see them become independent.

4. 寫作指導

第一段是引言，第二段用 although 做語氣轉折，再以 everyone would agree with the following observations 帶出下文。

5. 重要的字詞及文法提示

(1) While everybody likes a good child,...

while（雖然）連接兩個子句，用來比較不同的事物或情況。

例 While most people obey the law, some just ignore it.

(2) like their child to be obedient

不定詞 to be obedient 是受詞補語。類似的結構有：

want sb. to V

need sb. to V

例 I need all of you to support me.

(3) Although a consensus is hard to reach,...

to reach a consensus 指的是「達成共識」。

例 The study group reached a consensus on what the priorities would be.

(4) make an effort to

make an effort（努力）之後可接不定詞。

例 She made an effort to improve her English pronunciation.

類似的常用片語有：

make efforts to...	努力
make every effort to...	盡全力
make little effort to...	並無努力
make no effort to...	毫不努力
spare no effort to...	毫無保留、使盡全力

6. 造句練習：將各句譯成英文。

(1) 雖然很多人為了生活而工作，但有些人活著是為了工作。

(2) 關於為什麼而活，人們的看法很不一致。

(3) 當地的人努力維護這棟歷史性的建築物。

(4) 他不喜歡他的學生虛度光陰。

(5) 董事會在該如何解決這個問題上，無法達成共識。

（參考解答請見附錄 II）

7. 實力培養

What Does It Mean to Be a Good Child?

While everybody likes a good child, people's ideas may differ greatly regarding _____. Many people like their child to be obedient, but they don't like the child _____. Many people like their child to be creative, but they don't want the child's creativity _____.

Although a consensus _____, I think everyone would agree with the following observations. First, a good child is _____ _____. This may mean sharing household chores, such as dish washing and doing the laundry.

Second, a good child does not make unreasonable demands on their parents. A good child lives within _____.

Finally, a good child makes an effort to become independent. Although parents are always _____, they are usually glad to see them become independent.

8. 輕鬆寫作

提示

以 "What Does It Mean to Be a Good Child?" 為主題，寫一篇英文作文，說明你心中的好孩子應該具備什麼特質。以 "A good child means several things." 為開頭。

參考資料：

Qualities/traits/characteristics of a good child

(1) does not worry their parents—keeps parents informed of where they go, stays out of trouble

(2) is considerate—helps with household chores

(3) honors parents—makes an effort to make parents proud of them

Unit 37 Formulas for Life

題型：主題寫作

1. 試題

以 "Formulas for Life" 為主題，寫一篇英文作文，說明你的生活準則是什麼，並提出理由。文長至少 120 字，至多不超過 170 字。

2. 擬寫內容

生活準則

以下為我的生活準則。第一，持續努力。如果我們觀察大自然，我們會發現所有生物在變老和死亡之前都會努力活下去。為什麼我們人類要例外呢？朗菲羅 (Longfellow) 曾說過：「失敗可能是勝利的偽裝。」因此，我的第一個生活準則就是我們必須持續努力，無論我們的情況如何困難。

第二，順著我們的心意走。我們擅長什麼？真正喜歡做的是什麼？想成為科學家還是藝術家？雖然我們可能會遭受別人的反對，但是我們必須順著我們的心意走，做我們真正喜歡做的事。如果我們順著我們的心意走，快樂將隨之而來。

最後，與人並存並榮（我們要活下去也要讓別人活下去）。我享有自由和人權，還有很多其他的東西。別人也一樣。因此，當我們在做自己喜歡做的事時，也應該尊敬別人，包容他們做的事，並且在必要的時候能夠展現同情心。

3. 參考範文

Formulas for Life

The following are my formulas for life. First, carry on. If we observe nature, we find that all living things strive to stay alive before they get old and die. Why should we human beings be an exception? Longfellow once said, "Defeat may be victory **in disguise**."[1] Therefore, my first formula for life is that we should carry on, **no matter how difficult our situation may be**.[2]

Second, we should follow our heart. What are we good at? What do we really like to do? Do we want to be a scientist or an artist? We should follow our heart and do what we really enjoy doing, **in spite of**[3] possible objections from others. If we follow our heart, happiness will follow.

Finally, live and let live. **I am entitled to freedom and human rights**,[4] **among other things**.[5] So are others. Therefore, while we do what we like, we should respect others, tolerate what they do, and show compassion **when necessary**.[6]

4. 寫作指導

formulas 也可寫成 formulae，是 formula（公式、準則）的多數形式。一如其他的說明文，本文開門見山，不用冗長的引言，讓內容更為精簡。

5. 重要的字詞及文法提示

(1) in disguise

in disguise（偽裝的）是介系詞片語當形容詞用，修飾其前的名詞。

例 Although you lose the job, it might be a blessing in disguise. Now you have more time to enjoy life.

(2) no matter how difficult our situation may be

也可說成 however difficult our situation may be。

例 No matter how busy he may be, he never forgets to call me.

(3) in spite of

in spite of（雖然），因 of 是介系詞，所以之後接名詞或動名詞，也可以用 despite。如果用 although，因是連接詞，之後要接子句。

例 In spite of/Despite the bad weather, they went camping.

Although the weather was bad, they went camping.

In spite of/Despite the fact that the weather was bad, they went camping.

(4) I am entitled to freedom and human rights

be entitled to sth. 表示「有資格獲得某事物」。

例 After a long year's work, you are entitled to a rest.

(5) among other things

among other things（其中）用在提及某一大群體中的一個或數個人或事物時用。

例 We discussed, among other things, the future of our company.

(6) when necessary

> when necessary 是從 when it is necessary 簡化來的。

> 例 Add some coloring to the solution, when necessary.

6. 造句練習：將各句譯成英文。

(1) 身為中華民國的公民，你有言論自由權。

(2) 如果需要的話，可以使用另外一張紙。

(3) 失敗可能是成功的偽裝；因此，不要因之而氣餒。

(4) 儘管錢不夠，他們還是完成了那座橋的建造。

(5) 從計程車裡出來了一個衣衫襤褸的乞丐。 (Out...)

(6) 其中，他高度的幽默感深深吸引了我。

(7) 不管情況有多糟，他對人生都抱持著積極的態度。

（參考解答請見附錄 II ）

7. 實力培養

Formulas for Life

The following are my formulas for life. First, carry on. If we observe nature, we find that all living things strive to stay alive _____ _____. Why should we human beings be an exception? Longfellow once said, "Defeat may be victory in disguise." Therefore, my first formula for life is that we should carry on, _____ _____.

Second, we should follow our heart. What are we good at? What do we really like to do? Do we want to be a scientist or an artist? We should follow our heart and do what we really enjoy doing, _____ _____. If we follow our heart, _____ _____.

Finally, live and let live. I _____ freedom and human rights, among other things. So are others. Therefore, while we do what we like, we should respect others, tolerate _____, and show compassion when necessary.

8. 輕鬆寫作

提示　你有沒有終生奉行的準則？請列出一或兩項，加以説明，並舉一個例子來驗證。

參考資料：

Possible formulae for life:

(1) Practice what you teach

(2) Action speaks louder than words

(3) Honesty is the best policy

(4) Be prepared for rainy days

(5) Keep your promise

(6) It is better to give than to receive

Unit 38 The Importance of Sleeping

題型：主題寫作

1. 試題

說明

以 "The Importance of Sleeping" 為主題，寫一篇英文作文，說明睡眠的重要以及安眠的方法。文長至少 120 字，至多不超過 170 字。

2. 擬寫內容

睡眠的重要

　　睡眠對我們有多麼重要？嗯，睡眠佔了人生三分之一的時間。睡眠對我們是極為重要的。

　　睡眠帶給我們幾個好處。第一，恢復我們的體力。當我們非常累的時候，所需要的就是一夜好眠。睡醒後，我們會覺得神清氣爽。體力也就恢復了。

　　第二，修復我們的身體。例如，感冒的時候，最好的治療方法就是睡覺。睡眠似乎可以修復損壞之處並使其恢復正常。

　　第三，強化我們的免疫系統。有了充足的睡眠，我們會更健康、更有活力且較不易感染疾病。

　　確保睡得好的一個良方就是作息規律。另一個良方是在睡覺前做一些溫和的活動。例如，我們可以聽輕音樂，讓優美的旋律帶我們到進入夢鄉。

3. 參考範文

The Importance of Sleeping

　　How important is sleeping to us? Well, we **spend**[1] **a third of our life**[2] **sleeping.**[1] Sleeping is essential to us.

　　Sleeping does several things for us. First, it restores our strength. When we are very tired, **all we need is**[3] a good night's sleep. After we wake up from our sleep, we feel refreshed. Our strength is restored.

　　Second, sleeping repairs our body. For example, if we **come down with**[4] a cold, the best cure for our cold is sleeping. Sleeping seems to fix what goes wrong and make it right.

Third, sleeping strengthens our immune system. **With sufficient sleep,**[5] we **are** more energetic, healthier, and **less susceptible to**[6] diseases.

One good way to ensure good sleep is to **keep regular hours.**[7] Another is to do some mild activity before sleeping. For example, we can listen to soft music and let the beautiful melody take us to our dreams.

4. 寫作指導

用修辭問句做主題句,是有效的開頭方法。接著用「觀點 + 說明」的方式加以鋪陳,最後用「確保睡得好的一個良方就是作息規律」做結尾。

5. 重要的字詞及文法提示

(1) spend... sleeping

sb. + spend(花費)+ 時間或金錢 + V-ing 這句型中,V-ing 之前可以加上 in,但大多不加。

例 She spends most of her time (in) reading.

另外的句型是 sb. + spend + 時間或金錢 + on + N。

例 I spent a lot of money on books.

(2) a third of our life

英文表示分數的方法如下:

分子(基數)分母(序數;分子為 1 以上,分母要用複數形)。

例 a/one third　　三分之一
　　two thirds　　三分之二
　　three tenths　　十分之三

但以下用法是固定的:

例 a/one half　　一半
　　a quarter　　四分之一
　　two quarters　　二分之一
　　three quarters　　四分之三

(3) all we need is...

all we need is...(我們所需要的就是…)中 we need 是關係子句,修飾 all,we need 之前省略了當受詞的關係代名詞 that:all that we need is...

例 All (that) I ask of you is true love.

(4) come down with

come down with + 疾病為「得到某病」的意思。

例 She came down with an unknown disease and couldn't get out of bed.

(5) With sufficient sleep,...

with + sth. 常放句首，表示後面句子所陳述事實的原因。

例 With the advance of technology, life has become more convenient.

(6) are less susceptible to

be susceptible to sth.（易受某事物影響或侵害）即 be easily influenced or harmed by sth.。本句多個 less，就是比較不易受某事物影響或侵害。

例 These plants are susceptible to frost and snow.

(7) keep regular hours

keep regular hours（作息有規律）另外有一個類似片語：

keep early hours (= go to bed early and get up early)

6. 造句練習：將各句譯成英文。

(1) 有了好的記憶力，你會發覺背生字很容易。
(2) 生病的人容易受感染。
(3) 他得了流行性感冒，必須待在家裡。
(4) 這些孤兒想要的只是愛和關懷。
(5) 他把三分之二的收入捐給慈善機構。
(6) 他把整個晚上的時間都花在講電話。
(7) 這些動物中有五分之一將會絕種。
(8) 如果作息規律，就比較不容易生病。

（參考解答請見附錄 II）

7. 實力培養

The Importance of Sleeping

How important is sleeping to us? Well, we spend a third of our life sleeping. Sleeping is _____.

Sleeping does several things for us. First, it restores our strength. When we are very tired, _____ a good night's sleep. After we wake up from our sleep, we feel refreshed. Our strength _____.

第三章

Second, sleeping repairs our body. For example, if we come down with a cold, _____ is sleeping. Sleeping seems to fix what goes wrong and make it right.

Third, sleeping strengthens our immune system. With sufficient sleep, we are more energetic, healthier, and less _____.

One good way to ensure good sleep is to _____. Another is to do some mild activity before sleeping. For example, we can listen to soft music and let the beautiful melody _____.

8. 輕鬆寫作

提示 睡眠不足會令人很難受。用英文寫一篇作文，描述一次睡眠不足的經過及感想。

參考資料：

Some symptoms of lack of sleep:

(1) You may feel very tired
(2) You cannot study efficiently
(3) You are unable to concentrate
(4) You feel dizzy
(5) You may fall asleep when you shouldn't

第三章

Unit 39 My Favorite Book

題型：主題寫作

1. 試題

以 "My Favorite Book" 為主題，寫一篇英文作文，說明你最喜歡的一本書是什麼以及喜歡的原因。文長至少 120 字，至多不超過 170 字。

2. 擬寫內容

我最喜愛的書

在我曾讀過的許多書中，我最喜愛的是《荒漠甘泉》，作者是 Charles E. Cowman 夫人。正如書名所指的，當我口渴時，這本書為我解了渴。當我受到傷害時，它安慰我。當我絕望時，它給我希望。當我寂寞時，它給我友誼。當我害怕時，它給我勇氣。最重要的是，當我不知所措時，它為我提供見解。

讀這本書就好像在和一位智者談話。無論我陷入什麼狀況，這位智者總是有適當的一些話可說，以顯示她的關心，並且告訴我她了解。這本書對我來說就像是一位良師。《荒漠甘泉》將永遠是我最喜愛的書。

3. 參考範文

My Favorite Book

Of the many books I have read, my favorite is *Streams in the Desert*, written by Mrs. Charles E. Cowman. **As implied by its title**,[1] this book quenches my thirst when I am thirsty. It **offers me comfort**[2] when I feel hurt. It gives me hope when I am in despair. It gives me companionship when I am lonely. It gives me courage when I am afraid. **Most important of all**,[3] it provides me with insight when I don't know **what to do**.[4]

Reading this book **is like**[5] talking to a wise person. **No matter what I run into**,[6] the wise person always has something to say to suit the occasion, to show that she cares, and to tell me that she understands. This book is like a mentor to me. *Streams in the Desert* will be my favorite book forever.

第三章

4. 寫作指導

本文第一句點出最喜歡的書是什麼，接著以數個理由來鋪陳。
第二段進一步說明書本著者和本文作者的互動。

5. 重要的字詞及文法提示

(1) As implied by its title

as 之後可接過去分詞，表示「正如…所…」。

As implied by its title, this book quenches my thirst when I am thirsty. 原意為
This book quenches my thirst when I am thirsty, which is implied by its title.

例 As suggested by the president, education is the only way to improve
our lives. (Education is the only way to improve our lives, which was
suggested by the president.)

(2) offers me comfort

offer sb. sth. 也可說 offer sth. to sb.，至於用何者，端看訊息焦點為何，新
的、重要的訊息放後面。

例 He offers us all kinds of help.

He offers his help to all those who are in need.

(3) most important of all

most important of all（最重要的是）是個轉承語。

例 Education serves a lot of functions.... Most important of all, it helps us
learn how to live.

(4) what to do

what to do（該怎麼辦），是從 what I can/should do 來的。疑問詞 ＋ 不定
詞的結構通常是由疑問詞引導的名詞子句來的。

例 They don't know where they can go.

→ They don't know where to go.

He didn't tell us when to leave.

→ He didn't tell us when we could leave.

(5) is like

be like（就像）通常用來做比喻，like 是介系詞，所以其後接名詞或動名詞。

例 Learning English is like playing basketball. You have to practice often.

(6) No matter what I run into

No matter what...（不論…什麼）也可說 Whatever...。

例 No matter what you want, I'll get it for you.

→ Whatever you want, I'll get it for you.

run into sth.（遭遇某事）亦即 encounter，通常都是遭遇問題或困難。

例 If you continue to play with fire, you'll run into danger someday.

6. 造句練習：將各句譯成英文。

(1) 這些是英語學習者可能會遇到的困難。

(2) 如預期的，他們不到一個月就分手了。

(3) 為了學好英文，你必須多聽多看，但最重要的是，你應該開口說英語。

(4) 不論你聽到什麼，都要三緘其口。

(5) 使用毒品就像是在玩火。

(6) 當他看到他的夢中情人時，卻不知該說什麼。

(7) 那個小女孩似乎受到了極度驚嚇。

(8) 他的鼓勵給我繼續前進的力量。

（參考解答請見附錄 II）

7. 實力培養

My Favorite Book

　　Of the many books I have read, my favorite is *Streams in the Desert*, written by Mrs. Charles E. Cowman. _____, this book quenches my thirst _____. It offers me comfort when I feel hurt. It gives me hope _____. It gives me companionship _____. It gives me courage _____. Most important of all, it provides me with insight _____.

　　Reading this book is like _____. No matter what I run into, the wise person always has something to say to suit the occasion, to show that she cares, and to tell me that she understands. This book is like a mentor to me. *Streams in the Desert* _____ _____.

8. 輕鬆寫作

提示 以 "My Favorite Book" 為主題，寫一篇英文作文，說明你最喜歡的一本書是什麼以及喜歡的原因。

參考資料：

(1) You should provide the title of the book you have read.

(2) Tell your reader why you like the book.

(3) What information you get from this book.

(4) What help you get from reading this book.

(5) Does it entertain you?

(6) Does it give you information or make you more knowledgeable?

Unit 40　Why I Read

題型：主題寫作

1. 試題

說明 以 "Why I Read" 為主題，寫一篇英文作文，説明你為何喜歡閱讀。文長至少 120 字，至多不超過 170 字。

2. 擬寫內容

我為什麼要閱讀

　　人們為了不同理由閱讀。有些人閱讀是為了消磨時間，有些人是為了娛樂，有些人則是為了獲得資訊。就我而言，閱讀是為了成長。

　　閱讀對我來說就像是食物。沒有食物，我會停止成長，且會死於飢餓。就像食物滋養身體，同樣地閱讀滋養心靈。在我讀了好文章、好故事或好書之後，我通常覺得更有想像力、更有創意，甚至可以做更多事情。如果我很久沒有閱讀，我就沒有東西和朋友談論，也不再活躍，生命似乎枯竭了。

　　此外，書本帶領我進入世界。當我閱讀歷史，感覺像在時光隧道中旅行；當我研究物理，便可瞭解宇宙如何運作；當我學習數學，不得不讚嘆事物竟能如此精細。

　　總而言之，如果不閱讀，我們的生命就一點也不像是生命了。

3. 參考範文

Why I Read

　　People read for different reasons. **Some**[1] read to kill time, **others**[1] read **to be entertained**,[2] **and still others**[1] read for information. **As far as I am concerned**,[3] I read to grow.

　　Reading **is like food to me**.[4] **Without food**,[5] I cease to grow, and I will die of hunger. **As food nourishes the body, so reading nourishes the mind**.[6] I often feel more imaginative, more creative, and even more productive after I have read a good article, a good story, or a good book. If I don't read for a long time, I have nothing to talk about with my friends, I cease to be active, and my life **seems to dry up**.[7]

> Moreover, books take me into the world. When I read history, I travel through time; when I study physics, I understand how the universe works; when I learn mathematics, I wonder at how precise things can be.
>
> **In summary,**[8] our lives are not lives at all if we don't read.

4. 寫作指導

第一段第二句是「A 子句,B 子句,and C 子句」的結構。第二段用了一個明喻 reading is like food to me。第三段用 moreover 做轉承。結尾說出 reading 的重要性。注意,標題是名詞子句,句尾不加標點。

5. 重要的字詞及文法提示

(1) Some..., others..., and still others...

這個句型用來列舉不同的事實。

例 People enjoy doing different things. Some like to read, and others like to go mountain climbing.

People enjoy doing different things. Some like to read, others like to go mountain climbing, and still others like to go to the KTV.

(2) to be entertained

to be V-en 是被動的不定詞。

例 He hates to be bossed around.

(3) As far as I am concerned,...

as far as I am concerned(就我個人而言)通常用來表示說話者的看法。

例 As far as I am concerned, that proposal is unrealistic.

(4) is like food to me

be like(像是)用來做比喻,因為 like 是介系詞,之後接名詞或動名詞。

例 She is like a mother to me.

(5) without food

without(沒有)是介系詞,後接名詞或動名詞。

例 Without air, no creatures could live.

He left without saying a word.

(6) As food nourishes the body, so reading nourishes the mind.

「As + 子句,so + 子句」意思是「正如…,…也…」。

例 As air is to man, so water is to fish.

(7) seems to dry up

sth./sb. seem to（似乎）之後接原形動詞。

例　John seems to know the truth.

Her plan seemed to work.

此句型是從 It seems that S V 的句型簡化來的。例如以上兩句原是：

It seems that John knows the truth.

It seemed that her plan worked.

將 that 子句中的主詞提前，再稍做改變即可。

(8) In summary

In summary（總之）在做總結時使用。

例　In summary, smoking causes a lot of health problems. It would be better not to start that habit.

6. 造句練習：將各句譯成英文。

(1) 父母的愛像是冬天的陽光。

(2) 就我個人而言，一個人的成功取決於他對社會的貢獻。

(3) 每一個人都渴望愛與被愛。

(4) 正如人們會改變，國家也會改變。

(5) 總之，一個人的態度決定了他的生活方式。

(6) 每個人似乎都知道真相。

(7) 人們需要電腦的目的不同。有些人用它來計算，有些人用它來寫故事，還有些人用它來畫畫。

（參考解答請見附錄 II）

7. 實力培養

Why I Read

People read for different reasons. Some read to kill time, others read to be entertained, and ＿＿＿＿＿＿＿＿＿＿ read for information. ＿＿＿＿＿ ＿＿＿＿＿＿＿＿＿, I read to grow.

Reading is like food to me. ＿＿＿＿＿＿＿, I cease to grow, and I will die of hunger. As food nourishes the body, ＿＿＿＿＿＿＿＿＿. I often feel more imaginative, more creative, and ＿＿＿＿＿＿＿ productive after I have read a good article, a good story or a good book. If I don't read for a long time, I have nothing _____, I cease to be active, and my life seems to dry up.

_____, books take me into the world. When I read history, I travel through time; when I study physics, I understand how the universe works; when I learn mathematics, I wonder at _____ things can be.

In summary, our lives are not lives at all if we don't read.

8. 輕鬆寫作

 你喜歡閱讀關於哪方面的題材？寫一篇英文作文，說明你喜歡讀這種題材的理由。

參考資料：

Types of reading materials and possible reasons why you like them:

(1) the newspaper—you read the newspapers for current events, opinions, comments on books, movies; for sports results; for comic strips, and other reasons

(2) novels—you read novels for the story and what you learn from the story; you read light novels to be entertained

(3) magazines—you read magazines for a variety of reasons, such as to acquire knowledge you don't get from textbooks

Unit 41 Life at a University

題型：主題寫作

1. 試題

以 "Life at a University" 為主題，寫一篇英文作文，說明你對大學生活的了解，嚮往大學生活的原因。文長至少 120 字，至多不超過 170 字。

2. 擬寫內容

大學生活

有人告訴我，大學的生活是多采多姿並具有挑戰性的。首先，大學生活之所以多采多姿是因為有很多對新事物充滿好奇心的青年男女。和他們一起研究和討論議題一定非常令人振奮。第二，這些青年來自各處。彼此學習不同的文化和背景將是很有趣的。第三，有各種各樣的社團。參加這些社團給人無限的機會可以認識有相同嗜好的人。能夠分享共同的興趣會使人非常快樂。

大學生活充滿挑戰因為教授們可能對學生要求很多。除了出席課堂之外，學生可能被要求寫很長的報告或自己做實驗。

總而言之，大學的生活是多采多姿並具有挑戰性的，所以我等不及要當大學生了。

3. 參考範文

Life at a University

It is said that life at a university is colorful and challenging. It is colorful first because there are so many inquisitive young men and women. Studying and discussing issues with them **must be very exciting**.[1] Second, these young people come from everywhere. It is interesting to learn about different cultures and backgrounds from each other. Third, there are all kinds of societies. Participating in these societies **provides one with endless chances**[2] to meet **people having the same hobbies**.[3] Being able to share things in common makes us happy.

Life at a university is challenging because professors may put a lot of demands on students. Besides attending classes, students may be asked to write lengthy papers or to conduct experiments on their own.

> **To sum up,**[4] life at a university is colorful and challenging, so I can't wait to be a college student.

4. 寫作指導

本文以大學生活 colorful and challenging 為訴求,說明嚮往大學生活的原因。內容切題。

5. 重要的字詞及文法提示

(1) must be very exciting

must(必定)表示肯定推測,句型如下:

must + V　　　　　(對現在的推測)

must + have V-en （對過去的推測)

例 John is yawning. He must be very tired.

John is yawning. He must have stayed up again last night.

(2) provides one with endless chances

provide sb. with sth.（提供某人某物），另外也可說 provide sth. for sb.

例 Jack often provides me with timely help.

Jack often provides timely help for his friends.

一般原則是,將新的或者較重要的資訊放後面。

(3) people having the same hobbies

people having the same hobbies（有相同嗜好的人）是從 people who have the same hobbies 簡化而來。名詞除了可以用單字形容詞來修飾外,也可以用關係子句或分詞片語來修飾。

例 She likes to meet interesting people（單字形容詞）

She likes to meet people who share a lot in common with her.（關係子句）

She likes to meet people sharing a lot in common with her.（分詞片語）

She sympathizes with kids who are abused by their parents.（關係子句）

She sympathizes with kids abused by their parents.（分詞片語）

(4) To sum up,...

to sum up（總而言之）用來為文章做摘要性的總結。也可說 In summary。

6. 造句練習：將各句譯成英文。

(1) 總而言之，年輕的一代應該尊敬長者並從他們的經驗學習。

(2) 這個節目提供給我們科技上的新知。

(3) 你一個人在家一定很寂寞。

(4) 穿著藍色洋裝的那位女士看起來很高雅。

(5) 他一定早就知道她會離家出走。

(6) 他們提供給那些在戰爭中受傷的士兵最好的照料。

（參考解答請見附錄Ⅱ）

7. 實力培養

Life at a University

It is said that life at a university is colorful and challenging. It is colorful first because _____. Studying and discussing issues with them must be very exciting. Second, these young people come from everywhere. It is interesting to _____ _____. Third, there are all kinds of societies. Participating in these societies _____ to meet people having the same hobbies. Being able to share things in common _____ _____.

Life at a university is challenging because professors may _____ _____. Besides attending classes, students may be asked to write lengthy papers or to _____.

To sum up, life at a university is colorful and challenging, so I can't wait to be a college student.

8. 輕鬆寫作

以 "Why I Want A College Education" 為主題，寫一篇英文作文，說明你嚮往大學生活的原因。文長 120～150 字之間。

參考資料：

Reasons for wanting a college education:

(1) You may be too young to seek a career.

(2) You want to pursue advanced learning.

(3) You want to learn a job skill.

(4) You want to meet people having the same interests and hobbies.

Unit 42 How to Be a Good Neighbor

題型：主題寫作

1. 試題

說明

以 "How to Be a Good Neighbor" 為主題，說明好鄰居的重要，和如何做好鄰居。文長至少 120 字，至多不超過 170 字。

2. 擬寫內容

如何成為好鄰居

　　每個人都喜歡有好鄰居。首先是因為有需要的時候，好鄰居可以依靠。再者，好鄰居有助於構成良好的居家環境。然而，我們不能只是要求別人成為好鄰居。相反地，我們自己也必須是好鄰居。

　　要成為好鄰居，首先要會為別人著想。例如，晚上我們不應該把音樂或電視開得太大聲，以免噪音騷擾到鄰居。第二，除了要為別人著想外，我們還要親切有禮貌。我們每次遇到鄰居的時候都要打招呼。我們可以準備一些食物適時和他們分享。我們也要適時給予幫助。

　　總之，如果我們會為別人著想、有禮貌且待人親切，我們就是好鄰居。

3. 參考範文

How to Be a Good Neighbor[1]

　　Everyone enjoys having good neighbors. For one thing, good neighbors **can be depended on**[2] **in times of need**.[3] For another, good neighbors help give our neighborhood a good living environment. **However**,[4] we cannot simply ask others to be good neighbors. Instead, we have to be good neighbors ourselves.

　　To be a good neighbor, first we have to be considerate. For example, we should not play blaring music or turn up our TV too loud at night, otherwise the noise would bother our neighbors. Second, **besides being considerate**,[5] we can **try**[6] to be polite and kind. We can greet our neighbors whenever we meet them. We can prepare some food and share it with them at some appropriate time. We can offer our help when it is needed.

　　In summary, if we are considerate, polite and kind, we will be good neighbors.

4. 寫作指導

第一段：第一句是 topic sentence。topic sentence 之後用 for one thing 及 for another 申論，之後用 however 做轉折，instead 句則為第二段舖路。

第二段：第一句為 To be a good neighbor, we have to observe several things. First, we have to be considerate. 之合併。For example 是 to be considerate 之申論。We can greet... when it is needed 為 we can try to be polite and kind 之申論

第三段：利用重述主旨的方法作結。

5. 重要的字詞及文法提示

(1) how to be a good neighbor

疑問詞 (how, when, where, what, which, who) 接不定詞成為名詞片語，可充當 (a) 主詞，(b) 受詞，(c) 補語。

例 (a) How to be a good neighbor is my topic today.（主詞）

  (b) Please tell me how to be a good neighbor.（受詞）

  (c) My topic today is how to be a good neighbor.（補語）

類似的例子還有：when to leave, where to go, who to see, what to say, which to buy... 等。

(2) can be depended on

to depend on（依賴）這個片語除了主動、被動用法之外，尚有一些詞類變化的靈活運用：

例 John said he could be depended on. I don't know whether I can depend on him or not. If I am dependent on him, I am afraid something unexpected might happen as a result of my dependence on him.

同義片語：to rely on, reliance on

(3) in times of need

in times of need（在有必要時）相當於 when it is necessary/when necessary

例 My sister told me that she would help me when necessary.

  My sister told me that she would help me in times of need.

(4) However

However（然而）是轉承語，在前後文表示對照時使用。相似詞有 still, but, yet, nevertheless

(5) besides being considerate

besides 是介詞，此處用動名詞片語做受詞。

中文的「體貼」在英文是 considerate，它是一個形容詞。形容詞通常不作介詞的受詞，所以，就拿它原來的連繫動詞 be（在 we are considerate 中，are 是連繫動詞），以動名詞的方式，充當 besides 的受詞。

(6) try

此處解為「努力」。類例：John tried hard to please his girlfriend.「努力」的類似用語：

to attempt to do something

to make attempts to do something

to make an effort to do something

to endeavor to do something

to strive for something

6. 造句練習：將各句譯成英文。

(1) 每個人都想知道如何過快樂的生活。

(2) 請告訴我何時離開和該見何人。

(3) 關於這件事，你可以完全依賴我。

(4) 我愛我的父母。他們總是在必要時協助我。

（參考解答請見附錄 II）

7. 實力培養

How to Be a Good Neighbor

Everyone enjoys having good neighbors. _____, good neighbors can be _____. For another, good neighbors help give our neighborhood a good living environment. However, we cannot simply ask others to be good neighbors. _____, we have to be good neighbors ourselves.

_____, first we have to be considerate. For example, we should not play blaring music or turn up our TV too loud at night, _____. Second, besides being considerate, we can _____. We can greet our neighbors _____. We can prepare some food

and share it with them at some appropriate time. We can offer our help
_____.

In summary, if we are considerate, polite and kind, we will be good neighbors.

8. 輕鬆寫作

 本單元的命題，另寫一篇作文，第一段說明好鄰居的特質，可參考以下的資料，第二段用一個你所認識的好鄰居做實例來印證第一段的看法。

Other good qualities of a good neighbor:

(1) provides timely help—like babysitting for us, watching our house when we are away

(2) is like friends—shares our joys and sorrows, offers comforts when we are sad

(3) shares things—such as CDs, books, and cameras

Unit 43 | A Dream

題型：看圖作文

1. 試題

 說明
1. 依提示在「答案卷」上寫一篇英文作文。
2. 文長 120 個單詞 (words) 左右。

 提示
請根據以下三張連環圖畫的內容，以 "In the (an) English class last week,..." 開頭，將圖中主角所經歷的事件作一合理的敘述。

2. 擬寫內容

一場夢

　　上星期的英文課中，一件有趣的事發生在約翰身上。當時老師正在教第三十課「我們就是世界」的時候，約翰卻睡著了，並做了一個夢

　　當時是 2005 年 1 月 15 日，但約翰卻夢到當時是 2025 年的同一天。他夢見他在教文法。但他教得太沒趣了，以致所有的學生都睡著了。因此，他很生氣，要學生們醒過來。

　　事實上，生氣的是約翰的老師，他要約翰醒過來。老師要求他解釋。約翰說他前一晚熬夜，為了準備學科能力測驗。

　　這個時候，我目睹了整個事件的經過，覺得很好笑。

3. 參考範文

A Dream

In the English class last week, something interesting happened to John. While the teacher was teaching Lesson 30, "We Are the World", John fell asleep and had a dream.

It was January 15, 2005, but John dreamed that it was the same day in 2025. He dreamed that he was teaching grammar. However, he was so boring that all of the students fell asleep. Consequently, he got angry and wanted his students to wake up.

In fact,[1] **it was John's teacher who was angry**[2] and wanted John to wake up. The teacher demanded an explanation. John said he **fell asleep**[3] because **he had sat up the previous night,**[4] **preparing for the Scholastic Achievement Test.**[5]

Meanwhile, I witnessed the whole thing and found it hilarious.

4. 寫作指導

(1) 看圖作文需要想像力,將圖片內容作合理的解釋與結局。

(2) 這個題目的圖片是敘述文 (narration),上文將 where (in the English class), when (last week), why (why John fell asleep), and what (what did John dream about) 等都有清楚的交代,而且用結尾對整個事件加以評論,是一個好的敘述文例子。

(3) 為方便敘述,可為圖中的主要人物取個名字。

(4) 圖片上提供的資料要設法用在作文中,以使作文更為切題。例如圖一中有 We are the world, Lesson 30, 2005 年 1 月 15 日;圖二有 2025 年 1 月 15 日等、圖三有 wake up 等,都應該用到作文中。

5. 重要的字詞及文法提示

(1) In fact

in fact 是轉承語,用法如下

(a) 強調

例 Mary likes John. In fact, she wants to marry him.

(b) 反駁

例 "You didn't do your assignment." "In fact, I have."

(c) 澄清

例 People think that the painting is genuine; in fact, it is a fake.

本文用法屬於 (c)。

(2) it was John's teacher who was angry

這句話原結構是 John's teacher was angry. 用 it is/was N who/that 是強調句型，置於 be 動詞後的 N 是要強調的部分。

> 例　John bought a car last week. 本句可分別強調畫底線的部分：
>
> → It was John who bought a car last week.
>
> → It was a car that John bought last week.
>
> → It was last week that John bought a car.

(3) fell asleep

片語 fall asleep 表「睡著了」之意。

> 例　My grandfather often falls asleep on the sofa while watching TV.

(4) he had sat up the previous night

片語 sit up 表「熬夜」之意。

the previous night 前一晚（指過去某時的前一晚），不同於 last night（現在算起的昨晚）。

比較: tomorrow（明天）及 the next day（過去某時的第二天）。

(5) preparing for the Scholastic Achievement Test

preparing 是 and prepared 簡化後的分詞。

學科能力測驗，大考中心譯成 the Scholastic Achievement Test。

---

6. 造句練習：將各句譯成英文。

(1) 為什麼你這麼疲倦？你熬夜了嗎？

(2) 是的，我熬夜準備今天的期末考。

(3) 事實上，我直到凌晨三點才睡覺。

（參考解答請見附錄Ⅱ）

---

7. 實力培養

A Dream

In the English class last week, something interesting happened to John. While the teacher was teaching Lesson 30, "We Are the World", _____ _____.

It was January 15, 2005, but John dreamed that it was _____ in 2025. He dreamed that _____. However, he was so _____. Consequently, he got angry and wanted _____.

_____, it was John's teacher _____ and wanted John to wake up. The teacher demanded an explanation. John said he fell asleep because he had _____,
preparing for the Scholastic Achievement Test.

_____, I witnessed the whole thing and found it hilarious.

8. 輕鬆寫作

 請根據以上三張連環圖畫的內容，以 "In the/an English class last week,..." 開頭，用你自己的版本，將圖中主角所經歷的事件作一合理的敘述。

參考資料：

圖一

(1) Lesson 30

(2) "We Are the World"

(3) 2005 年 1 月 15 日

(4) the hero fell asleep during an English class

圖二

(1) 2025 年 1 月 15 日

(2) grammar

(3) a blackboard

(4) a lectern

(5) the hero dreamed he was teaching

圖三

(1) the narrator was giggling

(2) the teacher wanted the hero to wake up

(3) the hero wanted the students in the dream to wake up

Unit 44 | Breakfast Eating Habits

題型：看圖作文

1. 試題

說明　下列圖表為臺灣高中學生食用早餐的頻率統計，請依據圖表內容，撰寫一篇文長約 150 字的短文。文分兩段，第一段先就圖表當中學生食用早餐的頻率統計加以說明，第二段則描述自己的早餐習慣及其優缺點。

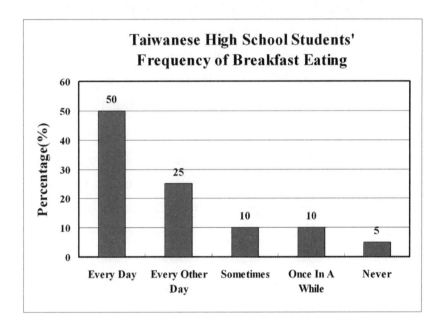

2. 擬寫內容

吃早餐的習慣

　　根據這張圖表，接受調查的所有學生中，百分之五十每天都吃早餐；百分之二十五，每兩天吃一次早餐；百分之十，有時候吃；另外百分之十，偶爾吃；百分之五，從來不吃早餐。

　　吃早餐的習慣因人而異。就我而言，我只是有時候吃。沒吃早餐，我很容易覺得累，而且我無法專心課業。這就是不吃早餐的缺點。另一方面，吃早餐，我覺得精力充沛，做起事比較有效率。這就是吃早餐的好處。

　　總之，吃早餐使我精力充沛、有效率；反之，不吃早餐容易疲勞且無法專注。所以每天吃早餐對我們有好處。

第三章

3. 參考範文

Breakfast Eating Habits

According to the chart, of all the students surveyed, 50 percent eat breakfast every day; 25 percent every other day; 10 percent sometimes; another 10 percent once in a while, and 5 percent never eat breakfast.

Different people have different breakfast eating habits. As far as I am concerned, I only eat breakfast sometimes. When I don't eat breakfast, I get tired easily, and I can't concentrate on my studies. This is the disadvantage of not having breakfast. On the other hand, when I eat breakfast, I feel energetic, and I am also efficient in **getting things done**.[1] This is the advantage of eating breakfast.

In summary, eating breakfast makes us energetic and efficient, while not eating breakfast makes us tire easily and makes us unable to concentrate. So, **it is to our advantage to eat breakfast every day**.[2]

4. 寫作指導

(1) 圖表題的寫作，首先要對圖表所表達的內容作正確的詮釋。

(2) 接著依命題要求寫作。

5. 重要的字詞及文法提示

(1) getting things done

get sth. V-en/adj. 用來表示使某件事完成或處於某狀態中。過去分詞也是形容詞用法，和形容詞一樣，用來當受詞補語。

例 He gets his hair cut every two weeks.

She often gets breakfast ready before her kids wake up.

如果是要某人去做某事，則用 get sb. to V...。

例 She got her kids to help with the housework.

(2) it is to our advantage to eat breakfast every day

Sth is to one's advantage 表示某事對某人有利。

例 The new policy is to everyone's advantage.

文中因為主詞是不定詞，用 it 代之。原句是：

例 To eat breakfast every day is to our advantage.

當主詞的不定詞移到句尾可達到強調的功用，然後用虛主詞 it 補位。

例 It would be to your advantage to concede a little.

主詞除了用不定詞外也可用 that 子句。

例 It is to our advantage that the two companies will merge.

6. 造句練習：將各句譯成英文。

(1) 考試盡量得高分對你有利。

(2) 你最好在開始寫報告前就把所有資料收集完成。

(3) 他總是如期地完成他的工作。

(4) 林老師吹著哨子要每個人往籃球場移動。

（參考解答請見附錄 II）

7. 實力培養

Breakfast Eating Habits

According to the chart, _____, 50 percent eat breakfast every day; 25 percent every other day; 10 percent sometimes; another 10 percent once in a while, and 5 percent _____ _____.

Different people have different breakfast eating habits. _____ _____, I only eat breakfast sometimes. _____, I get tired easily, and I can't concentrate on my studies. This is the disadvantage of _____. On the other hand, when I eat breakfast, I feel energetic, and I am also efficient in _____ _____. This is the advantage of eating breakfast.

In summary, eating breakfast makes us energetic and efficient, while not eating breakfast _____. So, it is _____ to eat breakfast every day.

8. 輕鬆寫作

 根據本單元圖表，用自己的版本寫一篇英文作文。

參考資料：

If you eat breakfast every day:

(1) You are lucky, because you live a regular life, and besides making you energetic and efficient, being regular will be to your advantage in life.

(2) You may have to get up earlier than if you don't eat breakfast.

If you never eat breakfast:

(1) You are at a risk, because you will suffer all the disadvantages of not eating breakfast, such as feeling weak in the morning, and you may even get sick.

(2) You can indulge in sleeping a longer while in the morning, but you probably go to bed later.

(3) You should think about changing your habits.

If you eat breakfast once in a while:

(1) You experience both the advantages and disadvantages of having breakfast.

(2) Perhaps you should try to be more regular so that you can have only the advantages of having breakfast.

Unit 45　The Best Way to Learn English

題型：主題寫作

1. 試題

說明　以 "The Best Way to Learn English" 為主題，說明你認為學英文最好的方法。文長至少 120 字，至多不超過 170 字。

2. 擬寫內容

學英語最好的方法

　　我的英文老師說學英文最有效的方法就是教英文。我非常同意這個觀點。我們經常為考試而讀英文。但是考試一結束我們就把所學的給忘了。這種學習英文的方法沒有效。

　　然而，如果我們學東西的目的是為了要能夠教，我們就會比為準備考試而做出更好的準備。能夠教意味者老師非常清楚教的內容。如果我們了解英文的某一個部分到可以教的程度，我們的英文肯定會進步。

　　誰會讓我們教呢？是這樣的。我們可以和同學或朋友解決這個問題。我們可以輪流教對方，不論是文法或閱讀。

　　試試這種方法。我向你保證，你會喜歡的，你的英文也會進步。

3. 參考範文

The Best Way to Learn English

　　My English teacher says that the best way to learn English is to teach it. I **can't agree more**[1] with that. Frequently we study English **in preparation for**[2] an examination. But as soon as the examination is over, we forget what we have learned. This is an ineffective way of learning English.

　　However, if we learn something in order to be able to teach it, we will be better prepared than if we just learn it for tests. To be able to teach something the teacher has to know it very well. If we know a certain part of English **to the extent that**[3] we can teach it, our English will definitely improve.

　　Who will listen to us teach, then? Well, we can work it out with our classmates or friends. We can take turns teaching each other, be it a grammar lesson or a reading selection.

　　Try it, and I **assure you that**[4] you will like it and improve your English.

4. 寫作指導

(1) 第一段的第一句是主題句，後面主要是鋪陳。

(2) 以對讀者提出邀請作結尾。

5. 重要的字詞及文法提示

(1) can't agree more

can't agree more 就是「非常同意」的意思。

例 I can't agree more that John is the best student in class.

(2) in preparation for

in preparation for sth. 的意思是「為某事做準備」。

例 We are collecting new data in preparation for the report.

(3) to the extent that

to the extent that（到達⋯的程度）之後接子句。

例 He loves her to the extent that he will sacrifice his life for her.

(4) assure you that

assure sb. that S V 的意思是「向某人保證⋯」。也可用 assure sb. of N。

例 I assure you of his innocence.

　　I assure you that he is innocent.

6. 造句練習：將各句譯成英文。

(1) 林老師向所有的教職員工保證我是誠實的。

(2) 他愛英文到了連做夢也說英文的程度。

(3) 我非常同意學生必須要可以自由使用圖書館。

(4) 他已連續三天熬夜為考試做準備。

(5) 如果你嫌開車太累，可換換搭飛機。

(6) 我可以向你保證他們是一個優秀的醫療團隊，而且你將會得到最好的照顧。

（參考解答請見附錄 II）

7. 實力培養

The Best Way to Learn English

My English teacher says that the best way to learn English is _____. I _____ with that. Frequently we study English _____ an examination. But as soon as _____ _____, we forget what we have learned. This is an ineffective way _____.

However, if we learn something _____, we will be better prepared than _____. To be able to teach something _____. If we know a certain part of English _____ we can teach it, our English will definitely improve.

Who will listen to us teach, then? Well, we can work it out with our classmates or friends. We can _____, be it a grammar lesson or a reading selection.

Try it, and I assure you that you will like it and improve your English.

8. 輕鬆寫作

提示

請你 (Paul) 將下文改以書信方式寫給你的筆友 Jordan，回答他你認為學英文的最好方法是什麼。

The Best Way to Learn English

The best way to learn English for me is memorization. First, I memorize how a word is spelt and what it means. Second, I memorize a sentence that tells me how the word is used. A word may have several meanings and, accordingly, different usages. But I just remember one meaning and one usage at a time. Similarly, I memorize what a phrase or an idiom means and how it is used.

Second, I memorize well-organized paragraphs. By well-organized I mean there is a topic sentence and relevant supporting details. Third, I memorize short, well-written passages, or essays. By short I mean less than 200 words. By well-written I mean there is a good beginning, development, and ending.

In summary, because memorization improves my overall proficiency in the four skills, for me memorization is the best way to learn English.

附錄 I　練 習 題 解 答

第一章　英文作文題型和寫作方法剖析

練習 1

1. A Windfall; who I would help with the windfall and the reasons why.
2. How To Remain Healthy; whether laughter is better than medicine and an example to support my position taken.
3. A Rainy Day; what I saw on a rainy day and how I felt about it.
4. Coping With Depression; how I cope with depression and an example to show why my method works.
5. A Class Reunion; when, where and how the reunion will be held and reasons for the activities planned.

練習 2

I.

1. John goes to school every day. （不是，不易帶出下文）
2. Going to school is essential for children. （是，下文說明 why going to school is essential for children）
3. Mike has many friends. （不是，不易帶出下文）
4. Baseball is a popular sport in Taiwan. （是，下文說明 why）
5. Helping other people can be challenging sometimes. （是，下文說明 why）
6. I am afraid of strangers for two reasons. （是，下文說明那兩個理由）
7. My favorite book is Harry Potter. （是，下文說明 why）
8. It's useless to regret what has already happened. （是，下文說明 why）
9. The movie I saw last week was unforgettable. （是，下文說明 why）
10. There are many cars running on the street. （不是，不易帶出下文）

II.

1. Topic: A Happy Ending
   Detail(s): Why my sister's romance with her boyfriend had a happy ending
   First sentence: My sister's romance with her boyfriend had a happy ending.

2. Topic: A Daily Item

   Detail(s): what that item is and how I depend on it

   First sentence: One daily item that I depend on very much is my bicycle.

3. Topic: Helping Others

   Detail(s): why and how I helped someone and how I felt about what I had done

   First sentence: I helped a friend last week.

4. Topic: Examinations

   Detail(s): What I think about having too many examinations

   First sentence: There are advantages and disadvantages in having too many examinations.

5. Topic: Qualities of a Good Friend

   Detail(s): The qualities I desire in a friend.

   First sentence: My friend must possess the following good qualities.

練習 3

I.

1. J   2. I   3. H   4. G   5. F   6. E   7. D   8. C   9. B   10. A

II.

First, Second, The third (reason), To sum up

練習 4

I.

1. C   2. D   3. E   4. B   5. A

II.

Learning to Ride a Bike

At fifteen I learned how to ride a bike. I remember that it was a sunny day and it was a holiday. I took my new bike to the park near my home to learn to ride it. <u>At the beginning</u>, I forgot I could use the brakes to stop the bike. <u>So</u>, I frequently ran into a tree or I had to jump off my bike to stop it. <u>As a result</u>, I often fell and got hurt. Although learning to ride a bike was difficult for me, I didn't give up. I tried again and again. Finally, I learned how to ride it.

練習 5

Learn it well, and you will be able to use it when you travel to other countries.

→　If we learn it well, we will be able to use it when we travel to other countries
其他地方的第二人稱 you 均改為 we, 以使敘事觀點一致。

練習 6

1. How to Save Electricity
2. My Favorite Season
3. Why I Love Dogs
4. One Thing I Have Learned in High School
5. An Appointment with My Dentist
6. An Interesting Incident
7. Taking a Positive Attitude Toward Life
8. Should We Help Our Enemy?
9. Incident on a Walk
10. How to Remain Healthy Throughout Life

第二章　如何寫出正確的英文句子

練習 7

1. The story is interesting.
　　主　　動　　主補
2. The story interests me.
　　主　　　動　　受
3. After searching for two days, the policemen finally found the stolen money.
　　　　　　　　　　　　　　　　　主　　　　　　動　　　受
4. The policemen finally found the stolen money buried in the woods.
　　主　　　　　動　　受　　　　　　　受補
5. Jim made a toy for his younger brother.
　　主　動　　受
6. Jane made Michael a good wife.
　　主　動　　間受　　直受
7. Jane made Michael a good husband.
　　主　動　　受　　　受補

8. What has happened?
　　主　　　動

9. You can't deny him his rights.
　　主　　　動　間受　直受

10. He bought his son a new pair of shoes.
　　主　動　　間受　　　　直受

11. You saved me a lot of trouble.
　　主　動　間受　　直受

12. Please tell me how to use this computer.
　　　動 間受　　　　直受

13. Please spare me my life.
　　　動　間受 直受

14. They called their daughter Jamie.
　　主　動　　受　　　受補

15. Whether ghosts exist or not remains controversial.
　　　　　主　　　　　　　動　　主補

16. She put on her coat.
　　主　動　　受

17. From five to seven is the rush hour.
　　　　主　　　動　　受

18. He who persists will win the race.
　　　主　　　　　　動　受

19. Please tell us whether you will come or not.
　　　動 間受　　　　直受

20. The sight of a huge spider in the kitchen surprised me.
　　　　　主　　　　　　　　　　　動　受

練習 8

1 ○	2 X	3 ○	4 ○	5 X 從屬子句
6 ○	7 ○合理片句	8 X	9 X	10 X
11 X	12 ○	13 ○	14 ○	15 ○
16 X	17 X	18 X	19 X	20 X
21 X	22 X	23 ○	24 ○	25 ○
26 ○	27 ○	28 X	29 X	30 X
31 X	32 ○	33 X	34 X	35 ○

36 ◯	37 ◯	38 ◯	39 ◯	40 ◯

練習 9

I.

1. and	2. and	3. or	4. or	5. nor
6. and/so	7. but/yet	8. for	9. yet/but	10. for

II.

2. He finished his work in time; moreover, he did it well
3. The house isn't big enough for us; furthermore, it is too far from the town.
4. You must pack plenty of food for the journey; likewise, you will need warm clothing.
5. He received the invitation; however, he did not go.
6. He is not very smart; nevertheless, we like him.
7. Study hard; otherwise, you may fail the course.
8. He was late for school; therefore, he was punished.
9. They have spent a lot of time learning English; accordingly, their English is very good.
10. The rain was heavy; consequently, the streets were flooded.

III.

2. He does not mind; in fact, he is very pleased.
3. My math teacher is a good guy; in addition, he teaches in an interesting way.
4. John tops his class academically; in addition, he is not proud.
5. Our teacher didn't say he would give us a test; on the contrary, he said he would let us watch a video.
6. Father did not let us go to the movie last Saturday; on the contrary, he ordered us to stay home and help with housework.
7. It is not cold; on the contrary, it is hot.
8. My father is very kind to us; on the other hand, he has a quick temper.
9. Patriotism is required of all; in other words, we must love our country.

IV.

2. Your car is new; mine is eight years old.
3. I don't feel well; I can't go with you.
4. Flora watches TV all night; she always comes to class late.
5. Peter is very kind; he is always helping others.

V.

1. Peter is a very lazy student; he is always late for class.
2. Study hard; otherwise, you won't make it to university.
3. I don't want to go to his party; I don't like him.
4. Because it was raining, we stayed indoors.
   It was raining, so we stayed indoors.
5. Though he likes her, he does not dare to tell her.
   He likes her, but he does not dare to tell her.

練習 10

I.

1. how   2. who   3. that   4. Whether, whether   5. Where

II.

1. I don't know whether or not I can go to a university.
2. But I know that I must work hard.
3. My father says that it doesn't matter whether or not I go to a university this year.
4. But I know that he hopes that I can pass the examination.
5. I know what I should do first.

練習 11

1. The building I live in has no elevator.
2. Romeo and Juliet were two lovers whose parents hated each other.
3. In my room there is a dictionary, which was a gift from my sister.
4. The chair I was sitting in suddenly collapsed.
5. The party will take place on Saturday, when more people can come.
6. Mr. Smith, who I had come especially to see, said he was too busy to speak to me.
7. His girlfriend, who he trusted absolutely, turned out to be an enemy spy.
8. This is the story of a man whose wife suddenly loses her memory.
9. We'll have to memorize a lot of words, which will be difficult.
10. The car crashed into a queue of people, four of whom were killed.
11. The man I was waiting for didn't turn up.
12. Most of the houses I saw were quite unsuitable.
13. This is where Mr. Smith works.
14. John didn't tell us how he did it.
15. You can call me Saturday afternoon, when I will be free.

16. There are no students but have to take tests.

17. This is the same watch as I lost.

18. The contest will be held on Sunday, when more people can participate.

19. Thank you very much for the gift you sent me.

20. I like to draw pictures of people I meet.

II.

1. My father often says that the lessons we learn from experience are very useful.

2. For example, he tells us that we cannot trust those who praise us to our face.

3. This is the most useful advice I have ever heard.

4. Last Sunday, when my father and mother were busy entertaining their guests, who come once a year, I went to see a movie.

5. The movie was about a famous writer, who was kidnapped by one of his admirers.

練習 12

1. When I was ten years old, I took part in a speech contest for the first time.

2. When it was my turn to make the speech, I slowly walked to the front.

3. However, when I was up front, all of a sudden I forgot everything that I had intended to say.

4. I had no choice but to walk back as soon as I could.

5. Strangely, once I was back to my seat, I recalled what I had intended to say.

6. Who takes the lead between the husband and the wife?

7. Some people say that wherever the husband goes, the wife should also follow.

8. Other people say that wherever the wife goes, the husband should also follow.

9. As far as I am concerned, wherever they may go, both the husband and the wife need to agree.

10. We usually do as what we are told by our coach.

11. One day he looked as if he had seen a ghost.

12. When he ordered that we run ten kilometers, we all ran home.

13. My father said that if we study as hard in college as we do in high school, we can have remarkable academic accomplishments.

14. In addition, the greater our accomplishments are, the stronger our motivation will be.

15. Consequently, I have decided to work as hard as I can after I go to college.

16. As students, we should read as much as we can. This is not because we are required to do so, but because reading will do us good.

17. When we read, we gain knowledge, and knowledge is power.
18. Now that we understand this, we should practice what we know.
19. My (elder) brother bought a car so that he can save time going to and from work
20. He drives his new car very carefully for fear that accidents might happen.
21. My classmate John is such a nice person that everyone likes him.
22. Yesterday in class he was so tired that he fell asleep.
23. If I won two million dollars in the lottery, I would help my father.
24. Unless we work hard, we won't learn anything well.
25. As long as there is life, there is hope.
26. What should we do in case of rain?
27. I will lend you my book provided that you return it in two weeks.
28. Whether we like it or not, we have to learn English.
29. Even if I am sick, I manage to learn something.
30. However old we may be, we should not stop learning.

附錄 II　練 習 題 解 答

第三章　輕鬆學會英文作文

Unit 1

(1) A strange thing happened to me this morning.

(2) I did not wear the school uniform. Instead, I wore casual clothing.

(3) However, my classmates did not seem to notice that I did not wear the school uniform.

(4) When it was time for me to go home, the school bus driver would not let me get on the bus.

(5) Luckily, a police car passed by, and I stopped it.

(6) The kind policemen took me home.

(7) This interesting incident turned out to be a dream.

Unit 2

(1) Reading has many advantages. Above all, it broadens our horizons.
Reading has many advantages. Above all, it increases our knowledge.

(2) It doesn't matter how much money you donate; what matters is the thought.

(3) The little girl is curious about what she will get for Christmas.

(4) At the end of the movie, all the passengers on the plane were saved.

(5) What we want to know is when we will run out of natural resources.

Unit 3

(1) Most parents do their best to bring up their children and ask for nothing in return.

(2) Learn to listen. Others' advice might be of great help to you.

(3) She was not discouraged; instead, she kept doing her research.

(4) While Susan was making a cake, her children were playing in the kitchen.

(5) Ted did very well on the test, so he looked forward to receiving the report card.

Unit 4

(1) The objective of this research is to understand the differences between men and women in using the library.

(2) The scenery here doesn't live up to expectations.

(3) How to protect wildlife is a hot issue.

(4) The topic of the article is how to improve memory.

(5) They haven't decided where to set up an orphanage.

Unit 5

(1) The government is working on bettering the living conditions of the farmers.

(2) I was tempted into buying that expensive car.

(3) A TV addict will gradually lose his creativity.

(4) Wars should be avoided by all means.

(5) Because he hung out all day long, he ended up a good-for-nothing.

Unit 6

(1) Mary took the medicine prescribed by the doctor; as a result, her headache was gone.

(2) Cell phones use a voice mailbox for callers to leave messages.

(3) I like cell phones, for they bring me great convenience.

Unit 7

(1) Who knows what the world will be like ten years from now?

(2) In sum, it takes everyone's effort to protect the environment.

(3) Is it likely that human beings will become extinct one thousand years from now?

(4) With the advancement of technology, modern people are better off.

(5) No one knows exactly what he did.

Unit 8

(1) I like to watch butterflies dance among flowers and hear birds sing.

(2) Whatever the reason, it is wrong to steal.

(3) To our surprise, he followed her advice instead of arguing.

(4) As far as I am concerned, nothing is impossible.

(5) He prefers staying home alone to hanging out with his friends.

(6) Although you have to spend all your time on this research, it is worth it.

(7) Whatever he said, don't take it too seriously.

(8) This book is worth reading. For one thing, its story is intriguing. For another, it is beautifully written.

Unit 9

(1) Whether you are rich or not, you can help those in need.

(2) He said nothing as to improving the working conditions.

(3) You can protect the environment by using fewer plastic bags.

(4) We need a good leader to follow.

(5) You hope that others will be honest with you. Likewise, you cannot cheat others.

(6) He likes challenges. It is no wonder that he took this tough job.

(7) Due to lack of love and care, he has difficulties staying mentally healthy.

Unit 10

(1) Generally speaking, teachers get a lot of respect.

(2) She is eager to live a life free from fear of violence.

(3) There are times when one must face death.

(4) This type of computer is not only expensive but (also) difficult to use.

(5) He not only takes care of his old parents but (also) raises five children.

(6) True happiness lies in appreciating what one owns.

(7) In conclusion, it takes everyone's effort to achieve/reach our goal.

Unit 11

(1) Even if they don't succeed, their hard work is (still) worthy of admiration.

(2) To reach an agreement, everyone should make some concession.

(3) The employer always has the welfare of the employees at heart.

(4) He looks on the bright side of things. Therefore, the world is always wonderful to him.

(5) There is a generation gap between parents and children. Similarly, there are differences of opinion between teachers and students.

(6) His proposal is practical and worthy of consideration.

Unit 12

(1) He drank a big glass of orange juice to quench his thirst.

(2) Without love, the world would be cold.

(3) He couldn't stand the hustle and bustle of the city. This was why he moved to the country.

(4) He is both an engineer and a poet.

(5) During the typhoon, it rains too much. As a result, there are floods everywhere.

(6) I like the plot and special effects of the movie. Most important of all, it inspired me to face the challenges in life.

Unit 13

(1) As a doctor, he has to attend to his patients' basic medical needs.

(2) He cannot take on such a challenging job. After all, he is seventy.

(3) There is no reason to expect everyone to yield to us.

(4) They took my tolerance for granted.

(5) We won't realize we shouldn't take our parents for granted until we need to be independent.

(6) We lost nearly $300,000, to say the least.

(7) Don't take it for granted that you will find a job after graduating from college.

(8) We didn't have a very pleasant weekend, to say the least.

Unit 14

(1) These government officials often criticize some policies constructively and provide some practicable advice.

(2) A journey without a destination often causes a waste of time.

(3) Finding he had no money to pay the bill, he felt very embarrassed.

(4) To conclude, environmental protection is an urgent matter, which requires everyone's assistance.

(5) His tedious lecture was very disappointing. The man sitting next to me left halfway.

Unit 15

(1) Racial discrimination generates hatred.

(2) Love will generate a lot of power.

(3) We considered him merciless until we found that he often helped the poor.

(4) His love of solitude alienates him from society.

(5) To cover up one's mistake is to make another mistake.

(6) Beckham is considered the most popular soccer player in the world.

(7) A mother's love is generally considered unconditional.

Unit 16

(1) The last thing I'd give up is my family.

(2) Reading more is the most effective way to increase your vocabulary.

(3) A self-centered person is the last person I'd like to marry.

(4) We completed the project efficiently by cooperating with each other.

(5) The last thing I want to do is to hurt you.

Unit 17

(1) As a result of overwork and long-term stress, he had a nervous breakdown.

(2) We should avoid spending money on unnecessary things.

(3) Since their separation, he has been avoiding his ex-girlfriend.

(4) Because of her diligence and capability, the business is prospering.

(5) People who often play with children stay young at heart.

Unit 18

(1) Looking at the stars in the sky, I could not but wonder how big the universe is.

(2) Whether it is a piece of music or a painting, art provides us with a rich mental feast.

(3) When I think of what my parents have done for me, I cannot (help) but say I love them more than anything else.

Unit 19

(1) Being able to forgive others brings inner peace.

(2) Naturally, English teachers are expected to have a good command of English.

(3) Reusing plastic bags is one way to protect the environment.

(4) On the one hand, he wants to use the air-conditioner; on the other hand, he doesn't want to spend too much money.

(5) A good command of four languages brings him a lot of job opportunities.

Unit 20

(1) How long has it been since men first landed on the moon?

(2) You can visit us whenever you like.

(3) I have been learning English for six years and I am making progress.

Unit 21

(1) I was pleased to listen to the performance of those world famous pianists.

(2) As soon as she graduated from college, she went abroad for further study.

(3) That dog will jump up and down as soon as it hears pleasant music.

(4) Mom's colleague came to pick her up, so she left her car with me.

(5) The philanthropist left all his money to that nursing home.

(6) No sooner had he heard the news than he ran out.

Unit 22

(1) Whenever I don't feel well, I go to see a doctor.

(2) Half of this class will major in literature and the other half, history.

(3) True love doesn't care whether the counterpart is well off/ rich/ wealthy or not.

Unit 23

(1) Success is made up of a few little victories.

(2) In the name of friendship, I won't cheat you or take advantage of you.

(3) Parents have the responsibility to impart proper values to their children.

(4) Like me, my fellow travelers were stunned by the magnificent scenery.

(5) Both work and leisure are important. The former gives us a chance to fulfill ourselves; the latter helps us to relax a bit.

(6) Mr. Wang likes to impart the latest information about teaching to his fellow teachers.

Unit 24

(1) Those who are pressed for time should learn to manage their time.

(2) It seems no one survived the fire. / No one seems to have survived the fire.

(3) The government should make and enforce stricter laws to regulate the traffic.

(4) He didn't do his homework, nor did he prepare for the test.

(5) At that moment, running away seemed to be the only way.

At that moment, it seemed that running away was the only way.

Unit 25

(1) Based on the book, human beings will be faced with a crisis caused by a shortage of resources in five years.

(2) He was so angry that he shook all over.

(3) She didn't enjoy his company at all.

(4) The students are asked to use as much English as they can in class.

(5) He was absent-minded in class. As a result/Consequently, he missed a lot of key points the teacher mentioned.

(6) They kept driving south and ended up in Kaohsiung.

(7) If you save ten thousand dollars a month, you'll end up a millionaire.

(8) A learned person is not necessarily a successful teacher.

(9) He didn't cultivate a hobby when he was young; as a result, he felt very bored after retirement.

Unit 26

(1) Make your life as simple as possible.
(2) All (that) you can do now is follow the doctor's advice.
(3) If I got SARS, I would have to stay home.
(4) The failure is a blow to him; nevertheless, he learned a good lesson.
(5) Many people see SARS as an incurable disease.
(6) If I were you, I would tell the truth instead of lying.
(7) The MRT is regarded as the most convenient public transportation.
(8) He takes a bus to work in order not to spend too much money.

Unit 27

(1) Since you know time is money, you should make good use of it.
(2) We wished them well as they left for the US.
(3) Besides fame and fortune, he won friendship.
(4) Summer vacation is a time when students explore new interests.
(5) Exercise relaxes us. Besides, it can help us keep fit.
(6) As a teacher, he tries his best to take care of every student in the class.

Unit 28

(1) Some children have difficulty learning to talk.
(2) When he was in his teens, he wanted to serve mankind. He made it his life's goal.
(3) His carelessness often makes his wife angry.
(4) He spends most of his time taking care of his old parents.
(5) She hopes to forget that unpleasant experience as soon as possible.
(6) If you want to have a good command of English, you have to read as many English books as possible.
(7) He has problems understanding abstract concepts.
(8) He has no difficulty (in) communicating in English.

Unit 29

(1) Even though he was very likely to lose, he still went all out.
(2) Those exposed to books have more knowledge.
(3) Dogs are known to be loyal.

(4) According to many reports, those who smoke are more likely to get lung cancer than those who don't.

(5) Although he lost a large sum of money, he won his friends' trust.

(6) I don't know whether I should go on to study at a graduate school.

(7) She is afraid of blood. Besides, she is not patient with patients.

(8) Based on her observation, these bears attack people only when they are frightened.

(9) It is said that the waste water from this factory will cause great harm to our bodies.

Unit 30

(1) I am determined to devote my life to education.

(2) He will finish writing the song he is going to dedicate to his mother by tomorrow.

(3) People always make New Year resolutions at the beginning of the year.

(4) When we are young, we should learn as many things as we can.

(5) He is determined to get married as soon as possible.

(6) I hope the MRT system near my home can be completed by the end of this year.

(7) The environmental group will manage to protect these endangered animals from hunters.

Unit 31

(1) He speaks slowly so that every student can understand his explanation.

(2) I want to build a website of my own.

(3) A person who always has his own way is not considerate of others.

(4) To protect yourselves from the cold, you need sweaters, coats, thick socks, and so forth.

(5) He is so tough that no one can persuade him to change his mind.

(6) When you arrive in a new place, you have to handle all the problems on your own.

Unit 32

(1) Once you make up your mind, you should persist.

(2) The new mayor spares no effort to crack down on drug trafficking.

(3) In a broader sense, the school can be counted as a community.

(4) I hope I can make a lot of contributions to our country as well.

(5) Those who come first will not necessarily receive the best service.

(6) In a way, our principal is a great educator.

(7) Beautiful women are not necessarily popular. Take my roommate for example. She

is beautiful, but very selfish.

(8) Once you become a well-recognized person, you will lose some freedom.

Unit 33

(1) He blushes whenever he feels embarrassed.

(2) When he was jogging in the park, he ran/came across a childhood friend.

(3) Students have to learn how to think for themselves.

(4) Good friends share experiences with each other, be they happy or sad.

(5) Remain calm when you face danger.

(6) Although they are in different places, they remain friends.

(7) While (I was) cleaning my drawer, I ran/came across the first love letter I received.

(8) Whenever I feel discouraged, this proverb encourages me to move on.

Unit 34

(1) You can buy dresses for all sorts of occasions in that boutique.

(2) Being understanding is one of her personality traits.

(3) Can two people who have nothing in common be good friends?

(4) Although my father has little in common with my mother, they can complement each other.

(5) Among all the qualifications for the job, the one the fewest people meet is the willingness to work overtime.

(6) Because they have a lot in common, they can read each other's mind.

(7) His greatest weakness is being indecisive.

Unit 35

(1) Since he went back to the US, I haven't heard from him.

(2) Of all the occupations, I think the most challenging is to be a teacher.

(3) However nervous you may be, you'd better pretend to be confident.

(4) Although I was angry, I managed to control my temper.

(5) As long as you keep working hard, your dream will come true in the long run.

(6) Because more people than expected will come, we need fifteen more chairs.

(7) This is the most interesting country I have ever been to.

(8) He has been working in a furniture factory since he dropped out of school.

Unit 36

(1) While many people work to live, some live to work.

(2) People's opinions differ greatly regarding what to live for.

(3) The local people make efforts to preserve this historical building.

(4) He doesn't like his students to idle away their time.

(5) The board could not reach a consensus on how to handle the problem.

Unit 37

(1) As a citizen of the ROC, you are entitled to the freedom of speech.

(2) If necessary, another sheet of paper can be used.

(3) Failure might be success in disguise; therefore, don't be discouraged.

(4) In spite of insufficient money, they (still) completed the bridge.

(5) Out of the taxi came a ragged beggar.

(6) Among other things, his good sense of humor greatly attracts me.

(7) No matter how terrible his condition is, he holds a positive attitude toward life.

Unit 38

(1) With a good memory, you'll find it easy to memorize vocabulary.

(2) A sick person is susceptible to infection.

(3) He came down with the flu and had to stay at home.

(4) All the orphans want is love and care.

(5) He donated two thirds of his income to charity.

(6) He spent the whole night talking on the phone.

(7) One fifth of the animals will become extinct.

(8) If you keep regular hours, you will be less susceptible to disease.

Unit 39

(1) These are the difficulties (that) an English learner may run into.

(2) As expected, they broke up in less than one month.

(3) To learn English well, you have to listen more and read more, but most important of all, you should open your mouth and speak English.

(4) No matter what you hear, keep it to yourself.

(5) Using drugs is like playing with fire.

(6) When he saw his dream lover, he didn't know what to say.

(7) That little girl seems extremely frightened.

(8) His encouragement gave me strength to move on.

Unit 40

(1) Parents' love is like the sun in winter.
(2) As far as I am concerned, one's success is determined by his contribution to society.
(3) Everybody is eager to love and to be loved.
(4) As people change, so countries change.
(5) In summary, one's attitude determines his way of living.
(6) Everybody seems to know the truth.
(7) People need the computer for different purposes. Some use it to calculate, others use it to write stories, and still others use it to draw pictures.

Unit 41

(1) To sum up, the younger generation should respect the elders and learn from their experiences.
(2) The program provides us with new knowledge in technology.
(3) You must be very lonely staying home all by yourself.
(4) The woman wearing a blue dress looks very elegant.
(5) He must have known that she would run away from home.
(6) They provided the best care for the soldiers wounded in the war.

Unit 42

(1) Everyone wishes to know how to live a happy life.
(2) Please tell me when to leave and who to see.
(3) Regarding this matter, you can fully depend on me.
(4) I love my parents; they always help me in times of need.

Unit 43

(1) Why are you so tired? Did you stay up?
(2) Yes, I did. I stayed up preparing for today's final exam.
(3) In fact, I did not go to bed until three this morning.

Unit 44

(1) It is to your advantage to score as high as possible on the exam.

(2) You had better get all the information collected before starting to write a report.

(3) He always gets his work finished on time.

(4) Mr. Lin blew the whistle to get everyone to move to the basketball court.

Unit 45

(1) Mr. Lin assured all the school faculty of my honesty.

Mr. Lin assured the school faculty that I was honest.

(2) He loves English to the extent that he speaks English even in his dreams.

(3) I can't agree more that students must have free access to the library.

(4) He has stayed up three days in a row in preparation for the exam.

(5) If you think driving is too tiring, you can try taking the plane.

(6) I can assure you that they are an excellent medical team and that you will receive the best care.

 附錄 III

歷年英文作文試題及作答示例

71年大學聯考

The National Flag and I

例文：

The National Flag and I

I have always loved the national flag. When I was in junior high school, my art teacher wanted us to draw the flag on a piece of paper and add colors to it. Following the teacher's instructions, I began drawing and coloring the flag. When it was finished, I took it to my teacher for a grade. I got an "A" for my work. I was very happy. Since then, I have felt attached to the national flag in an artistic way. (83 words)

72年大學聯考

A Taxi Ride

例文：

A Taxi Ride

My last taxi ride was a frustrating experience. I needed to buy some food for my friends, but I didn't know where to go. So I took a taxi, and I asked the driver to drive me around until I found a place. The driver said that since I was not sure where I was going, he did not have the time to drive me around slowly. As a result, as soon as he saw a food shop, he asked me to get out. Although I was frustrated, I could not do anything about it. (95 words)

73年大學聯考

How I Spent Yesterday Evening

例文：

How I Spent Yesterday Evening

I spent yesterday evening preparing for my exam today. I wanted to do well on my English test, so I spent most of the evening reviewing English. At about ten o'clock, my mother prepared a snack for me. I thanked her and ate the food. Then I took a shower. After the shower, I continued studying until about one o'clock in the morning. Then I went to bed. This was how I spent yesterday evening. (75 words)

74年大學聯考

用英文簡要敘述一件在高中階段一直想做卻沒有做到，因而想在進大學以後盡情去做的休閒活動（例如旅遊、運動、看電影、聽音樂、讀自己所喜愛的書等）。把文章分為兩段：第一段說明高中階段未能做到的原因；但二段敘述進大學後如何去做這一件事。文章以 80 字為度，不要太長或太短。

例文：

The Thing I Want to Do Most after Entering College

The thing I want to do most after entering college is to have a boyfriend. The high school I attended was a girls' school. The students in my school were all girls, and everybody thought that a student in a girls' school with a boyfriend was abnormal. So I didn't have the courage to have a boyfriend.

But when I enter college, there must be many male students. Besides, to have a boyfriend in college is very reasonable. Since there are many chances to meet boys in college, I'll choose a tall and handsome boy to be my boyfriend. (98 words)

75年大學聯考

用英文簡要敘述你上街買東西的經驗。全文分為兩段。第一段（約三十個詞＜words ＞說明買東西（例如：書籍、衣服、禮物等）的理由、商店的所在地、往返的交通工具等。第二段（約五十個詞）敘述買東西的經過情形、東西是否買成功、買了以後是否感到滿意等。文長以 80 個詞為度，不要太長或太短，並參考後面的評分指標。文章寫在「非選擇題試卷」上。

例文：

A Shopping Trip

On my brother's birthday, I went shopping for a present for him. I took the bus to a good department store in the downtown area.

I looked at many things at the department store. Finally, I decided to buy my brother a Nike T-shirt. My brother likes to play basketball, so I thought the shirt would suit him well. I paid the money and gladly took the bus home. My brother thanked me for the gift and I felt happy because I had chosen the right gift for him. (89 words)

76年大學聯考

　　一般來說，中國學生功課負擔，無論是上課時間或家庭作業，都比美國學生為重。請寫一篇八十字（words）左右的短文，敘述你對功課沉重的看法。文章寫在「非選擇題試卷」上，並參考下面的評分指標。

例文：

Comments on Heavy Schoolwork

　　Heavy schoolwork has an advantage and a disadvantage. The advantage is that students with a heavy workload tend to do better academically. Accordingly, they will be better prepared for college. The disadvantage is, since students are almost fully occupied with their studies, they have little time for extracurricular activities. As a result, their high school life is often boring. Therefore, a balance is needed to make high school life more interesting. (73 words)

77年大學聯考

　　寫一篇大約八十個英文字（words）的英文作文，說明樹木對人類的重要。第一段描述樹木對人類的益處，第二段說明如何保護樹木，每段約四十字。文章寫在「非選擇題試卷」上，並參考下面的評分指標。

例文：

The Importance of Trees

　　Has it ever occurred to you how important trees are? Trees offer us building material, provide us with fuel and fruit, beautify our environment, and help preserve the soil. Indeed, trees are important to us. (35 words)

　　Since trees are important to us, we should do what we can to protect them. We should plant more trees where we can. We can use trees for our needs, but we should not fell them excessively. Most important of all, our government should make laws to protect the trees. (83 words)

78年大學聯考

　　寫一篇大約八十個英文字（words）的短文，敘述你上學途中看到什麼、聽到什麼、想到什麼。把文章分成兩段，第一段敘述你怎麼上學、在上學途中遇到那些人、見到那些事物、景象；第二段就所見所聞敘述你的看法。文章請寫在「非選擇題試卷」上。

例文：

On My Way to School

I go to school by bicycle. On my way to school in the early morning, I usually see a lot of cars and motorcycles. These vehicles carry people to where they work. At the same time, these vehicles also produce lots of smoke that pollutes the air.

I am happy to see that many people are heading for work. This shows that our people are industrious. On the other hand, I feel sad to see so much car exhaust polluting our environment. I hope something can be done to improve the air quality of our city. (96 words)

79年大學聯考

台灣多山，氣候溫和，有很多珍貴的野生動物，但是有些人卻濫捕濫殺。請寫一篇大約一百個英文字（words）的短文。短文分為兩段；第一段說明台灣野生動物越來越稀少而濫捕濫殺卻不斷發生的情形；第二段討論我們應該怎麼樣保護野生動物。

例文：

Protecting Wild Animals

The mild climate of Taiwan makes it possible for many precious wild animals to exist. However, these animals have become smaller in number because of unreasonable killing. For example, people kill Taiwanese black bears for their gall.

I think wild animals should be protected, because their existence is an indication that we have a healthy environment. Moreover, if wild animals are completely wiped out, our environment may become dangerous for us without our being aware of it. Accordingly, we should make laws to protect wild animals, and those who disobey the laws should be heavily punished. (99 words)

80年大學聯考

寫一篇有關鐘或錶的短文，分成兩段：第一段談鐘或錶對我們生活的重要性；第二段談你最喜歡的一個鐘或錶。文章寫在「非選擇題試卷」上，長度以不超過 100 個單字為原則。

例文：

My Favorite Watch

Almost everyone has a watch. This is because we depend on our watches for our everyday activities. For example, we have to know how much time we have before the train leaves. We rely on our watches simply because they are convenient timepieces. Similarly, in our home or our offices we have clocks, which regulate the activities of the people in the home or the office.

My favorite watch was given to me as a present by my father. He gave it to me when I entered high school. Because it looks good on my wrist and because it keeps good time, I have been wearing it. I will probably continue to wear it for several years to come. (119 words)

81年大學聯考

寫一篇大約 100 個單字（word）的英文作文，題目是 "Time"。分成兩段： 第一段第一句必須是 "Lost time is never found again." 第二段第一句必須是 "Now I have a new plan for using my time wisely." 文章請寫在「非選擇題試卷」上。

例文：

Time

Lost time is never found again. Many old people wish that they could be young again, but they can't. This fact tells us that we should cherish every minute we have and that we should make the best use of time. In this way, we will have fewer regrets when we get old.

Now I have a new plan for using my time wisely. First, I will make a to-do list. If I do not finish doing the items on the list, I won't watch TV or spend time on entertainment. Second, I will do my best to take advantage of all the chances I have in life. In this way, I am sure I will live a happy life. (120 words)

82年大學聯考

寫一篇大約一百個單字（word）的英文作文，分成兩段，題目是 "Near-sightedness"（近視）。第一段的第一句必須是主題句 "Near-sightedness is a serious problem among the youth of our country" 第二段的第一句必須是主題句 "I have some suggestions for solving this problem."。文章請寫在「非選擇題試卷」上。

例文：

Near-sightedness

Near-sightedness is a serious problem among the youth of our country. Probably because of too much schoolwork or because of watching too much TV, many of the youth of our country get near-sighted and have to wear glasses. It can be very inconvenient if one is near-sighted. Therefore, something should be done about it.

I have some suggestions for solving this problem. First, prevention is better than cure. Those who have normal eyes should take good care of their eyes. For example, they should always read under sufficient illumination. Second, those who are near-sighted should seek treatment. They can improve their vision by wearing glasses. In summary, our eyes are important to us and we should take good care of them. (122 words)

83年大學聯考

寫一篇大約 100 到 120 個單字的英文作文，題目是 "A House Is Not a Home"。分成兩段：第一段先解釋 house 和 home 兩個字，及使用上意思可能相同的情況。第二段說明 house 和 home 這兩個字的涵義有何不同。文章請寫在「非選擇題答卷」上。

例文：

A House Is Not a Home

The words "house" and "home" can both refer to a place where people live. For example, we can say that somebody has a beautiful home or a lovely house. Or, we can say that a house or a home is for sale.

However, these two words can have different meanings. For example, the word "home" carries the sense of belonging. Be it an apartment, a flat, or a house, people go home to rest. In other words, apartments, flats, or houses are all homes if one finds comfort in them. On the other hand, one may live in a house without the feeling of a home. (106 words)

84年大學聯考

寫一篇大約一百二十個單字左右的英文作文，分成兩段，題目是 "Making Decisions"。第一段的第一句必須是主題句 "Growing up means making my own decisions." 第二段的第一句必須是主題句 "The hardest decision that I ever made was＿＿＿"，同時自行在空格中填入自己所作的決定。文章請寫在「非選擇題答案卷」上。

例文：

Making Decisions

Growing up means making my own decisions. When I was younger, I relied on my parents for everything I needed. Gradually, I realized I had to learn to make my own decisions. For example, my mother would take me to a department store and ask me which shirt I liked. In this way, I gradually learned to make decisions.

The hardest decision that I ever made was to quit my piano lessons in order to prepare for the university entrance examination. I used to have two piano lessons every week. And I practiced a lot. Since I love music, playing the piano makes me very happy. However, my parents said that I needed more time to prepare for the exam. So I had to quit my piano lessons. I hope the exam will be over very soon and I can start playing the piano again. (145 words)

85年大學聯考

　　寫一篇約一百二十字的短文，一段或兩段皆可。文章必須以下面的英文句開頭：" You win some; you lose some. That is life" 人生中，每一個人都會有得有失。文章中必須舉出你自己有所得（win）又有所失（lose）的一個實例。請寫在「非選擇題答案卷」上。

例文：

Winning and Losing in Life

　　You win some; you lose some. That is life. You can't have a pie and eat it at the same time. I remember last year my good friend Mandy and I both entered an English speech contest. Both of us worked very hard for it, and we practiced a lot. On the day of the contest, both of us did very well, except that Mandy coughed once halfway through the speech. As a result, I won first place and she second. Mandy didn't take the result very well. She kept thinking that she would have won the first place if she had not coughed. After that, we were not as close as we had been before.

　　The above example shows that although I won the contest, I lost a friend. That is, you win some and you lose some. This is life, and we should learn to accept it. (149 words)

86年大學聯考

　　下面有兩個英文問題，和你的未來計畫有關，每個問題請用大約六十個英文單字回答。答案請寫在「非選擇題答案卷」上，同時務必標示題號。

Why do you want to enter college?

What else would you do if you should fail to enter college?

例文：

　　(1) I want to enter college for two reasons. To begin with, I am still too young and too inexperienced for work. College is a good place for me to get older and become more mature. Second, I need to specialize in something; that is, I need to learn a job skill. College is a good place for me to learn more advanced skills

for work. (65 words)

(2) If I should fail to enter college, I would still try to further my education and learn a job skill. Perhaps I could enter a military school and become a professional soldier. If I should fail again, then I could always wait for one more year and try to take the university entrance examination again. I believe that as long as I persevere, I will succeed in the end. (69 words)

87年大學聯考

請以 Saying "Thank you" and "I'm sorry" frequently will make you a happier person. 為起始句,寫一篇約一百二十個單字的英文作文。答案請寫在「非選擇題答案卷」上。

例文:

How to Become Happier

Saying "Thank you" and "I'm sorry" frequently will make you a happier person. We human beings are social animals. In our daily life, we are frequently in contact with other people. We don't want to be considered impolite or rude. Similarly, we don't like impolite or rude people. Not saying "Thank you" or "I am sorry" makes us impolite or even rude. Being impolite or being rude generates an uncomfortable atmosphere that tends to suffocate.

On the other hand, a simple "Thank you" shows appreciation and an "I am sorry" shows that there is no bad intention. If we say "Thank you" and "I am sorry" frequently, we will be considered polite people and will be socially welcome. In consequence, we will certainly be happier than otherwise. (127 words)

88年大學聯考

請以 "A Happy Ending"(快樂的結局)為題,寫一篇約一百二十個單字的英文作文。你可以從你所讀過的故事、看過的電影或親身的體驗中去找題材。描寫完快樂的結局以後,並寫幾句你的感想。答案請寫在「非選擇題答案卷」上。

例文:

A Happy Ending

Nobody in my family thought that my elder sister Janet could marry the Frenchman she fell in love with, but it had a happy ending.

Janet was a French major at a private university in Taipei. When she was a junior, she met her French professor. We didn't think the professor was suitable for Janet. For one thing, the professor was much older than Janet. For another, nobody in my family speaks French except Janet.

However, the professor managed to learn to speak some Chinese. And we found that he was a gentleman and was serious about Janet. So, when he proposed to Janet after her graduation, Janet as well as the family consented. They are happily married now.

Personally, I think intercultural marriages can enhance understanding between different cultures. I am glad that my sister's love with the French professor had a happy ending. (145 words)

89年大學聯考

請以 "The Difficulties I Have with Learning English" 為題，寫一篇約一百二十個單字的英文作文。文分兩段，第一段寫出你修習英語過程中某些學習上的困難；第二段說明處理這些困難的經過及結果。

例文：

The Difficulties I Have with Learning English

The difficulties I have with learning English are many. First, I don't know how to write well. Second, there are a lot of new words I don't know when I take reading comprehension tests. Third, I can't spell correctly. Fourth, I don't speak well.

But I have to learn English, anyway. So, I try to solve my problems one by one. To become a good writer, I practice a lot. To increase my vocabulary, I memorize whatever I come across. To improve my spelling, I practice writing the new words I learn on a computer and let it tell me whether I have spelt them correctly or not. Finally, to practice speaking, I memorize many essays and try to recite them. I use a tape recorder. In this way, I have gradually improved my English. (135 words)

90年大學聯考

請以 "My Favorite Retreat" （我最喜歡去的僻靜處所）為題，寫一篇約一百二十個單字 (words) 的英文作文。人在繁忙或苦惱的時候，常會找一個地方靜下心來，好好休息，好好思考，使自己放鬆。描述這樣一個能讓你身心寧靜或放鬆的地方，並且說明在什麼情況下，你會到這個地方去。這個地方可以在市區內，也可以在郊區，例如公園或河邊等。

例文：

My Favorite Retreat

My favorite retreat is the city park near my home. The park is medium in size, with lots of trees, a green lawn, a playground for small children, and some open spaces for activities.

Whenever I feel distressed, disappointed, or sad, I like to go to the park to gather myself together. I usually sit on one bench, looking at the people going in and out of the park. Some come for a stroll, others to walk their dog, still others to do shadow boxing or to folk dance. To me, it is interesting to see people full of energy. The people who come to the park don't seem distressed, disappointed, or sad. They seem to come to enjoy what the park has to offer—an open space for activities. In this way, I am reminded that life is for us to enjoy. There is no room for distress, for disappointments, or sadness. I soon get over my low mood. The park is my favorite retreat. (166 words)

83年學科能力測驗

Things Are Not As Difficult As They Appear

在成長的過程中，有些事情在開始的時候你可能覺得很難，但經過一番努力後就不再認為困難了。請寫一篇至少一百二十個單字的英文作文，描述一個親身的經驗。文章的頭兩句必須是：

Things are not as difficult as they appear. I have a personal experience to prove this.

例文：

Things Are Not As Difficult As They Appear

Things are not as difficult as they appear. I have a personal experience to prove this. When I was a freshman in high school, because I was learning how to use the computer, I wanted to learn to type. That is, I wanted to learn how to use the keyboard more efficiently. Instead of using my index finger all the time, I wanted to use all the fingers and the thumbs of both hands.

Following a guidebook, I began practicing typing on the computer. At the beginning, I was often awkward, and was not able to use my fingers as I wished. But gradually, after some practice, I found that I was beginning to make progress. My fingers hit the right keys at the right places. Now I can type without looking at the keyboard. You see, things are not as difficult as they appear. (145 words)

84年學科能力測驗

　　高中生王治平收到美國筆友 George 的來信，告訴治平他要隨父母到台灣來住兩年左右，並問治平："Can you give me some advice and suggestions so that I know what I should do and what I should not do when I am in Taiwan?"

　　現在請你以治平的身分，擬一封適當的回信給 George，歡迎他來台灣，並且針對他的問題，提出一些具體的建議。

例文：

February 20, 1995

Dear George,

　　I'm really glad to hear that you're coming to Taiwan. During your stay here, there are a few things that you should know. First, you will be invited to dine with local people. So, you should know how to use chopsticks. Your host and hostess will be pleased that you can handle the chopsticks.

　　Second, you should know the public transportation system. In Taipei, you have several choices if you want to go somewhere. You can take the bus, the subway, or you can take a taxi. Most taxi drivers are friendly and are eager to help you even though they may not speak English. But do not flag down taxicabs that are not clean. Filthy taxicabs may indicate that the drivers are not professional ones, and accordingly, they may be unsafe. Don't give these drivers a chance.

　　Finally, you can do some sightseeing and take strolls to the night markets. There you can get a taste of local foods.

　　I will tell you more when you are here. See you soon. (173 words)

Your friend,

Chih-ping

85年學科能力測驗

背景提示：

　　西元 1939 年紐約世界博覽會前夕，主辦單位在會址的地底下埋了一個時間膠囊 (time capsule)，裡面放了許多最能代表當時生活方式的物品，如電話機、開罐器、手錶、香煙、以及一塊煤炭等。這個密封的盒子，要等到西元 6939 年才打開，以便讓五千年後的人知道 1930 年代的生活型態。

　　現在有一個國際性基金會也預備舉辦類似的活動，要將一個真空密閉的時間膠囊埋在地底，膠囊中的東西都不會腐壞，好讓一千年以後的人知道 1996 年世界各地區的生活方式。該基金會公開向各國人士徵求建議。

提示：

　　請你寫一篇英文短文前往應徵，提出最能代表我國人民生活現狀的物品兩件（體積不限），說明你選擇這兩件物品的理由，並以 "The two things I would like to put in the time capsule are..." 作為短文的開頭。

例文：

The Time Capsule

　　The two things I would like to put in the time capsule are a telephone and a TV set. Nowadays almost every household has at least one telephone. The telephone plays an important role in our life. People use the telephone to greet each other, to inform each other of the latest happenings, to gossip, to make appointments, and even to conduct business. It is obvious that the telephone is an important item in our era.

　　Another item I would put in the capsule is a TV set. Almost every living room I know is centered round a TV set. This means that TV is the main entertainment in most homes. Indeed, children and adults all spend a lot of time watching TV. Consequently, I would choose to put in the capsule a TV set, to let people in the future know how important it is to our daily life.

86年學科能力測驗

提示：

　　你同意 "Laughter is better than medicine" 這種說法嗎？以你自己或親朋好友的經驗或你所知道的故事為例，加以說明。你的論點無論是正面或是反面都不會影響你的得分。

例文：

Laughter Is Better Than Medicine

　　To remain healthy, laughter is better than medicine. People who laugh a lot are likely to be more positive and tend to maintain an optimistic attitude toward life. It is said that with this attitude, their immune system is strengthened. As a result, they get sick less often and tend to live longer.

　　A distant relative of mine was diagnosed as having terminal cancer. Her doctor told her that, even with the best medical treatment, she had only a few months to live. But what the doctor did not know was that she is an extremely optimistic person and that she laughs a lot. Instead of feeling desperate, she laughed at her cancer and faced it bravely. It has been five years now and she is still alive and well.

The above example shows that it is indeed true that laughter is better than medicine.

87年學科能力測驗

提示：

每個人在不同的情況下對雨可能有不同的感受。請寫一篇短文，敘述你在某一個下雨天的實際經驗或看到的景象，並據此描述你對雨的感覺。

例文：

A Rainy Day

It had not rained for a long time. If it did not rain soon, our rice field would dry up and we would suffer great losses. Fortunately, the sky became cloudy and it finally rained.

On the rainy day, I saw people deliberately go outdoors to get wet. They reached their hands to the sky and shouted excitedly. The ducks came out of their shelter and joyfully played in the rainwater. Suddenly, there was a world of colorful umbrellas. Although the rain brought some inconvenience, people seemed happy with it.

I like rain. It is nature's gift to us. For one thing, it fills up water reservoirs so that we won't run short of water. For another, most plants depend on the rain for growth. Without rainwater, many plants would die. In summary, the rain does us a lot of good, so I like it.

88年學科能力測驗

提示：

A

MARKETING PROFESSIONALS

A major US corporation in the health and nutrition industry has announced the opening of its direct sales division in Taiwan.

The company offers the most lucrative compensation plan in the industry and has paid over *$3.5 billion NTD in commissions* in just 6 years in the US. We are a group of top earners. Applicants should meet the requirements:
(1) Taiwan citizen
(2) Have interest or experience in marketing
(3) Aggressive, energetic, and willing to learn

If you believe you have what it takes to develop this business, please call 2742-6996

B

An international company requires a

Service Technician

To service and maintain electronic medical equipment.

Applicants should possess degree in electronics. The selected candidate will undergo a training program to be conducted by our manufacturer's trained technical personnel.

Interested candidates please apply immediately with resume to P.O. box 594. Or telephone Ms. Chang at 2945-0027 for an immediate interview.

C

Wanted: Reporters & Editors

Qualifications:
% Strong command of English language
% Chinese speaking and reading ability a must
% A university degree
% Journalism education and/or experience a plus

Flexible working hours (30 hours per week)
Good work environment and great co-workers
Medical insurance, etc.

Fax resume and work samples, if any, to
The China Post at (03) 2595-7962.

D

Southeastern Travel Services

OPENINGS *************************

TOUR GUIDES

Duties: To conduct escorted tours for foreign visitors; to assist with travel and transportation arrangements.

Qualifications: Good appearance. High school diploma. Good knowledge of English. Outgoing personality.

Call 2703-2172 after 3:00 PM. Ask for Gary.

根據以上四則求職廣告，寫一篇英文作文。文分兩段：第一段寫出你認為這四種工作中那一種對你而言是最好的工作，並説明理由；第二段則寫出四種工作中你最不可能選擇的工作，也説明理由。假如這四種工作你都不喜歡，則在第一段説明都不喜歡的理由，在第二段寫你喜歡什麼工作，並説明理由。

例文：

The Job I Like

Of the four jobs offered in the ads, I would like being an editor and reporter the best. I have been enjoying writing and editing since I was in elementary school. Editing requires a lot of patience and skill. I am patient and I have the skills needed for the job. Besides, being a reporter is challenging. I would be exposed to many strange things and I would enjoy reporting them to my readers.

On the other hand, I wouldn't like being a service technician. In the first place, I am not interested in electronics. Second, I don't like to work with machines. To sum up, if I could, I would choose to be an editor and reporter. I wouldn't like to be a technician or a marketing professional. (128 words)

89年學科能力測驗

請寫一篇英文作文，主題為 "Weight Loss"：以你個人或你熟悉的人（朋友、親戚）為例，說明造成這個人體重過重的原因，並提出你認為理想的解決之道。

例文：

Weight Loss

The term "weight loss" is fairly new in Taiwan. Here many people think that to eat is to enjoy life. As a result, many of them become overweight and they risk high blood pressure and heart problems.

My classmate Jack is an example. His mother thinks that if he is too thin, it may mean that she is not a responsible mother. Consequently, she has been overfeeding him since he was a baby. Moreover, he has become very fond of food. He eats all kinds of food and does not do exercise. It is no surprise that, at the young age of 18, he already weighs 250 pounds.

As mentioned above, being overweight can bring about many health problems. I think it is better for Jack to lose weight, simply for the sake of good health. To lose weight, I think first he has to resist the temptation to overeat. He should carefully count the calories he takes in and do exercise to consume excessive ones. In this way, he can reduce his weight. In summary, the way to lose weight is to burn more calories than one takes in.

90年學科能力測驗

請以 "Something Interesting about a Classmate of Mine" 為題，寫出有關你一位同學的一件趣事。這位同學可以是你任何時期的同學，例如中學、小學或幼稚園的同學。

例文：

Something Interesting about a Classmate of Mine

Something interesting about a classmate of mine—Jack—happened when he was a small child. When Jack was a kid, he liked to play with elevators. He would get in an elevator, press all the bottons, and ride the elevator up and down until he was satisfied.

One day, his parents were busy entertaining guests and had no time to look after Jack. So he left his apartment and started playing with the elevator again. He pushed all the bottons, as usual. However, this time the elevator got stuck and would not move either up or down, and Jack was locked inside the elevator. Because it was during office hours, nobody needed to ride the elevator that afternoon. As a result, nobody knew that the elevator was out of order and Jack was locked inside for a long time. Jack could not get out until the superintendent found out about the malfunction and rescued Jack.

When his parents realized what had happened, they scolded Jack for being so naughty. It was an interesting incident that Jack had. (175 words)

91年學科能力測驗(1)

以 "The Most Precious Thing in My Room" 為題，寫一篇英文作文，描述你的房間內一件你最珍愛的物品，同時並說明珍愛的理由。(這一件你最珍愛的物品不一定是貴重的，但對你來說卻是最有意義或是最值得紀念的。)

例文：

The Most Precious Thing in My Room

The most precious thing in my room is a tape recorder with a built-in radio. It is precious to me because I have been using it to listen to Studio Classroom. I wanted to improve my English, and I found listening to the radio a good way to accomplish my goal. Each day, I record the program. Then I listen to it again and again until I fully understand what has been said. In this way, my listening comprehension has been greatly improved.

Besides using my tape recorder for English, I also use it to improve my speech. I usually read to the recorder and record my own speech. Then I play it to see if there is room for improvement. I have found the tape recorder a tremendous help. In summary, for these reasons, the most precious thing in my room is my tape recorder. (146 words)

91年學科能力測驗(2)

以 "Growing up is a/an ＿＿＿ experience" 為題，寫一篇英文作文，描述你的成長經驗是令人興奮的 (exciting)、令人困惑的 (confusing)，快樂的 (happy) 或是痛苦的。除了這些形容詞之外，你也可以用其他的形容詞來描述你成長的經驗。請務必提出具體的例子以描述你成長的經驗。(注意： 如果你用的形容詞以子音起始，請選擇冠詞 "a"，如 "a confusing experience"；如果你用的形容詞以母音起始，請選擇冠詞 "an"，如 "an exciting experience"。)

例文：

Growing Up Is an Exciting Experience

Growing up may mean different things to different people. For example, to children in poor families, growing up may mean increased responsibilities. As far as I am concerned, growing up is an exciting experience.

When I was a child, I could only let my parents take me wherever they went, and there wasn't much I could do except follow their orders. But now that I am older, I am allowed more freedom to go places and do more of what I like. For example, I enjoy reading science fiction. My parents usually let me read as much as I want so long as I keep up with my schoolwork. It is exciting to explore the imaginative world. I would not be able to do this if I were younger. Therefore, I think growing up is an exciting experience. (139 words)

92年學科能力測驗(1)

請以 "Music Is an Important Part of Our Life" 為題，說明音樂 (例如古典音樂、流行歌曲、搖滾音樂等) 在生活中的重要性，並以你或他人的經驗為例，敘述音樂所帶來的好處。

例文：

Music Is an Important Part of Our Life

It is obvious that music is an important part of our life. Many of us have never traveled abroad, but every one of us has some experience with music. For example, in school we learn to sing or to play a musical instrument. In our free time, we listen to music, or go to concerts for entertainment. We sing songs when we are happy. These are evidences that music is indeed an important part of our life.

Through years of listening to music, I have learned to appreciate music. Personally, I think the advantages that music brings are several. First, the beautiful sounds of music delight us. Second, the stories in popular songs touch us. Third, music reduces our tension and it releases our emotions. In summary, music plays such an important role in my life that I simply can't do without it. (144 words)

92年學科能力測驗(2)

請以自己的經驗為例，描述當你感到不快樂或情緒低落時，(除了簡答題選文中所提及的方法外，)你最常用哪一種方法幫自己度過低潮，並舉實例說明這個方法何以有效。

例文：

Coping with Unhappiness

It is inevitable that people sometimes feel unhappy or low. I am no exception. During such times, instead of getting angry or feeling helpless, I always know how to cope with it. First, I try to identify the cause of my unhappiness or my low mood. For example, is it because I have not done well on an exam? Once I identify the cause, I will normally feel better. Then I make a decision. That is, I will not make the same mistake again. It is in this way that I get over my unhappiness or my low mood.

At the end of last semester, I felt unhappy. Then I realized it was because I did not do well on the final exam. I had spent too much time watching TV. I decided to do something about it. I gave up watching TV and concentrated all my energy on my studies. As a result, my grades improved. By not making the same mistake again I have now overcome my unhappiness. In summary, to identify the cause and then do something about it is indeed an effective measure to cope with unhappiness or a low mood. (194 words)

93年學科能力測驗

試題及例文見第三章 Unit 1 An Embarrassing Incident。

94年學科能力測驗

試題及例文參考第三章 Unit 43 A Dream。

95年學科能力測驗

說明：

1. 依提示在「答案卷」上寫一篇英文作文。

2. 文長 100 個單詞左右。

提示：

根據下列連環圖畫的內容，將圖中女子、小狗、與大猩猩 (gorilla) 之間所發生的事件作一合理的敘述。

例文：

A Surprise

Mary had a surprise one day. Mary invited her boyfriend Allan to her apartment to have dinner together. That evening, Mary was in the kitchen cooking dinner, and her dog Daisy was watching her, hoping to get something to eat.

Suddenly, a gorilla entered the kitchen. The sight of a gorilla in the kitchen shocked Mary and the food she was cooking fell on the floor. Daisy rushed to the food and enjoyed eating it.

Then, the gorilla took off its mask and held a bunch of flowers in his hand. It was Allan, who had disguised himself as a gorilla. Seeing that the gorilla turned out to be her boyfriend, Mary smiled and they spent a pleasant evening together.

96年學科能力測驗

説明：

　　1. 依提示在「答案卷」上寫一篇英文作文。

　　2. 文長 120 個單詞 (words) 左右。

提示：

　　請以下面編號 1 至 4 的四張圖畫內容為藍本，依序寫一篇文章，描述女孩與貓之間的故事。你也可以發揮想像力，自己選定一個順序，編寫故事。請注意，故事內容務必涵蓋四張圖意，力求情節完整、前後發展合理。

例文：

Cat Trouble

One day Jamie ran into a stray kitten in the park. Jamie took a ball of yarn out of her pocket and played with the kitten. The kitten was so cute that Jamie wanted to keep it.

So, Jamie picked up 'Kitty,' as she called it, and started walking home. However, what she didn't know was that several other stray cats were following her.

When Jamie got home, she asked her mother whether she could keep Kitty. Her mother finally consented.

Jamie was very happy and took Kitty to the living room. Meanwhile, the other stray cats had slipped into the house and made a mess of the living room. On the floor were paw prints, fish bones and a roll of toilet tissue. Worse still, the sofa was scratched all over. Jamie had a hard time deciding whether she should keep Kitty or throw her out with the rest of the cats!

91年指定科目考試

文章請以 "If I won two million dollars in the lottery, I would help..." 開始，敘述如果你或妳贏得臺灣樂透彩新臺幣兩百萬元之後，最想把全數金額拿去幫助的人、機構或組織，並寫出理由。

例文：

Helping My Family

If I won two million dollars in the lottery, I would help my family. First, I would help my father buy a car. It takes a long time for him to go to and from work. With a car, he could save much time.

Second, I would help my brother with his college expenses. My brother is a law student. He is working his way through college. I am sure if he didn't have to work part time, he could concentrate better on his studies.

Third, I would help my sister with her piano lessons. My sister has a tutor come every week to give her piano lessons. The fee is very high. If I could help her with that, it would reduce my father's burden somewhat.

In summary, if I won two million dollars in the lottery, I would help my father, my brother and my sister. (148 words)

92年指定科目考試

提示：

　　小考、段考、複習考、畢業考、甚至校外其他各種大大小小的考試，已成為高中學生生活中不可或缺的一部分。請寫一篇 120 至 150 個單詞左右的英文作文，文分二段，第一段以 Exams of all kinds have become a necessary part of my high school life. 為主題句；第二段則以 The most unforgettable exam I have ever taken is ... 為開頭並加以發展。

註：92 年指定科目考試英文作文試題有欠妥當。其一，參加考試的絕大多數考生應已高中畢業。但提示中卻規定「第一段以 Exams of all kinds have become a necessary part of my high school life. 為主題句」，視考生仍為高中學生。若改為 "Exams of all kinds were a necessary part of my high school life."，似較為妥當。其二，提示中又規定「第二段則以 The most unforgettable exam I have ever taken is ... 為開頭並加以發展」，動詞 "is" 應以過去式 "was" 為佳。這裡提供的例文係依據命題而寫。

例文：

Examinations

　　Exams of all kinds have become a necessary part of my high school life. In every class period, I have a quiz. At the end of the day, I have a daily examination. Each week, I have a weekly exam, followed by monthly, mid-term, and final examinations. Exams are a major part of my high school life.

　　The most unforgettable exam I have ever taken is the university entrance examination. It is unforgettable for three reasons. First, it took the longest time—three years—for me to prepare for it. Second, it was the exam that would make or break me. My future depended a lot on the success of the exam. Third, it was the one that gave me the greatest pressure—I could not afford to disappoint my parents and those who love me. (134 words)

93年指定科目考試

提示：

　　請以 "Travel Is the Best Teacher" 為主題，寫一篇至少 120 個字的英文作文。第一段針對作文主題，說明旅行的優點，並在第二段舉自己在國內或國外的旅行經驗，以印證第一段的說明。

例文：

Travel Is the Best Teacher

Travel is the best teacher for two reasons. First, travel enables us to learn about different cultures and meet different people. Our horizons are expanded. Second, travel strengthens family bonds. The common experience family members have provides them with something to talk about, they can recall a beautiful time had together. The bond is strengthened.

I was told that the US is a spacious country. But I did not know what that means until my family and I actually traveled to America. We rented a car, and drove from city to city. Unlike in Taiwan, where cities can be reached in a matter of hours, some big cities in the US take days to reach. This gave me an idea how big the country is. The journey has expanded my horizons. Furthermore, because we traveled together, after we got back from our trip, we had a lot in common to share with each other. Our bond was strengthened.

94年指定科目考試

提示：

指定科目考試完畢後，高中同學決定召開畢業後的第一次同學會，你被公推負責主辦。請將你打算籌辦的活動寫成一篇短文。文分兩段，第一段詳細介紹同學會的時間、地點及活動內容，第二段則說明採取這種活動方式的理由。

例文：

參考附錄IV第一篇範文。

95年指定科目考試

提示：

人的生活中，難免有遭人誤解因而感到委屈的時候。請以此為主題，寫一篇至少120字的英文作文；第一段描述個人被誤解的經驗，第二段談這段經驗對個人的影響與啟示。

例文：

Remedying a Grievance

A year ago I got a ticket for running a red light. As a result, I had to pay a fine. My father reprimanded me for not observing traffic regulations. I told him that I didn't break any regulation, nor did I run a red light, but he wouldn't listen. He paid the fine for me, but, as punishment, I wasn't allowed to ride my motorcycle for the rest of the year.

What actually happened was that the policeman made a mistake in judging my case. And his mistake not only made my father punish me when I didn't deserve it, but also caused great inconvenience in my daily life. I could have nursed the grievance and let bitterness pile up. But I chose to forgive the policeman. Only by forgiving others can we have peace of mind. My mom always tells me that to err is human, but to forgive, divine. I found this to be a great chance putting this wisdom into practice.

96年指定科目考試

說明：

　　1. 依提示在「答案卷」上寫一篇英文作文。

　　2. 文長 120 個單詞 (words) 左右。

提示：

　　你能想像一個沒有電 (electricity) 的世界嗎？請寫一篇文章，第一段描述我們的世界沒有電了以後，會是甚麼樣子，第二段說明這樣的世界是好是壞，並舉例解釋原因。

例文：

A World Without Electricity

If there were no electricity, our world would be different in at least three ways. First, we would not be able to enjoy the many comforts electricity offers us. There would not be air-conditioning. We would suffer cold in winter and heat in summer. Secondly, we would not be able to enjoy the many conveniences electricity offers us. Communication by telephone would not be possible. Rapid transportation of passengers and goods would not be possible. The pace of life would certainly slow down. Third, technology would suffer, too. For example, machinery that operates on electricity would no longer be available.

A world without electricity is undesirable for one simple reason. It would be very difficult for humanity to go back to the days when there was no electricity. Without electricity, it is very likely that our civilization would come to a halt. I am afraid that we would not be able to survive. Many people would die as a result.

 這樣的作文可得幾分？

1.

A Class Reunion

Since I have the honor to hold our first reunion, our team, including me and a few other classmates, have finally decided how this party will go. First, considering that we girls are definitely going to get very wild and noisy, therefore we choose to hold the party at the Cashbox KTV, next to our school rather than a high-class restaurant.

As to how the party will go, we have decided several games, including singing, of course, gift-exchanging, and most importantly, the girl chat. Also the date will be on July 10th, from 1 pm to 5 pm. The reason why we chose this date is that we think you girls might want to have some personal time with your family and friends; therefore we set the date on mid-July. That's how our first reunion will go. Remember, it's on July 10th, start from 1 pm, and don't be late. Also don't forget to bring your little present.

項目	內容	組織	文法	用字拼字	格式	總計
得分	4.5	4.5	4	4	2	18-19

說明

(1) 第一段可再加三個字，使 decided how this party will go 成為 decided when, where, and how this party will go。

(2) 第二段開頭可加轉承語Second。

(3) 取自聯合晚報。

2.

Winning and Losing in Life

You win some; you lose some. That is life. Life without adventure is not life. You won't win all things all the time, nor will you lose forever. Wins and loses make your life more colorful. When you lose, do not be frustrated. Work harder and you will win next time. Besides, you can always learn something from your failure. The important thing is, you should always improve yourself and be prepared for the next challenge.

Take myself for example. When I was a junior in senior high school, I was chosen by my teacher to participate in an English speech contest. I spent so much time preparing for this contest that I neglected my schoolwork. Although I finally won first prize in the contest, I failed my mathematics and had to lose my weekends for additional mathematics lesson. Since then, I have learned the meaning of the saying "You win some; you lose some. That is life."

項目	內容	組織	文法	用字拼字	格式	總計
得分	5	5	4	4	2	20

 取自閱卷手冊。

4.

Ways of Environmental Protection

Because of the progress of science and culture, men have destroyed their living environment for two hundred years. Although the earth is a young planet in the solar system, it looks like an old one. It's apparent that people hurt her so heavily.

Now people can't scorn this problem they make. Everyone must take the responsibility on the mistake. The nature has objected the pollution we produce. If we continue to enjoy our life but waste the energy of the earth, it follows that people perish. Many scientists have done research in environmental protection. They exert themselves to some new method to solve the pollution and look for the best energy. But it's not this few men's work. Everyone inhabit in the world is under obligation to join the assignment.

How do we do for the earth. It's very easy in practice. We only notice the resource around us, take a look that it's used or not. Sometimes we also decrease the use of energy because it's limited in the earth. Only by doing so we can help the earth continue to exist. We have no time to consider now let us do in time.

項目	內容	組織	文法	用字拼字	格式	總計
得分	0	0	0	0	0	0

 本文不切題。取自大考中心研究報告。

Ways of Environmental Protection

There are roughly two ways to protect our environment. First, there should be environmental protection laws and they should be enforced. If there are no laws that restrict people from destroying our environment, people will do whatever they want with the environment. As a result, our environment will not be a safe one for us to live in. For example, there may be air and water pollution, which endanger our health.

Second, a good education on environmental protection helps. All people, children and adults alike, should be told the importance of environment protection so that they won't risk breaking environmental protection laws for selfish purposes.

To sum up, if there are environmental protection laws and if people are educated to obey them, our environment will be protected. (127 words)

項目	內容	組織	文法	用字拼字	格式	總計
得分	5	5	4	4	2	20

3.

Living in a Big City

In the recent years, the improvement of industry and commercial brings us citization. First of all, the effects attract more and more people who want to find a job, elevate our living-standard, and refine our living environment.

Because of this, most people like to live in a big city, and I do, too. I have livied in Taipei and I like it so much. I have to say that Taipei has many drawbacks, but I love it for it is my home town.

項目	內容	組織	文法	用字拼字	格式	總計
得分	0.5	0.5	0.5	0.5	0.5	2.5

說明　取自大考中心研究報告。

 **97 年學測和指考作文解答**

97年學測

> 説明： 1. 依提示在「答案卷」上寫一篇英文作文。
>
> 　　　 2. 文長 120 個單詞 (words) 左右。

提示：你（英文名字必須假設為 George 或 Mary）向朋友（英文名字必須假設為 Adam 或 Eve）借了一件相當珍貴的物品，但不慎遺失，一時又買不到替代品。請寫一封信，第一段説明物品遺失的經過，第二段則表達歉意並提出可能的解決方案。

請注意：為避免評分困擾，請使用上述提示的 George 或 Mary 在信末署名，**不得使用自己真實的中文或英文姓名。**

February 2, 2008

Dear Adam,

　　I am sorry to tell you that I lost the cell phone I borrowed from you. I was going on my first date with my girlfriend and wanted to impress her. I thought your cell phone would do the trick and it did. We talked about cell phones in the restaurant, and I showed her yours, pretending it was mine. But when I got home, I found that the phone was missing. I must have left it somewhere. So I went back to where my girlfriend and I had been, trying to find it, but in vain.

　　I know the phone means a lot to you because it was a gift from your cousin. I am sorry I lost it. But don t worry; I am going to borrow money from my parents and buy you another one. We can meet tomorrow and you can pick out any phone in the shop. I will work part time to pay my parents back. Let me know when you want to meet.

Regretfully,

George

97年指考

> 説明： 1. 依提示在「答案卷」上寫一篇英文作文。
>
> 　　　 2. 文長至少 120 個單詞。

提示：廣告在我們生活中隨處可見。請寫一篇大約120-150 字的短文，介紹一則令你印象深刻的電視或平面廣告。第一段描述該廣告的內容（如：主題、故事情節、音樂、畫面等），第二段說明該廣告令你印象深刻的原因。

An Impressive TV Commercial

Of the many TV commercials I have seen, the most impressive one is perhaps the one by Chien-ming Wong, speaking for Acer computer. The commercial has an Acer computer on one side, and Wong on the other. Wong speaks for Acer to the effect that it faces the most difficult challenges therefore it is the best. Also, the commercial has background music, to which Wong dances.

The commercial is impressive for two reasons. First, it features Chien-ming Wong. As we all know, Wong is currently a top pitcher with the N.Y. Yankees. He won 19 games for two years. In the first year he was even nominated for the Cy Young Award, given to the best pitcher of the year. Since Wong is an international sports star, Acer picked him for the commercial. It was a wise choice. Second, Wong stands for excellence. To be good at something should be the goal of life. If we are good at something, we can better serve our society. Wong reminds me of this. For these two reasons, I think the Acer commercial is impressive.

98 年學測和指考作文解答

98年學測

提示：請根據右方圖片的場景，描述整個事件發生的前因後果。文章請分兩段，第一段說明<u>之前</u>發生了什麼事情，並根據圖片內容描述<u>現在</u>的狀況；第二段請合理說明接下來可能會發生什麼事，或者<u>未來</u>該做些什麼。

An Earthquake

Wearing a large hat and carrying a basket on his back, farmer George was picking tea leaves on his tea plantation one sunny afternoon, when he felt the ground shaking violently and realized it was a terrible earthquake. He left his work half finished and rushed home to see what the quake had done to his house. He was shocked to see the walls collapsed, the roof toppled, and debris scattered everywhere.

George's home had been destroyed. Fortunately, his family was away visiting his wife's parents, so there were no casualties. However, George would have to rebuild his home. For the time being, his wife and children could stay with his parents-in-law. As for the money, he could borrow some from his rich in-laws. Also the government had a program to help quake victims rebuild their homes. George was sure his life would return to normal soon.

98年指考

提示：如果你可以不用擔心預算，隨心所欲的度過一天，你會怎麼過？請寫一篇短文，
第一段說明你會邀請誰和你一起度過這一天？為什麼？第二段描述你會去哪裡？
做些什麼事？為什麼？

A Wonderful Day

If budgeting was not a problem and I could have one day the way I want it, I would invite my family to spend the day with me. I want to do this for two reasons. First, I can show my appreciation for what my parents have done for me. They raised me and sacrificed a lot, but they do not expect anything in return from me. Second, my family is very dear to me. They share my sorrows and my happiness in everything I do. I can use this day to make them happy.

I will take my family to Las Vegas. We will stay in a big room at a luxurious hotel. Room service will bring us breakfast. As soon as we finish eating, we will go out to explore the city. First, I will take them shopping. My father longs for a sports car. I will take him to a car dealer and let him choose one that he likes. Second, my sister wants a good piano. I will take her to a piano shop and fulfill her wish. Then we will go to a department store and shop to our heart's content. In the afternoon, we will try our luck at a casino. Since we have an unlimited budget for a day, we will play blackjack. We will bet the amount of money we need. For example, I need about a million NT for my college expenses, so that's what I would bet. If we lose, we can double our bet. We will not be greedy, and we will not play long. As soon as we win once, we will quit. In this way, I am sure to get the million NT for my college expenses and my family can get what they need. In the evening, we will watch the shows. I am sure we will all have a great time.

99 年學測和指考作文解答

99年學測

> 說明： 1. 依提示在「答案卷」上寫一篇英文作文。
>
> 　　　 2. 文長 120 個單詞 (words) 左右。

提示：請仔細觀察以下三幅連環圖片的內容，並想像第四幅圖片可能的發展，寫出一個涵蓋連環圖片內容並有完整結局的故事。

An Unexpected Incident

One day, something unexpected happened in a noodle shop. The shop owner was serving behind the counter and her son, Johnny, was doing homework in front of her. Meanwhile, a middle-aged man, who wore glasses and looked plump in his business suit, was having noodles a seat away from Johnny. On the seat between them was a bag, which the customer had put there before he started eating, and which seemed full of stuff. It looked like the man said something to Johnny.

The man finished his noodles and headed for Xin-chu train station, leaving his bag behind. A while later, Johnny and his mother noticed the forgotten bag and opened it. To their surprise, they found the bag full of thousand-dollar notes.

When the absent-minded man arrived at the train station and needed money for a ticket, he suddenly realized that his bag was missing. Where could it be and how could he get it back? The man was extremely nervous.

Back in the noodle shop, Johnny and his mother wondered how to deal with the situation. Should they keep the bag and wait for the man to claim the money? But what if the money was stolen? On second thought, they decided to turn the money over to the police and let them handle it. In this way, if the money was not stolen, the man could still claim it. If the money was stolen, it could be returned to the original owner.

99年指考

> 說明：1. 依提示在「答案卷」上寫一篇英文作文。
>
> 　　　2. 文長至少 120 個單詞。

提示：在你的記憶中，哪一種氣味（smell）最讓你難忘？請寫一篇英文作文，文長至少 120 字，文分兩段，第一段描述你在何種情境中聞到這種氣味，以及你初聞這種氣味時的感受，第二段描述這個氣味至今仍令你難忘的理由。

An Unforgettable Smell

I remember when I was a child, my mother made a chocolate cake to celebrate my tenth birthday. It was the first time my mom made a chocolate cake, and it smelled wonderful. I had chocolate candy and other kinds of chocolate before, but I had never smelled chocolate giving off the aroma that my mom's cake did. It was probably because my mother had a secret recipe, or because the occasion made the smell special. The smell of the cake, together with the gifts from my parents, made me extremely excited and content on that day.

The smell of that chocolate has stayed with me since the first time I smelled it. I look forward to that smell on every birthday. The smell reminds me of the happy times I had during my childhood. It reminds me of my mother's love. I am what I am today largely because of her love.

100 年學測和指考作文解答

100年學測

> 說明：1. 依提示在「答案卷」上寫一篇英文作文。
>
> 　　　2. 文長約 100 至 120 個單詞（words）。

提示：請仔細觀察以下三幅連環圖片的內容，並想像第四幅圖片可能的發展，寫出一個涵蓋連環圖片內容並有完整結局的故事。

The Masquerade

Something interesting happened to Jim during a masquerade last week. Wearing a pair of crescent shaped glasses, Jim attended a masquerade, during which he met a pretty girl. With her hair past her shoulders, the girl wore a necklace and a crown on her head. It seemed like Cupid had shot an arrow, making the two fall in love at first sight.

Jim decided to pursue his love. Carrying a guitar, Jim appeared in front of the pretty girl's apartment building on a starry night. With the crescent moon hanging in the sky and the stars twinkling above, the atmosphere seemed romantic. So, accompanied by his guitar, Jim started singing love songs to court the pretty girl.

Apparently, Jim's singing annoyed the people in the building. One stared angrily at him while the other yelled at him to stop. A third person looked out of the third floor window, totally confused. Jim was surprised and didn't know what to do. To his disappointment, the girl he fell in love with did not come out to meet him.

Later, Larry, a guy living on the third floor, realized what had happened. He realized that the singing boy was the one he had met at the masquerade. And obviously, the guy mistook him to be the pretty girl. His disguise had been a success. To avoid further misunderstandings, Larry decided to find Jim and explain to him about the mistake at the masquerade.

100年指考

> 說明：1. 依提示在「答案卷」上寫一篇英文作文。
>
> 　　　 2. 文長至少 120 個單詞（words）。

提示：你認為畢業典禮應該是個溫馨感人、活潑熱鬧、或是嚴肅傷感的場景？請寫一篇英文作文説明你對畢業典禮的看法，第一段寫出畢業典禮對你而言意義是什麼，第二段説明要如何安排或進行活動才能呈現出這個意義。

The Graduation Ceremony

Different people have different opinions regarding whether the graduation ceremony should be an occasion of sadness, warmth, joy, excitement or liveliness. In my opinion, the graduation ceremony should be both an occasion to celebrate our past achievements and an occasion to plan our future. If we reflect for a moment on what has happened to our lives so far, we will realize that we have spent most of our time preparing for something. After we achieve our goal, we immediately start to prepare for our next goal. Since the graduation ceremony marks the end of high school, it is fit and proper that we should celebrate our achievement of having obtained a diploma. The graduation ceremony is an occasion to plan our future because it is also called commencement, which means the beginning. Although we have completed our high school education, the new life ahead of us is just beginning. Accordingly, while we celebrate, we should also think about what to do next.

附錄 V

In view of the above discussion, if I were to organize the commencement, I would probably do two things. First, to celebrate our achievement, I would make sure that those who had done well were rewarded, including teachers and students. Moreover, there should be a party for all to express their thanks, their gratitude, their joy, to cherish the last moment together, and to be carefree. For after this, each will bide another goodbye. Second, to prepare for our next goal, Iwould like our teachers. or our elders with their accumulated wisdom. I'm sure we would benefit a lot from this.

101 年學測和指考作文解答

101年學測

説明： 1. 依提示在「答案卷」上寫一篇英文作文。

2. 文長 120 個單詞 (words) 左右。

提示：你最好的朋友最近迷上電玩，因此常常熬夜，疏忽課業，並受到父母的責罵。你（英文名字必須假設為Jack或Jill）打算寫一封信給他/她（英文名字必須假設為Ken或Barbie），適當地給予勸告。

請注意：必須使用上述的Jack或Jill在信末署名，<u>不得使用自己的真實中文或英文名字</u>。

Dear Barbie,

As you are aware, the university entrance examinations are drawing near and everyone in our class is working hard in preparation for them. Our future depends on the success of the exams. Therefore, we should do all we can in order to do well.

However, I realized that you have recently become addicted to computer games and often sit up all night playing. Your parents have scolded you for neglecting your studies. As your friend and classmate, I would like to give you some friendly advice. Firstly, we should know better than to waste our time on unimportant things. You may get some fun out of playing computer games, but you must know that you are paying a high price for the fun, which is very unwise. You will be sacrificing your health and your future if you continue to play like this. If you really cannot give up playing computer games, I suggest that you put them off until a later time, at least until after the exams.

Secondly, the zeal for computer games is momentary. Soon you will find that they have lost their intellectual challenge. So I recommend that you stop playing now and re-direct your attention to your studies. In this way, you can still have a chance to do well on the exams. Thirdly, I would hate to see you full of regret in your future life. Most importantly, I want to continue to be your best friend and go to college together. I don't want to go to college alone.

Finally, you are a sensible person and I don't think you will be offended by my advice. I wish you success.

Sincerely yours,

Jack

101年指考

說明：1. 依提示在「答案卷」上寫一篇英文作文。

2. 文長至少 120 個單詞（words）。

提示：請以運動為主題，寫一篇至少120個單詞的文章，說明你最常從事的運動是什麼。文分兩段，第一段描述這項運動如何進行（如地點、活動方式、及可能需要的相關用品等），第二段說明你從事這項運動的原因及這項運動對你生活的影響由。

Sports

My favorite sport is jogging. I jog almost every day. When I get home after school, I put on my sneakers, go outside and start jogging. I like jogging because it is easy to do and does not require expensive gear. All I need is a pair of sneakers and a T-shirt. I can jog almost any place. Most often I jog along the outdoor track at the school in our neighborhood. Running around the track, it is easy to count the distance I have covered. Sometimes I jog along the road to a destination like a business building, a memorial hall or other landmark in the city, and then I jog back. Sometimes I jog with a friend and follow his or her route.

I jog because it makes me happy and because it keeps me healthy. After I jog for about twenty minutes, my body releases endorphins and I begin to feel high. After jogging, instead of feeling tired, I often feel energetic and can better concentrate on my studies. Because I jog, my immune system is strengthened and I am sick less often. I am a healthier person. For these reasons, jogging is my favorite sport.

102 年學測和指考作文解答

102年學測

二、英文作文（占 20 分）

> 說明：1. 依提示在「答案卷」上寫一篇英文作文。
>
> 　　　2. 文長至少 120 個單詞（words）。

提示：請仔細觀察以下三幅連環圖片的內容，並想像第四幅圖片可能的發展，寫出一個涵蓋連環圖片內容並有完整結局的故事。

Jason is a high school student. He goes to school by MRT. One day, he took the MRT as usual. However, he paid no attention to the Priority Seats sign, sat down and was busy with his iPhone. Moreover, when a senior citizen stood in front of him, he pretended he didn't see him and continued with his iPhone, without offering his seat to the senior citizen. The people around him were furious, but Jason didn't seem to be aware or mind.

After Jason got to school, he had a PE class. He played basketball. The weather was good, with the sun shining in the sky. Everyone on the basketball court was having a good time. Unfortunately, Jason tripped over the ball, fell to the ground and hurt his ankle. His classmate Peter, wearing Number 3 T-shirt, saw what happened and helped take Jason to receive treatment.

After the accident, Jason's ankle hurt and he walked with a crutch. When he was on the MRT as usual, he hoped that he could sit down so that he would not feel so much pain. But nobody seemed to care. The young lady sitting on the priority seat in front of him didn't offer her seat.

Seeing that nobody cared about his need, Jason suddenly realized something. It dawned on him that he had been a selfish person. He just cared about himself. He now understood that if everybody behaved like him, there would be no love and the world would be a terrible place. So, instead of blaming the young lady for not offering her seat to him, he decided to change. From now on, he would not be selfish, not to mention occupy a priority seat.

102年指考
二、英文作文（占20分）

> 說明：1. 依提示在「答案卷」上寫一篇英文作文。
>
> 2. 文長至少 120 個單詞（words）。

提示：以下有兩項即將上市之新科技產品：

產品二：智慧型眼鏡
（smart glasses）

穿上後頓時隱形，旁人看不到你的存在；同時，隱形披風會保護你，讓你水火不侵。

產品一：隱形披風
（invisibility cloak）

具有掃瞄透視功能，戴上後即能看到障礙物後方的生物；同時能完整紀錄你所經歷過的場景。

如果你有機會獲贈其中一項產品，你會選擇哪一項？請以此為主題，寫一篇至少120個單詞的英文作文。文分兩段，第一段說明你的選擇及理由，並舉例說明你將如何使用這項產品。第二段說明你不選擇另一項產品的理由及該項產品可能衍生的問題。

Of the two scientific products, if I had to choose, I would choose the smart glasses. When I play hide and seek, I would certainly wear the smart glasses. With the smart glasses, my playmates cannot hide from me. I like adventures. When I explore a new place, I would like to know what is lurking behind a huge tree, or in a cave. Is there a rattle snake? Is there a jaguar? With the smart glasses, I could take precautions. My adventure will be more interesting. But, on the other hand, the smart glasses would take away the atmosphere of suspension and mystery. There would be no surprises at all.

I wouldn't choose the invisibility cloak because it may be used for evil purposes. For example, a criminal can wear it and enter a bank to commit robbery. A peeping Tom can wear it and hide in a bathroom to watch others bathe. The invisibility cloak endangers the neighborhood too. Thefts will be hard to prevent, there will be no use for security check points. People will have no privacy because they will have no way of knowing whether there is someone around or not.

103 年學測和指考作文解答

103年學測

二、英文作文（占 20 分）

> 說明： 1. 依提示在「答案卷」上寫一篇英文作文。
>
> 　　　 2. 文長至少 120 個單詞（words）。

提示：請仔細觀察以下三幅連環圖片的內容，並想像第四幅圖片可能的發展，寫一篇涵蓋所有連環圖片內容且有完整結局的故事。

　　Lily and Sam are siblings. They are used to going to school together. They have to walk through a park in their neighborhood. One day, on their way to school, they walked through the park as usual. However, they were not paying attention to where they were. Lily was busy with her cell phone and Sam was listening to music on YouTube.

　　Concentrating on her cell phone, Lily bumped into a tree. She was terribly hurt. A lady and her child walking behind Lily saw what happened. When she saw Lily bump into the tree, the lady wondered how such a thing could have happened. She came to Lily and asked her whether she needed help.

Meanwhile, Sam was focusing on the music he was listening to and was not aware of what had happened to his sister. He continued walking toward his destination. Because he was so absorbed in music, he wasn't aware that he was now on a main street and he didn't hear the horn from the car behind him. The driver of the car was angry because Sam didn't pay attention to him. He made an emergency stop before his car hit Sam.

The angry driver got out of his car and gave Sam a lecture. Sam apologized and after he made the apology he tried to find his sister, only to realize that she was not around. So Sam rushed back to the park to look for Lily. Fortunately, he found her sitting under the tree she bumped into, crying.

103年指考

二、英文作文（占20分）

> 説明：1. 依提示在「答案卷」上寫一篇英文作文。
>
> 　　　2. 文長至少 120 個單詞（words）。

提示：下圖呈現的是美國某高中的全體學生每天進行各種活動的時間分配，請寫一篇至少120個單詞的英文作文。文分兩段，第一段描述該圖所呈現之特別現象；第二段請說明整體而言，你一天的時間分配與該高中全體學生的異同，並說明其理由。

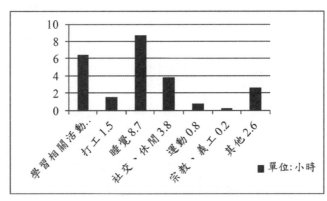

From the time allocation chart we learn that the students spend the greatest amounts of time in resting (8.7 hours) and studying (6.4 hours). They spend 3.8 hours socializing or pursuing hobbies. They spend 1.5 hours working part time and 0.8 hours exercising. They spend 0.2 hours being a volunteer or being religious. They spend about 2.6 hours doing other miscellaneous stuff.

On the whole, my daily routine differs from that of these high school kids. I sleep less hours and study more. I don't work part time during the semester. I seldom socialize or engage in leisure pursuits. Instead, I attend cram schools, hoping to improve my grades. I don't do volunteer work and I am not involved in religious activities. While my grades in school seem to be my only concern and I think the American students do not study as hard as I do, their life seems to consist of more variety

104 年學測和指考作文解答

104年學測

二、英文作文（占 20 分）

> 說明：1. 依提示在「答案卷」上寫一篇英文作文。
>
> 　　　2. 文長至少 120 個單詞（words）

提示：下面兩本書是學校建議的暑假閱讀書籍，請依書名想想看該書的內容，並思考你會選擇哪一本書閱讀，為什麼？請在第一段說明你會選哪一本書及你認為該書的內容大概會是什麼，第二段提出你選擇該書的理由。

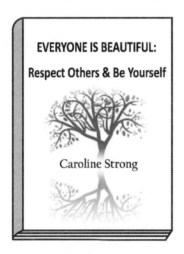

By looking at the titles of the two books, I would probably choose to read the one by Strong, *EVERYONE IS BEAUTIFUL: Respect Others & Be Yourself*. This book is possibly about ethics, about personal relationships, especially in the area of boundary setting. Why is everyone beautiful? If it is really so, why are there beauty contests every year? Why are fair ladies and handsome guys frequently preferred? They say that beauty is in the eyes of the beholder. They say that each person is unique. They say that beauty is skin deep. And they also say that don't judge others by appearance. But saying and believing are two different things. There must be many people suffering from not having a good appearance. It is probably because of these facts that the theme of beauty needs to be dealt with. It will take some time before we realize that everyone is beautiful, that everyone, no matter who they are, what job they have, what background they are from, is worthy of respect, because each one is unique. And because each one is unique, we don't have to admire other people for what we don't have, we can just be ourselves.

I would choose to read this book because the issue of appearance bothers many people. This is why plastic surgery is so popular nowadays. People want a higher nose, bigger eyes, and rounder hips. I personally think that appearances are deceiving. What we need is to cultivate inner beauty, pursue moral excellence, and develop good relationships with ourselves and with others. This is what is appealing. Not just appearance. Beauty, like a flower, blooms and then fades. But our inner beauty and moral excellence last a lifetime.

104年指考
二、英文作文（占 20 分）

> 說明：1. 依提示在「答案卷」上寫一篇英文作文。
>
> 　　　　2. 文長至少 120 個單詞（words）。

提示：指導別人學習讓他學會一件事物，或是得到別人的指導而自己學會一件事物，都是很好的經驗。請根據你過去幫助別人學習，或得到別人的指導而學會某件事的經驗，寫一篇至少120個單詞的英文作文。文分兩段，第一段說明該次經驗的緣由、內容和過程，第二段說明你對該次經驗的感想。

In school I was good at English. This was because I had had a passion for learning the language well. I would study on my own. I read as much as I could and took note of new words that I ran across. Whenever there was something in my reading that I did not understand, be it grammatical or cultural, I would ask someone who was better at English than I was. When they answered my question, I thanked them and was full of gratitude. It was in this way that I gradually made progress in my English. I wouldn't say that I have learned English, but I would say that I have managed to learn English reasonably well.

Being helped is like a need satisfied. For example, you are thirsty and someone kind gives you a glass of water. Your thirst is quenched. It is also like fixing a problem. For example, you cannot start your motorcycle. Someone comes along and fixes the problem. Because of the help, you can continue your journey. When I got stuck with my learning, I found it hard to go on. This is my reflection of being helped and helping others. I am forever grateful to those who have helped me, and am willing to help those who need help.

105 年學測和指考作文解答

105學測作文

提示：你認為家裡生活環境的維持應該是誰的責任？請寫一篇短文説明你的看法。文分兩段，第一段説明你對家事該如何分工的看法及理由，第二段舉例説明你家中家事分工的情形，並描述你自己做家事的經驗及感想。

Sustaining the Home

As the proverb goes, "East, west, home is best." In other words there is no place like home. The place we call home is our refuge, where we get recharged when our energy level is low. However, as precious as home is, there are many chores to be done and they should be shared. We cannot take our home for granted. With the exception of babies, everyone should have a share in doing the chores. Young children can be responsible for keeping their rooms tidy. Teenagers should be responsible for dumping the garbage, clearing the floor, doing the laundry, and washing the dishes. Food preparation usually belongs to adults, although children can help by cleaning vegetables. By sharing chores, children grow up to be responsible adults and learn to take care of themselves in the process. Parents should encourage their children to share chores. It is a bad idea to have a maid doing all the chores for the family, where children do nothing but play and study.

At my home I clean up the table after meals, and I do the dishes. I sort the laundry and put it into the washing machine. Then I hang them up to dry.

I also help mop the floor sometimes. Every year we repaint our walls. I help my dad with the repainting. Though sometimes we get dirty, it is a lot of fun. We feel a sense of achievement after we have finished painting the home. I think sharing chores is good for me. My relationship with my parents is better as a result. And we become more intimate with each other. I also learned many useful things during the process, like how to thin paint. Most importantly, I learned to be a useful member of our family.

105指考作文

The job of a waste collector in Taiwan does not require a master's degree. The fact that fifty degree holders compete for the position of waste collector tells us that jobs are hard to find. In order to survive, these people are willing to put aside their expertise and take whatever is available. It is sad that a well-educated person becomes a square peg in a round hole. Or, perhaps these degree holders do not have real passion for learning. If they did, they would not give in so easily. They would keep looking for a more suitable job until they finally found one. If I can go to university, I will pursue my interest in three areas. First, I will learn all I can at the department I will be studying in. I will seek academic excellence by preparing myself to become an expert in the field I specialize in. Second, I will join a club to develop a hobby like filming or painting. Clubs are places to meet people with similar hobbies. Third, I will make use of what I learn by taking part-time jobs during holidays. This will strengthen my interest in my field of learning. To sum up, I want to be really good in my field. Attending university will make my dreams come true.